RECOLLECTIONS OF MURDER

DAVID HOWARD

ISBN: 1533510776
ISBN-13: 978-1533510778
ASIN: BO1HCMNJH4

This is a work of fiction. Names, characters, places and incidents either are
products of the author's imagination or are used fictitiously, and any
resemblance to actual persons, living or dead, businesses, companies,
events or locales is entirely coincidental.

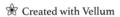 Created with Vellum

For VICKI and JESSICA
forever and always

1

"IT'S THE FLAW THAT MAKES THE MAN," LIZA THOUGHT AS SHE watched Joe Brandt unconsciously toy with the ragged scar on his upper lip. She wondered what she found so attractive about his most visible defect, maybe the fact there was some mystery attached to it. He claimed he'd taken a line drive to the mouth in Little League, but his evasiveness about adding more detail left the point open in her mind. She had long ago noticed his habit of rubbing a finger over the scar's ridges while his dark eyes stared far into some unknown past. It was this, Joe's recurrent escape from the moment, which intrigued yet confounded Liza Upman.

To everyone else in the courtroom it looked as if Joe were intently watching his star witness shuffle forward with the help of her guardian. The girl walked uneasily over the worn floor of the old and austerely handsome courtroom in downtown St. Paul. Its dark wood paneling, jury dock, railings and judge's bench all gleamed from decades of hand-rubbed polish which left a faint, sweet aroma. Despite the care and upkeep, the room itself absorbed light, leaving a sense of somberness. People's futures were decided here and neither the place nor its inhabitants was meant to take that charge lightly. Just now Joe Brandt was most serious about putting prison into the future of the defendant and his prosecution strategy hinged on his ability to extract the right half dozen words from his brain-damaged and under-aged charge.

Joe was first chair for the Ramsay County District Attorney and Liza vaguely knew she should resent being second chair. She had slight seniority over him, but when she watched him work with victims, she never flattered herself into bitterness. Joe was brilliant at burrowing into family violence, he seemed to understand it almost like a savant. He connected somewhere below a conscious level with life's casualties, especially children like Lydia Church – innocents who had been victimized by those closest to them. As always Liza watched him intently, trying to discover his secret, but it was like the scar: she could see it, she knew it had a cause, and yet the underlying truth remained elusive.

Joe had no awareness he was touching his scar as his eyes followed Lydia bumbling her way onto the witness stand. The nearly unimaginable traumas in her short life had compounded by the year, but unlike her previous ordeals, this part of her nightmare she had been forced to anticipate. She had become terrified about having to speak in front of so many people. And with good cause. Joe could hear the gasps of the jury as his broken six-year-old witness turned to face the court with even more anxiety than he had feared she'd feel. Sadly, it was perfect.

Lydia did her best to be sworn in properly while the judge explained that she was promising to tell the truth. Lydia clutched her doll in one hand and her court-appointed guardian's hand in the other until Judge Swander insisted gently that Mrs. Driscoll had to leave her alone. Joe knew this would cause the girl more suffering, but unhappily his case was built on displaying her physical and emotional debilities. He needed and depended upon Lydia's distress.

As he appeared to watch Lydia, Joe contemplated the power it took to drive the brain against the skull with such force it caused permanent and profound tissue damage. In the first two days of the trial he had drawn out testimony from experts about brain traumas as well as the fact that shaken baby syndrome could impact children as old as seven, well beyond Lydia's age when she was removed from her mother's care. Throughout that discussion of brain damage, Joe was repeatedly reawakened to thoughts he had spent most of his life avoiding. He had never known what to trust of his own unwanted nightmares, whether they were genuine recollections or imagined traumas. He had aggressively tried to escape them through excess activity, an obsessive drive to achieve and relentless efforts at getting justice for others who had been severely wronged. Like Lydia.

WHEN HE FELT A NUDGE, Joe jolted back to the present and the trial of Helena Church. At twenty-eight, Joe was physically compact, but when combined with his obvious mental gifts, evident shyness, apparent lack of organization and his hopeless attempts to dress suitably, his flawed good looks made him quite sympathetic in the jury's eyes.

"Hello, Lydia," Joe said as he cautiously approached the stand. Squarely in front of the girl he stopped and smiled. "Do you remember me, Lydia? I'm Joe. Joe Brandt."

Lydia smiled and drooled as she said something meant to be "Joe." To the jury it sounded like gibberish.

"I'm glad to see you and Wendy again," Joe said.

The courtroom disappeared for Lydia who broadened her crooked smile and held up her blonde doll, clutching it with one trembling hand while her other groped about to find it.

Liza followed her hand-written script of their witness strategy and was pleased to see how natural Joe made it seem despite their hours of preparation for this delicate and crucial moment. She knew Lydia would either convict her mother in the next ten minutes or set her free forever. Despite her focus on her notes, a prickling at the back of her neck forced Liza to look around. With alarm she discovered the district attorney standing at the rear of the room, intently watching Joe and Lydia.

Mike Westermann never attended the trials of his assistants. Liza thought, 'Why would he come here today?' When she turned back to her legal pad, all she could see was her shaking hands as she began to fear Joe might stumble if he spotted Mike. She hoped he wouldn't realize they were under such unprecedented scrutiny. Even seasoned prosecutors faltered when their extremely demanding boss watched. Mike was not an easy man to please.

The District Attorney looked like a model: perfect suit, perfect teeth, perfect hair and a regal, commanding presence. He stood a head taller than the bailiff at the door who gave him deference he didn't currently want. Mike wished to be unnoticed, to observe, not be observed. Maybe it was a dead end anyway, Mike thought unhappily. This little girl on the stand was clearly in love with Joe Brandt. He'd had more than a few witnesses infatuated with him over the years, but one of Mike's ironclad rules had been to keep every ambiguous nuance from being obvious to the jury.

Here was Joe Brandt, the reputed boy wonder, trotting

out the affections of his witness for all to see. Granted, the girl was only six. Having her eating out of his hand was a significant achievement for his assistant prosecutor, a feat Mike could not envision any of his other ADAs successfully pulling off. His prosecution chief had bragged about this guy, saying she was bringing him along quickly, but she had still insisted Mike decide about Joe for himself.

This testimony from a child, the toughest witness there is, was what had dragged Mike from his office and into a courtroom. How unusual, he mused as he watched a prosecution no one else in his office had wanted. Only Joe had lobbied to get it, as if he thought prosecuting a rich and handsome mother with only an unreliable witness to work with was a plum. Mike had never believed this case would come to trial. He had thought it would be plea bargained into probation and loss of custody for the mother, county dependence for the little girl. Yet here were the courtroom, the jury, the guilty-as-sin mother and her accuser perched on the edge of her chair, hanging on every word from an ADA who hadn't known enough to know he couldn't win the case. So he'd pursued it it with a passion.

"How is Wendy today? Is she feeling strong?" Joe asked the trembling girl in the witness stand.

Lydia nodded and managed to say, "Good."

"I'm glad," Joe said. "Do you remember we talked about coming here today so you could tell what happened to you?"

Lydia shot a panicky look toward Mrs. Driscoll, then nodded. There was a pretty six-year-old girl inside Lydia who had been lost forever. Half her face was slack, as if she'd had a stroke; she drooled and one eye was wayward.

The more agitated she felt, the more she shook as she nervously tried to flatten her own curly and unruly hair.

Joe stepped aside so Lydia could now see her mother. Helena Church stared glumly ahead. She was elegantly dressed, every hair was in place and she sat with a rigidity that flawlessly supported Joe's prosecution strategy. Mrs. Church looked supremely unforgiving and one glance at Lydia proved how unsatisfactory she would seem to a perfectionist.

"Do you recognize the woman sitting there, Lydia?"

"Mommy," Lydia said with a slur, while drool darkened her frilly pink dress. It was said without acrimony and Joe knew the girl couldn't possibly make a verbal accusation, but he hoped she'd complete the picture he had been drawing.

"Can you tell us what your mommy did to you, Lydia?"

Lydia tried to form a word, but failed and Mrs. Driscoll was instantly out of her seat. Joe signaled for her to sit back down and Lydia tried again, "Shhhhhhh..."

"What did your mommy do, Lydia?" he asked softly.

Lydia clutched the doll and stared with gaping eyes.

"I know it's hard, Lydia," Joe said, "but could you put it in a word? Do you feel like you can say a word?"

Lydia finally looked Joe squarely in the eye before saying, "Yes," clearly.

"Thank you, Lydia. You're being very brave," he said as Lydia intently straightened the doll's slightly wayward hair.

"What word tells us what your mommy did?"

Lydia started to speak and then stopped, started, then clammed up completely. Joe looked at Judge Swander. "Your Honor, may I...?" Joe indicated the doll. The judge nodded.

"Could you show us with Wendy, Lydia?"

Lydia looked at the doll sympathetically, then held it

up in both hands and began to shake it. The agitation became so hard and so fast, one hand couldn't keep up. Lydia kept shaking one-handed until the doll flew right past Joe onto the courtroom floor. Lydia leapt up, crying and reaching for it in such a heart-wrenching panic that Mrs. Driscoll had her in an embrace before Joe could retrieve the doll.

Mike Westermann smiled to himself, he loved the impossible wins. There was nothing left to do but let this tea steep, Mike thought. Mrs. Church was on her way to jail. Maybe his chief of prosecution was right about Joe, which meant now he'd really have to think about her suggestion of using this young guy. It was risky, but Mike had never been accused of being risk averse.

"Are you saying your mother shook you and hurt you?" Joe asked as he handed the doll back to Lydia.

Lydia looked right at Joe and said "Yes" emphatically.

"Thank you, Lydia," Joe said, "No further questions, Your Honor. The state rests."

"Let the record reflect that Lydia Church shook her doll violently," Judge Swander said to the stenographer.

Before he got to his seat, Lydia blurted out a fully understandable, "Joe." He gave her a warm smile and sat back down beside Liza, who had somehow remained stoic. She'd never once gotten through a bonding session with Lydia without crying, but her silent terror of the DA watching had stifled any chance of tears today.

"We can't just stop there," Liza whispered as she pointed to the rest of the script on her legal pad.

"She just gave us everything we need."

Liza hated it when Joe improvised, but when she looked at Phil Thompkins, Helena Church's lawyer, he looked crushed. Phil knew Joe had killed him. When she looked back to Mike for any encouraging signs, he was already gone.

Thompkins asked Lydia if she loved her mother, which she claimed she did, then began what Joe felt could only be an ineffectual defense in the face of such damning direct testimony – character witnesses. A monotonous stream of friends and associates agreed Helena Church was a wonderful, kind, charitable and energetic woman, one with a big heart and a great smile. Joe knew all of it was true except when it wasn't true. There was a demon inside Mrs. Church which could not tolerate her daughter's slowness.

Judge Swander stopped Thompkins between character witnesses to break for lunch and no sooner were the judge and jury out of the courtroom than Joe was loosening his necktie.

"What is it with you and ties?" Liza asked as he pulled the tied loop over his head. He hated having anything around his neck, it felt like he was being choked. A primal fear of strangulation was one of several unwanted thoughts he'd spent his life sidestepping. He had no real idea of the source of this phobia and no desire to discover it.

JUST OUTSIDE THE COURTROOM DOORS, Joe and Liza were shocked to find Mike Westermann waiting for them. Liza immediately flushed and wished she'd told Joe their boss had watched, but mostly she worried about how much trouble they were in. Mike looked disapprovingly over Joe's rumpled old suit, his missing tie and those god-awful shoes, then smiled at Liza and said, "You need to find another lunch companion today, Liza. I have to steal Joe."

Liza nodded, shot a supportive look to Joe and mimed

'Call me' as the elevator doors opened. She left them with a sense of both relief and boundless curiosity.

Joe stared at the handkerchief in Mike's suit pocket, it was matched to his tie. They were at eye level for him. He told himself he wasn't obsessed about it, but Mike's size gave him pause as he awaited his fate. Never once in his nearly three years with the district attorney's office had the DA waited for him outside court. Mike didn't wait for people, he made them come to him and wait.

"So here's the deal, Joe," Mike finally said when they were alone. "I want you to look at a crime scene, I want you to nose around, talk with everyone and form your own opinions. There's a boy there and I want you to get close to him and give me your ideas about how he can be effectively used. Then tell me this afternoon what you think. I've got a huge decision to make and it might include you."

"I have to be back in court after lunch, sir."

"I'm taking Judge Swander to a long lunch, Joe."

"Really, sir?" Joe didn't know whether to be scared or excited. "What's the case, sir?"

"Byron Enright will update you on the drive," Mike said. "Introduce yourself to him and get up to speed." He pressed the elevator button for Joe. "The moment Swander gavels, come to my office. I have to get out front of this in time for the end of the news cycle." He let the door close between them, leaving Joe mystified.

Until this moment, life as a prosecutor had been simple. Joe was a good guy who put bad guys in jail. He had never once thought about a news cycle or advising his boss.

JOE FOUND the Courthouse and City Hall lobby noisier than usual. There was a phalanx of aggressive news crews from local and national television stations and newspapers. They spotted him and shrank back in disappointment, he wasn't who they were looking for. Joe only understood the full scale of the media assault when he found news vans outside with satellite dishes on cranes and more news people all hungering for a meal they did not expect to find with him. Joe remained virtually unnoticed.

One man spotted Joe and slipped up to usher him toward a large black SUV which was illegally parked and being guarded by a uniformed policeman. Byron Enright, Chief Investigator for the district attorney's office, held out a huge hand to shake and nearly crushed Joe's hand as he introduced himself. Joe knew who he was, but the cases Enright handled for the DA were more important than the ones Joe was usually assigned so they had not worked together. Joe was still trying to fathom what he'd done to have been put in the hands of Byron Enright and hijacked to a mysterious crime scene in the middle of a trial day.

"You got anything in your stomach?" Enright asked.

Joe shook his head and hoped they wouldn't stop for greasy fast food on the way.

"Keep it that way," Enright said as they climbed into the car and he signaled thanks to the cop who had guarded it for him. "What I hear, either it starts empty or becomes that way pretty quick."

"Where are we going, Byron?"

"A place where mere mortals like you and me rarely go, Paramount Hills." When he saw Joe looking puzzled, he added, "Didn't you see any news this morning?"

"Prep for testimony, then in court. What'd I miss?"

"A river of blood in the back garden of a castle."

2

BYRON ENRIGHT LOOKED LIKE A COP, WHICH IN FACT, HE HAD been for twenty years. Big, beefy and florid, there was an unmistakable aura about him, don't mess with Byron. He was mid to late forties and couldn't run as well as younger men, but he thought faster and with greater understanding of the criminal mind than most of the young, hot-shot prosecutors for whom he supposedly worked. In reality he worked for Mike. Among the ADAs, it was widely known that the most important cases could easily be identified, they were the ones Enright focused on. Right now his crosshairs included Joe's shortcomings. The investigator looked him over during the drive and said, "You need to let a woman into your life."

"What makes you think there isn't one?" Joe asked.

"A kid who buys that suit, those shoes and the tie you're hiding in your pocket, he's a guy who shops alone."

Joe knew it was meant to put him in his place and, against his better judgment, it did just that. He'd never learned how to buy clothes – or much of anything else, he realized – but most people politely avoided mentioning his failings to his face. It wasn't like he'd ever had someone to teach him about clothing, he told himself in his own defense. Even Byron Enright, no clothes horse himself, had had a mother and a father and, no doubt a wife, who guided him and told him the rules and secrets, whatever they were. Joe hadn't known who to ask. Rather than face these dilemmas head-on, he'd hidden behind studying and practicing.

"Your tie come pre-stained or you artfully arranged that mustard on your own?" Joe asked, deadpan.

Byron Enright looked him over with a smirk. He didn't need to glance at his tie to know it was true. "Am I going to like working with you or am I going to grind you into dust?"

"Are we going to work together?" Joe asked in surprise.

"Mike didn't send you out on this for fun. This won't be fun," Enright said. "So I'm guessing you're part of it."

"Mike said the jury was out until I meet the boy and give him my impressions," Joe said.

Enright drove in silence as they got onto Highway 61 heading north. "Guess we better go form some good impressions."

Joe was about to thank him for sounding as if he were on his side, but the sentiment didn't last long as Enright began to tell him what they were up against. They had a butchered victim, a mysterious killer the eyewitness suggested was the husband and a husband who was documented to have been in a hotel for the duration of the crime. That same presumed-but-impossible suspect was perhaps the richest man in the state of Minnesota and the witness who called 911 was nine years old. The boy was son of the suspect, son of the victim, heir to the empire and so well hidden in the mansion it took police hours to locate him and many hours to extract him.

"Did I mention," Enright went on, "the boy hasn't said a single word since the 911 call?"

With downtown St. Paul behind them they drove into the northern suburbs which were in the full and scenic bloom of mid-summer. Joe finally asked the question which had been bugging him, "Why would Mike put me on a case like that?"

"Be realistic, Kid, he shouldn't," Enright said, "but there's a boy at the center and word is you're good with kids. Probably because you can look 'em right in the eye."

Joe marveled there was any word at all around the DA's office about him and that Byron Enright knew who he was prior to their meeting. Enright pointed at a billboard they were approaching and said, "That's him."

As they passed, Joe caught a fleeting look, but he was already familiar with the sign's content, though not the fact this murder had something to do with Dusan Tanovich. His last name, with the cross on the T forming a roof over the rest of the letters, was visible everywhere in St. Paul. Most neighborhoods had a Tanovich development of single family homes. Dusan Tanovich was a local institution.

"Hurry in, the real estate market is heating up..." Joe said, "He's the husband?"

"Widower, as of this morning," Enright said.

"Holy shit."

"See why you're not getting the case, Kid?" Enright said as a statement of fact, this was the big league.

"He'll have millions for his defense," Joe marveled.

"That and he's already got an ironclad alibi."

JOE HAD ONLY HEARD about Paramount Hills, he'd never seen the gilded fortress where the very wealthiest of the astonishingly rich lived. Even prominent elected officials couldn't afford it unless they had made millions before running for office. One of the richest towns in the U.S., Paramount Hills was so exclusive even the streets were private property. Thinking about the media sideshow downtown, Joe wondered how the collision of a free press with the privacy of the phenomenally wealthy would be decided. He guessed property rights would trump the Bill of Rights.

They drove through Maplewood, a nice, modest bedroom community that was home to people Joe could understand, working people. Then they entered White Bear Lake, a lovely, semi-rural, heavily wooded area of nice suburban homes along the shores of the lake, great high school football teams and a basketball team he'd scored twenty-one points against his senior year. White Bear was filled with professionals and was where normal people aspired to live. Joe couldn't quite place himself there, but at least he knew people who might fit in.

Financially, Paramount Hills could not even be seen from White Bear Lake. People there ran huge hedge funds or headed corporations. Or they oversaw family foundations giving away the billions great-granddad amassed as a robber baron. Or they just hoarded their family's wealth.

'Welcome to Paramount Hills,' said the sign at the guarded front gate. The SUV inched toward the booth through a mass of news crews that were clearly not welcome inside. Score one for rich people's right to privacy.

"How many entrances are there?" Joe asked.

"Only this for residents and guests," the guard said as he offered a guest pass. "There's also a service entrance."

Joe asked for a map and discovered it outlined every street and parcel and listed a few of the association rules which were mostly about privacy and quiet. The map didn't indicate if there was a perimeter fence, but on paper Paramount Hills seemed like an armed compound.

Byron saw him looking at the security cameras as they drove into another universe. "Security recordings are all impounded and being logged. The service entrance is closed after 9pm and also has a camera."

"If I were picking a place to commit murder, a gated and guarded community would be low on my list," Joe said.

"Theory goes that our killer lives at the scene."

"At least we're going in with open minds," Joe said.

Enright laughed. "Last word on the 911 call from the boy was 'Dad.'"

"Sounds like a good theory then."

"Question is, you got all the money in the world and want to get rid of the little lady, why hack her up in the back yard yourself? Why not hire someone?"

Enright drove through a forest dotted with storybook homes. Some were nice homes worth a few million dollars, but others were faux palaces on lots as big as a city block. Even the gardeners drove expensive trucks. Impressed more than he cared to be, Joe watched Enright openly marvel. "No wonder they keep us riffraff out," he said. "I heard they won't let Google Maps in and now I see why. They only show off for each other, we're not even on their radar."

At the end of a road they found a palatial estate with a dozen city and county vehicles out front. Both men were speechless. It was a castle. Stone and more stone, towers and an intricate slate roof, bay windows and cantilevered balconies. Tanovich made his millions selling starter homes in subdivisions, but he spent them presenting himself as king. Lord over all he surveyed.

"Bitt," Enright shouted past the stream of city and county workers heading back and forth from the rear of the house to trucks and cars in the crowded street.

Detective Ed Bittinger was a thin man with a narrow, old-fashioned mustache and a fountain of nervous energy. Seasoned by too many years on the St. Paul Police Force and jaded by the worst that humans could do, Bittinger's first smile of his day came when he spotted them. He warmly shook hands with Byron Enright, so by association, Joe was afforded quite a warm welcome as well.

"I'll be with you soon's we get the prince out and safe so we can get down to real business in the house," Bittinger said as he broke loose, signaling for them to stay in place. The detective hurried to the hand-carved oak front door as a crowd of officials began to emerge. The first wave included a couple strong cops wrestling a frantic woman out the door. The hysterical woman – dark haired, pretty, not properly dressed for the day and out of control with anxiety to get back inside – was not touching the ground as she was ushered in the arms of the police toward a city van. Joe couldn't imagine what she had to do with the case until the second wave of cops sidled out the door carrying someone wrapped in a blanket despite the fact it was a sunny, warm summer day.

The woman, Nicola Patterson, screamed at the boy in the blanket with such visceral and desperate torment, "Billy" cut through every heart in the cul-de-sac.

For Joe the anguish was worse than for most because he had heard that exact tone far too many times. It was an unnatural, yet universal sound, the kind made only in circumstances of horrific loss and suffering. He knew the primal, animalistic torment all too well and he hated it.

As if frozen, Joe watched them set down the boy beside a

Social Services van. The blanket fell away from the decidedly handsome boy, as the police tried to get him inside the van. Billy Tanovich, skinny with a mass of dark, dusty hair, was inert as he stood there, staring blindly. He wore Minnesota Twins pajamas which were covered in dust that billowed away in the light breeze. He seemed utterly unaware as he was bundled toward the van door.

Before he fully realized he had become unfrozen, Joe broke across the lawn in a desire to meet the boy. It was a visceral move, the sort of thing Joe had done too many times across too many ordeals. None had been quite like this one.

Next thing he knew, Joe was face down in the grass.

It was a disorienting moment before he realized he'd been tackled. He was held down by a cop the size of a Mack truck as he watched the boy being put in the van. Finally, he saw a hand extended down and Bittinger helped him to his feet. "No more fast moves, okay, Kid?" the detective said as he dusted off Joe while Billy was driven away in the van.

"I have to speak with the boy," Joe blurted out.

"Not gonna happen," Bittinger said as Enright joined them and the two older men shared a look which seemed to say, we going to have a problem here?

"The district attorney sent me to meet with the boy."

"You've seen everything there is to learn from that boy today," Bittinger said. "He wouldn't make a sound and it took forever just to find his hiding place. The kid crawled inside the heating ducts. Then he wouldn't cooperate when we wanted to get him out and even his aunt couldn't get him to come out after we brought her to help. Hell, she scared us all half to death, so I don't blame the boy."

"The boy's now in the system," Enright said. "He's safe and we got his voice on the 911 tape."

"Last words he spoke," Bittinger added. "Maybe ever."

Joe watched Nicola Patterson, the aunt, sobbing as she was led to a separate van, then noticed Enright standing in his line of vision, pointing at his watch. "Don't you have a trial?" he said.

Joe nodded and called Liza, triggering her second chair into first chair action. She would have to sit through the character witnesses and hyperbole on her own. He promised to be back soon, though he knew he had the ordeal of a lifetime between him and the courtroom. He had the crime scene.

3

BITTINGER THREADED THEM THROUGH THE POLICE AND CRIME scene techs crowding outside the garage and then toward the tents at the back of an 'out building' that was bigger than the house Joe grew up in. He learned it was called a potting shed, though who repotted plants in it was a mystery. One of many. Bittinger wasn't overly concerned about Enright enduring the murder scene, but this novice prosecutor, he could be a problem. Even a veteran detective like Bittinger was still reeling from seeing it all. Enright had noticed that Bitt was uncharacteristically muted; he hadn't made a single sexist joke yet. A new first.

As an officer wrote their names in the crime scene log and gave all of them green booties for their shoes Joe's misgivings began to kick into high gear. He'd seen lots of blood before – his own, other people's, loved ones' blood, strangers' blood. Part of the life he had chosen had necessitated more than an average tolerance for blood, if not the violence which usually spilled it. But if what was outside the tents was any indication, he was in for a truly horrific crime scene. Clear plastic sheeting stretched out from under side-by-side twelve foot square tents and it was heavily trampled in blood. Several news helicopters hovered at the prescribed height and distance from the site, like mosquitoes outside a camper's tent, lurking and ready to strike.

"Listen, Kid," Bittinger said with a solicitous hand on Joe's shoulder. "This is as rough as they get. Worse 'cuz she is...this lady was a seventy-two on a scale of one to ten." He handed both Joe and Enright airline barf bags. "Please don't spoil my crime scene."

Bittinger led the way, nodding to workers hurrying out of the tent. No one stayed inside longer than they needed. Enright felt his anger rising. No matter the victim or the offense – real or imagined – between them, there was nothing which could forgive this level of brutality.

Bittinger wasn't looking at the site itself – he'd seen more than enough. He was watching his new charge as Joe stepped inside the tent. Joe was overwhelmed at first by the silence. Crime scenes had a lot of people working side by side, jockeying for access, kidding each other, telling jokes, flirting even, to let off steam. But no one here said a word. The choppers could be heard in the distance, but there were no human voices as the men and women went about their work. Joe tried to force his mind to comprehend what his eyes were relaying. This was the moment Bittinger was watching for, the moment when so many seasoned crime scene workers had rushed out of the tent.

Joe was able to sharpen his focus step by step, from the white of the tent sides to the red pools and spatters of blood to the shine of the clear plastic under all the devastation. Plastic sheeting had been placed atop the grass, clearly laid out before the murder as if to contain it. To capture the blood and the violence.

Finally, after what seemed an eternity, Joe was able to

recognize something. It was a calf. Ankle to knee. White, slim, shapely, drained of blood which had seeped onto the plastic. The calf was by itself without a foot or a body. Coming to recognize it made Joe gasp. Everyone had done the same thing at that same moment of comprehension.

There were parts of Sienna Tanovich's body strewn about helter skelter, blood spatter over much of the plastic sheeting and there was a blood-drenched reciprocating saw at the center of it. He spotted a foot then the lower half of a slender thigh with a fragment of blue knit cotton stuck to it by dried blood. The femur was hacked in half and the chopping of the serrated knife-like blade of the recip saw could be seen in the flesh and bone.

Joe tugged at his scar, because it helped him focus his mind until he noticed Bittinger watching closely.

"The boy saw this?" Joe finally said.

"We don't really know what all he saw," Bitt said.

"We gotta destroy this fucking bastard," Enright said.

"M.E. says all the cutting was post mortem," Bittinger said as if it were a smidgeon of solace. "At least she wasn't alive for it. Six-inch knife to the heart first."

"What a nightmare," Joe said as he looked from part to part. It was even worse than his own bad dreams which had begun in childhood. He'd glanced at the blonde hair mottled with blood, but hadn't been able to bring himself to look directly at the head yet. Severed legs and arms, feet and hands. The torso was quartered, with guts streaming out, but still some remnants of blue cotton clung to the quadrants.

"It's like he just cut fast and moved on," Bitt said.

"The electric saw was for efficiency," Joe said. "But it looks like he didn't finish what he had in mind."

Bitt shook his head and gave an approving nod to Enright as if to say, 'Kid's okay.'

"What was the five-gallon bucket for?" Joe asked, pointing at a crescent of dried blood which outlined the bottom rim of a large container, though no bucket was there.

"Don't know," Bittinger said. "He took the bucket and some kind of sizeable power tool, but left body parts everywhere. Can't figure out his thought process."

Joe noticed Enright was studying the plastic sheeting that rose up the back of the potting shed and was doubled under the body parts. Then he squatted to get a look at something outlined in blood. "A wrench?" he asked.

"Yeah, can't figure out what for," Bitt said, "but it doesn't go with the recip saw, that much we know."

It looked as if Joe was about to hurry out of the site, but at the entrance flap he turned back to assess the scene. The greatest concentration of blood spatter was underneath the spotlight at the corner of the potting shed and the strung-up plastic seemed to have caught every single drop. At first her body pieces appeared to be just strewn about with no relationship to each other. Then Joe noticed the smaller parts like the feet were together, the bigger parts like the thighs, both of which had been cut in two, were near each other. He finally dared to look at her head and was forever grateful she was not facing him.

Joe stepped outside and looked up toward the news choppers still hovering. Enright was close on his heels and finally able to walk off his tension. "Stay on the paper, Byron," Bittinger said. There were streams of white butcher paper stretched across the lawn, each marred with bloody footprints.

"Those body parts would each fit in a five-gallon bucket," Joe said as Enright finally quit pacing.

"Yeah, don't know why, but they would," Bitt said.

"I hate this guy," Enright said as Bittinger led them on a tour of what he had tracked in the backyard. They walked on the trampled white paper that had been laid out to preserve the important parts of the scene. He pointed out the killer's footsteps leaving the plastic, the imprint of a large duffle bag in the grass, the impression of a fairly heavy machine indented in the plastic, the footsteps disappearing in the well-tended lawn leading to the forest which grew right to the edge of the massive back yard. No neighboring house could be seen from the back yard.

The crime scene team had been thorough at recreating where the killer had walked and where he'd taken off at least two layers of plastic booties like the ones they all wore. There were no blood droplets more than ten feet from the plastic and those only from whatever the man must have worn. No spatter had flown that far. Bittinger theorized the killer had worn a hazmat suit which went along with the boy's 911 call about the 'man in orange.'

Joe asked if there was a fence around Paramount Hills and learned there was only the forest, nearly a half mile of woods. It was mid-summer and the woodlands would be dense except along the manicured walking paths the Paramount Hills Association maintained for residents. Those paths didn't cut through the county road beyond the woods. The owners didn't make it easy to trespass on their sacred privacy. To get through, someone would have to push through a thicket of summer-growth forest and underbrush and pass dozens of 'No Trespassing' signs. On the manicured paths, there were no identifiable footprints, no blood, no signs of five gallon buckets having been set down. All traces of the killer stopped by the middle of the lawn.

If the killer had driven, Bitt told them, he hadn't parked on Valley Road which had no shoulder. That two-lane county road was the limit of Paramount Hills' property and the killer couldn't have left a car for himself out there, it would have been seen and towed for blocking the lane.

"Are we thinking he did his cutting first and was going to arrange it into a display or something?" Joe asked.

"A serial killer kind of fantasy?" Enright said.

"We're pretty open to theories," Bittinger said as he watched Joe sink inside himself, brooding. Joe knew from too much personal experience that people were capable of doing unspeakable things. Even so, this scene formed a new category all its own. He'd seen horrors inflicted which nearly rivaled this. He'd seen first hand violence of almost comparable brutality. He'd experienced similar sociopathic indifference to others. He'd looked into the eyes of men capable of things just as bad as this. Even so, this was entirely new to him.

He hadn't expected to discover all this violence and evil among the rich. The privileged, he had previously believed, escaped such depravities.

"He didn't intend to leave it this way," Joe said at last and Bittinger shook his head. "He didn't want to leave any blood on the potting shed. He planned to clean everything up, maybe leave no trace at all."

"Agreed," Bittinger said. "What he wanted to do makes no sense to me, but this fucker had a plan," Bittinger said.

"His plan is how we'll catch him," Joe said.

JOE REALIZED he'd already stayed too long and if he got the case, he'd be back before the day was over. Still, he wanted to see where the boy had been when he witnessed all this horror and had called 911. He looked toward the house from the side of the crime scene tent, but it was almost entirely blocked by a magnificent oak tree.

Joe was told the boy had been in the basement with his train set when he called 911. Bitt explained that one little basement window was the only place in the house which overlooked the murder scene and suggested he see the spot for himself. That was when Joe changed his mind. He decided he wanted to see the boy's bedroom instead, telling Enright and Bittinger that if he were brought aboard, it would be to work with Billy. He needed to understand the boy.

Joe failed to mention that he hadn't set foot in a basement of any kind in twenty years.

While Bittinger led Enright downstairs to inspect the basement, Joe was guided toward the front entryway which was built to highlight a crystal chandelier that cost more than most houses. The foyer looked more like a movie set than a home and Joe couldn't imagine actually living in such a house. Real people didn't live this way.

'How completely fucked up must this boy be?' Joe wondered as he climbed the front, arcing stairway. He stepped around crime scene techs taking photos and finger-prints and realized those things weren't going to be decisive in this case. Everything already hung on the boy.

The curved marble stairs, which owed some of their heritage to Scarlett O'Hara, gave way to thick pile carpet in the upstairs hallway. It felt like walking on a cloud, Joe thought, as he looked in on a tech working in Sienna's bedroom. Too big, too nice, too much of everything, yet it had a sense that an actual human being lived in it. The art was tasteful and probably original. The woman's bathrobe, which was draped over the chair at an overstated, crystal-topped vanity, was plain terrycloth. It seemed to go with the cotton knit pajamas the victim had been wearing when she had been butchered. A few hours ago, Sienna Tanovich had pulled something comfortable on to her much-admired body and had gone to sleep in that bed.

He noticed there was no sign of the husband's presence in the room. Separate bedrooms. Her idea? Joe wondered.

He ventured down the hall and discovered the boy's room. Billy Tanovich was his mother's son, there was too much of everything. Until this moment, it had never occurred to Joe that a child's room could have 'areas.' This one had a play area, an art and study area, a sleeping area and a dressing area, with enough room left over to hold a school dance.

The huge bed covered in a train print looked as if it had fitfully been slept in, with the bedding twisted in a knot. While there were framed posters from Minnesota Twins and Timberwolves players, the play area looked as if everything was perfectly placed on display. Toys and a painting easel and sports paraphernalia were all carefully positioned. Almost nothing in the room gave it a personal touch excepts a Twins schedule taped to the wall.

Joe looked out the window and his view of the potting shed was entirely blocked by the dense foliage of the oak.

Finally, on the far side of the bed, Joe found something personal. He guessed it was the boy's secret place. On a piece of cardboard cut from a shipping box was a little model house hand-made with cardboard, popsicle sticks, buttons and white glue. Trees and grass and roofing had been colored in crayon and it had a boy-built look Joe could recognize. It hadn't come from a kit, just found materials. It showed a simple, lopsided house on a scale an actual person could live in.

Joe looked under the king-sized bed where he found more models in a similar vein and a shoebox filled with well-used crayons and other building materials. The boy had a secret life. Billy Tanovich had ignored his expensive playthings and built something of his own. Maybe this rich kid wouldn't be so difficult to relate to after all.

He sat down between the bed and the wall, beside the little model and studied it. He knew a lot about not wanting to be present in one's own house, about needing to find escapes and secrets, about having to take over control of his own life much earlier than most children. He worried that he was reading far too much into the difference between Billy's secrets and the perfection of the untouched parts of the room. But in his gut he knew the boy had sat in this very spot escaping. There was a reason and that could be his entrée to the child's life and to communicating with him.

Joe liked the shoebox. Utility knives and strong scissors, a metal ruler and little clamps, tapes, bottle caps and found objects, bits of stiff colored plastic stripped from long-forgotten toys. The boy inside Joe still liked all these things, it was the kind of stuff no parent provided. Billy Tanovich had gathered it for himself. There was some truth about the boy in that box and under that bed. The rest was for show.

"Joe?" surprised the hell out of him and he rather sheepishly got up from behind the boy's bed to find Enright looking for him. "Find any more bodies?"

ON THE DRIVE BACK, Enright regaled Joe with an account of the boy's train set in the basement, he said his own sons would love it. He talked about where the boy had stood on the back of a couch to peer out the basement window into the back yard and the clarity of his view from there, but he might not have seen every last detail. They would find out tonight when they recreated the scene in the dark and tested the visibility from the basement window.

Bittinger had told Enright no neighbor had heard or seen anything. It was Enright's opinion that rich people never went outside, they paid fortunes for yards they didn't use, for patios they didn't entertain in and vistas they rarely looked at. The seclusion of the killing point had been perfectly chosen for the crime.

Joe listened, but more of his attention was taken with thinking about this boy. So young to have secrets, Joe thought, then reflected on his own early life, secrets had kept him safe. The same for Billy, he decided.

Now the poor kid was going to have people digging into every detail of his world. Billy's life would never go back to the simplicity of hiding his secrets behind his bed.

Joe felt more than a tinge of comfort knowing that his own life had never been subjected to such scrutiny.

4

Joe opened the courtroom door as quietly as he could and tiptoed up the center aisle. Liza was listening intently as Phil Thompkins questioned another character witness while Joe slipped into the chair beside her. Under the watchful eyes of the bored jury, he handed her a note and nodded grimly. It said, 'This has to convince the jury I had to be away working on our case. Nod solemnly. I'll tell all later.' Liza read the note twice, nodded with great earnestness and never quite looked at Joe as she kept her attention apparently directed on the useless witness. It worked, Joe could sense it. They were a team.

Liza had raised no objections while Joe was missing in action since nothing presented had any relevance to the repeated assaults on Lydia by her mother. Joe wanted her to remain in first chair so he had time to think about what he would tell Mike. He could no longer focus on the Church case and was already obsessed with Billy Tanovich and his own desire to be part of the prosecution of his mother's killer.

Before the afternoon was out, the defense rested without

seriously challenging the prosecution case. Judge Swander
gave the order for prosecution and defense summations to
be delivered at ten o'clock the next morning, warned the
jury against discussing the case and dismissed everyone.

At last, Liza thought, she'd have a chance to satisfy her
burning curiosity about Joe and all that was going on. To
her chagrin, Joe jammed his papers into his aged briefcase
and dashed out of the courtroom.

JOE PUSHED through crowds of increasingly impatient
reporters, both inside and in front of the City Hall and
Courthouse Building. Once he got across Wabasha Street he
arrived outside the Ramsay County Government Center
West where the District Attorney offices were. As always, he
did not take the tunnel which connected the two buildings
even when there was heavy traffic or bad weather, for which
St. Paul was justifiably famous. Today, with news crews
crushing the intersection and obstructing his way, he picked
a path unnoticed through the throng.

Once past the press, he used his ID on the stairway security pad and finally dashed up the one flight of stairs to the
eighth floor of RCGC West. He caught his breath as he
emerged into the hallway outside the DA's main offices.

The building had been built into the side of the cliff
where St. Paul stood sentry over the Mississippi River. The
street entrance was on the seventh floor and the basement
emerged on Shepard's Road near the river below. He always
thought the building was like the DA's office itself. It only
presented a couple levels to the public, but it kept going
deeper and deeper into the heart of the city. St. Paul may
have begun simply as a fort guarding the convergence of the
Mississippi and the Minnesota Rivers, but it had grown far

more complicated than that very quickly. The resources of the upper Mississippi had brought power and prosperity. This led to a disproportionate influence, creating layers of intrigue far deeper than the city seemed to present to the world.

The rest of RCGC West was utilitarian, but the eighth floor was wood paneled and its glass doors led to bright offices. Mike Westermann liked things to look good and that extended from his suits and the décor of his offices to the lovely new receptionist. Joe had forgotten her name. At the last second he spotted her brass nameplate. "Hi Christie, Mike wanted to see me as soon as I finished in court."

"I'll let him know you're here, Mr. Brandt."

As he sat on the astonishingly soft leather couch and waited to fight for a place in the prosecution of the case, Joe looked toward the walnut doors to Mike's office. He seemed to recall someone once saying the doorway to hell was the most exquisite place on earth, it had been made as an irresistible enticement.

Joe wasn't so sure. The hell he'd known had a shitty door, one he still had to venture through on a regular basis. There had been only one attractive feature of that hell, it had eventually ended. There remained a few hazy memories, but the torment of his personal hell had ceased.

Billy Tanovich, on the other hand, had a beautiful door to his hell, plus chandeliers and an expansive yard. There would be no way to escape the images in his mind and the nightmares that would plague his existence. Joe knew too much of Billy's future from his own unfortunate past.

BEFORE HE HAD a chance to review his thoughts about the case, the murder scene and the site visit, plus his talks with

Enright and Detective Bittinger, Joe was shown into Mike's office. It was not the meeting he had hoped for. Ronald Sheldon and Bruce Baldamino sat before Mike who was on two cell phones at the same time.

Ronald was Assistant Chief of Prosecution and copied Mike in every way he could. His handkerchief and tie were color-matched and his suit cost more than all the clothes in Joe's closet. To be like Mike he just needed more size, more charm, more brains, more guts and more success. Ronald had steadily risen to his level of incompetence and everyone knew he would never move up. As a result, he was perpetually pissed off. He had identified Joe as a threat and worked to undercut him whenever he could.

Bruce claimed to have prosecuted more murderers than anyone in the office besides Mike and saw major homicides as his domain. Though he might not be an enduring enemy like Ronald, Bruce would not yield a big homicide to an upstart like Joe without a fight, either overt or covert.

Joe didn't have an ally in sight.

When he sat beside the grown-ups with their nice suits and Florsheims, he noticed a grass stain on the knee of his old suit from being tackled on the lawn.

He was relieved when the office door flew open and in sprang Stacy Whitcomb. She was Chief of Prosecution and Joe's immediate boss. She had also apparently been the person to recommend him for the case. In some capacity.

She had played for the other team right out of Harvard Law when she'd moved to the Twin Cities while her husband went to medical school at the U, as everyone in the state called the University of Minnesota. But the moment he was earning enough, Stacy quit working for the defense. She said she was tired of being on the wrong side, but the truth was, she loved winning and most of the clients she'd defended were guilty. Some of them even got convicted.

She slid into a chair, caught her breath and smiled all around the table. "What'd I miss?" she said.

Now that he faced losing the fantasy of having the big case, Joe became nervous because he realized how badly he wanted it. There was something worse about getting close and failing than not being in the running at all.

Joe realized it wasn't the notoriety or career boost this case would bring that was most compelling for him. He had started to believe he truly was the best person in the DA's office to help Billy put his father away forever. Unfortunately, he couldn't present it that way. He couldn't tell them he was a kindred soul, a fellow traveler among the unfortunate sufferers of parental abuse in all its forms. None of his colleagues knew – or would ever know – why he would be able to connect better with the boy than they could.

As they watched Mike finish off a one-handed text on one phone and end the conversation on the other, Joe avoided the frowns from Ronald and the superiority emanating from Bruce.

"Dusan Fucking Tanovich is not going to beat us in an election year," Mike said as he stood up from his desk. They all knew enough not to interfere.

Mike Westermann strode to the corner windows offering a fabled view of the stately, flag-draped Wabasha Bridge which led down to Harriet Island in the middle of the Mississippi River. Not far across the river, a gleaming white private jet took off from the nearby Downtown Airport. Mike had been a middle linebacker for the University of Minnesota Golden Gophers and only a senior year knee injury kept him from playing in the NFL. Tough break for Mike, but tougher break for Minnesota's criminals. Instead of going professional, he went to law school and straight into public life.

Mike had started for the Gophers' defense until two guards, two tackles and a center quintuple-teamed him on a fourth down from the half-yard line. The touchdown was stopped but so was Mike's football career. He was noted for playing defense as if it was offense and always said a smart defender could make the other team change their play at the last second. Every campaign the voters of Ramsay County were reminded how lucky they were this defender decided to put his talents to work for the people.

He had also been noted for putting on a clean uniform at halftime. Nearly all players wore the mud and grass stains of the first half as a badge of honor, but Mike liked to look good. He still did, as evidenced by the hand-sewn suit that somehow brought his huge frame into even greater focus without making him seem monstrous.

Byron Enright slipped in and pulled up a chair behind Stacy. Joe caught a look from him and what he believed was half a smile. He might have an ally in the room.

"Lobby, parking garage and elevator surveillance tapes, the room service waiter and the in-room porn movie all prove Dusan Tanovich never left the hotel during the time his wife was being butchered," Mike announced from the corner windows.

"He really didn't do it?" Ronald marveled.

Mike let the horrible news sink in before asking, "What did you find out, Joe?"

Nothing he had planned to say overcame any of those obstacles. All he could do was use the tactic he'd learned in debate. He laid out the reasoning in order to discover what he really had in mind – and its underlying logic – as it came out. It was a risky strategy with any jury and this group was the toughest jury ever. He was surrounded by nothing but superiors, each with good cause to discount everything he had to say, all with reason to know better than he did.

He began with what he felt would be taken as news – whoever committed the murder had had a plan he had not completed. Joe led them through the sorting by size of the body parts, the potential use of a five-gallon bucket to hold them for some unknown reason, the mysterious wrench and puzzling power tool the killer had chosen to take with him while leaving body parts. He told them of his feeling the killer had expected to leave no trace of a murder having been committed.

Joe discussed the boy's still unexplained presence in the basement at one o'clock in the morning. He told about the boy's room and found himself discussing Billy's detachment from his home and family, his need for a secret place and hidden creations. Halfway through, he realized he could be talking himself right out of a position on the case, but he was now committed. And maybe this was really what he thought. Billy Tanovich had been a lonely, maybe unhappy nine-year-old boy who had not been comforted by his family's wealth. He had tried to escape, had kept his life behind his bed and, perhaps, had kept a secret life in the basement or the air ducts as well. His secrets were clues to his make up.

He wrapped up by urging that the boy be assigned to Katherine Nolan, a psychological therapist for Ramsey County Social Services, telling them he had worked well with her in the past. She was the best the county had and with her help, he'd find a way to work with the boy, delve into those secrets and wrangle a cogent statement out of him.

"Who do you think did it?" Mike asked in the silence that followed Joe's presentation.

"Dusan Tanovich," Joe said instantly.

"Obviously that can't be right," Ronald said. "We have proof he was nowhere near the crime scene."

"The boy did say 'Dad' on the 911," Bruce said.

"We'll have to unravel the alibi" Joe admitted. "We either believe the hotel surveillance tapes or the 911 call."

"That's a pretty big 'we,'" Bruce said, then turned to Mike. "My people tell me Tanovich hired Marty Chesler, so he's going to be as well defended as a virgin in a convent."

"What do you think of the boy? He a good witness for us or is he too much like his daddy?" Mike asked Joe.

"Police haven't let me near him yet..." Joe said.

"And, man, did he try," Enright added with a grin.

"Billy Tanovich comes from all the money in the world, but he wants to make his own things out of cardboard and glue," Joe said. "There's something almost normal about a boy who wants a train set. He's in complete shock at the moment, but I think he can be reached."

Ronald laughed to himself as Joe noticed Stacy hanging up her cell phone. He hadn't seen her make a call.

"Joe's had good luck with kids," she said quietly, then nodded to Mike as she pocketed her phone.

"The boy's been assigned to Katherine Nolan," Mike said.

"This case has me and Bruce written all over it, Mike," Ronald said insistently. "We got people in social service, we got experience and maturity. Let us at this kid and we'll have the killer in stir for the rest of his unnatural life."

"I appreciate your input Ronald, Bruce," Mike said.

Bruce knew that time was up. He stood to go and said, "No one knows your job better than you do, Mike. If you want to switch paddles somewhere downstream, I'll be happy to come aboard and help." Without a glance, Bruce went to the door, leaving Ronald hanging. That man was an anchor he didn't need.

Ronald made an embarrassingly long exit trying to cajole Mike into relenting but the boss's mind was made up. When Ronald left at last, Mike turned to Enright.

"How'd he do at the scene, Byron?" Mike asked.

"His open field running could improve," Enright said, pointing out the grass stain on his suit, "but his inside game is solid and I think he might understand kids."

Mike sat on the front edge of his desk and looked down on Joe like a stern father. "Three things, Joe," Mike said. "I like your theory it was a job left unfinished and the tools he took could open that up for us. I like that you're already trying to think like the witness. Work that out with this Katherine Nolan and we're good as gold."

Mike straightened his already immaculate tie, buttoned his perfect coat and started to head toward the door. "And last thing, Joe. Like everyone else who ever met this woman, I remember Sienna Tanovich. Vividly. This is staying news for a long time, so make us look good."

Mike turned to Stacy as he opened the door, "Give me five minutes, Stacy, then join me over there."

Joe looked from her to Mike and back, then realized he was standing. "Okay, but, that is...who's first chair?"

"You are," Mike said calmly.

5

JOE WATCHED THE DOOR SHUT BEHIND MIKE, THEN LOOKED from Stacy to Enright in utter disbelief.

"I'll be your second," Stacy said as if it were natural for the Chief of Prosecution to be an ADA's second chair. As far as Joe knew, it had never happened before. Half her time was spent administrating and overseeing all prosecutions, half was spent taking the toughest and most important cases.

"Bring in the boy, Joe. Just keep your eye on that prize," she said as she ushered him out the door.

Enright followed them into the elevators, but didn't get off with them on the seventh floor.

Joe was surprised to find the lobby free of journalists and cameras. "There'll be a lot of razzle dazzle, especially with a vulture like Marty Chesler for his defense counsel," Stacy said, "but it will only ever be about the boy. Do that for us, for Mike. Bring in the boy."

Joe nodded as they stepped out of the RCGC West and discovered that the entire media frenzy had moved across the street to the City Hall and Courthouse. Unfortunately, that was exactly where Stacy was leading him.

"Overall strategy, all investigative directions...check with me," Stacy said as they crossed the street, still being ignored by the press. "I'm your second chair but I'm still your boss and I'm in on every decision. Only place you are a hundred percent in the lead on this is Billy Tanovich."

"I can live with that" he said almost to himself.

"You better. Our asses are on the line and I like my ass just the way it is," she said.

He resisted the joke and nodded.

"You do the Church summation tomorrow, then clear the rest of your calendar. This is your only case from now on," Stacy said. "Anything else you got, let Liza take over."

The press blocked their way and Stacy said, "Welcome to the shark tank." She caught the eye of a policeman and he grabbed a couple more uniformed men. Together they pushed through the crowd into the building. Joe was surprised when cameras snapped photos of him and Stacy.

After they were processed through the metal detectors, the journalists were finally behind them and Stacy stopped. She adjusted Joe's tie and eyed his suit with disapproval.

"Where are we going anyway?" Joe asked at last.

"To have our pictures taken several thousand times." She adjusted his rumpled shoulder. "Don't be surprised if the word 'eccentric' is applied to you by the media, Joe."

THE BEAUTIFUL AND ornate City Hall lobby, now restored to its Art Deco splendor, was filled with an overflow of local and national news crews who were all pressing farther into the building, trying to enter a room behind the lobby. The four story Memorial Hall had rising black marble pillars on three sides and the soaring white onyx 'Vision of Peace' sculpture which depicted five tribes of American Indians native to Minnesota on the fourth.

Over the heads of the crowd, they could see Mike speaking as Stacy led the way toward their boss around the crush of press. When they got to him, Mike held a hand up to halt Stacy and Joe while he finished, "Mr. Tanovich is not under indictment, let's keep that clear. Yes, he is of interest to us at the moment, but let us grant him his right to the presumption of innocence until proven guilty."

A reporter shouted out, "When will you indict him?"

"We will indict him only if we become convinced that he killed his wife and can prove it beyond a reasonable doubt."

"Is it true Tanovich chopped her into seventeen pieces?" a reporter shouted.

Mike held up his hands to the crowd, then beckoned Stacy. She pulled Joe onto the wooden platform where Mike stood on the lowest step, then manhandled him until he was one step up from Mike. Even so, the DA still appeared taller, but at least now Joe was visible to all the cameras.

"I would like to introduce our Chief of Prosecution, Stacy Whitcomb, and the young man who will be lead prosecutor for the Ramsay County Attorney's Office, Joseph Brandt." Joe felt he was growing red with embarrassment.

"Have you seen her body? Was it really chopped up in little pieces? Is this a jigsaw murder?" reporters yelled.

Mike raised his commanding hands. "Ladies and Gentlemen, as much as I realize you want sound bites and quick decisions, there is a legal process in this country and I think we are all grateful for that. Joe will lead the investigation for us and we will present his findings to the grand jury if we decide to go for an indictment. Joe?"

Joe hated having it thrown at him, but leaned up to

speak, "I think Mr. Westermann has been very clear. First we investigate, we find evidence, we apply the rule of law, we grant suspects their rights and we do everything in the state's power to stand up for the victim. In due time, we will find the killer, we will indict the killer and we will convict the killer. More than that, we can't say today."

Joe found Mike's hand offered to shake and realized they were having hundreds of photos taken at that moment. He hoped they didn't look like a terrified boy and his dad.

When Mike headed down the steps, it was easy to see his past as a linebacker, the dense crowd parted around him. Joe joined Stacy in the slipstream behind him, all the way out the doors. Before he knew it, he was stuffed into the backseat of a big black SUV where he was joined by Mike, while Stacy took the front passenger seat.

"Fucker's guilty as sin and I wish we could go for the death penalty," Mike said as he slumped into the rear seat. The death penalty had been outlawed in Minnesota in 1911 but Mike's was a common lament in the most despicable cases.

"Stacy lay out the parameters for you, Joe?" Mike said as he plopped down news print-outs: 'Jigsaw Killer' 'Builder's Wife Foreclosed' 'Tanovich Subdivides.'

"I have to bring in the boy," Joe said but was startled by the aggressive throng of journalists outside the car windows as they pulled away.

"These guys are crows," Mike said. "They make a lot of noise, pick over everything you drop and could give a shit whether you win or lose, they get sound bites either way."

"Be kind to the press, Mike," Stacy soothed.

"You're so good with the press, Mike," Joe said.

"Yeah, and who got the best sound bite of the month?" Mike and Stacy exchanged a look and both laughed. "You sounded like Winston Fucking Churchill, 'We will find the killer, we will indict the killer and we will convict the killer.'" Mike nudged Joe. "You're a natural. Tell Mom and Dad to record the news, their boy is gonna be on TV."

THE CAR DROVE around the block simply to deposit Mike and Stacy back across the street at RCGC West unmolested. As they climbed out, Joe sat alone in the back, overwhelmed with racing thoughts. He'd actually gotten the case.

"You gonna ride back there like I'm your chauffeur?" Enright said from behind the wheel. Joe was surprised to see him again so soon and hurried out and back in to the front seat before the car pulled away.

Enright drove past the press unnoticed and then said, "I was so caught up with the train set, it never crossed my mind that it was a sign of being a normal boy to want one."

"It might have been bullshit," Joe said.

"That it might," Enright said, "but it got you the case of your career. So it wasn't the shittiest bullshit."

"You do know how to fill a guy with confidence."

"You ever prosecuted a murder, Kid?" Enright asked.

"One," Joe said. "Guy killed his son in front of a crowded McDonald's."

"So you just babysat a foregone conviction?"

"Yet another reassurance, Byron."

"So I asked a few more people and for whatever reason, they say good things about you," Enright said. "Since we're on this together, we better set some ground rules."

Joe thought about the relationship between experienced sergeants and greenhorn lieutenants and wondered if this was what Enright had in mind. He felt like telling him to fuck off, but he needed all the help he could get. He listened.

"One, I don't like being told to do obvious shit like check bank and phone records. Two, I will not hold back a single thing from you. If you have to lose something for a while in order not to give it to the enemy in discovery, you lose it on your own. That shit don't roll on me."

"We are on the same team, are we not?" Joe asked.

"Three, I interface with the police. They know me, respect me, remember when I was one a them and I'll get ten times more cooperation than anyone else. Anything you want, tell me, I decide if we ask our friends or do it in house."

"I've played sports that have fewer rules than you."

"Okay, I'll throw you a bone, Kid. I want you to call me any time, day or night you have a fucking brilliant idea. I don't have a life aside from turning over rocks to unearth scumbags. I get a hard on for midnight brilliant ideas."

"You really don't have a life?"

"Well, I got a wife and three boys, coach soccer and hand carve duck decoys, but you know what I mean."

"You need help getting a hard on in the middle of the night, that it?" Joe said, then wondered if Enright recognized it as a joke. Maybe he just made an enemy.

"So," Enright finally said, "we clear?"

"No," Joe said. "Haven't told you my rules yet."

Enright scowled and made a big show out of listening.

"One, it's Joe, not Kid, not Boy, not Stretch. Two, I am disgustingly, aggravatingly, compulsively and obsessively honest, so I don't lose anything in discovery and when I win, it's on the merits and quality of my work, our work."

"I believe the aggravating part," Enright said.

"Three, much as I'm disturbed by any connection,

however tangential, to your nocturnal erections, I'll banish that image from mind and call you with my brilliant ideas."

Enright laughed out loud and Joe relaxed just a bit.

THE MIDSUMMER SUN was still high in the sky and there would be a considerable wait until everything was set up to duplicate the conditions Billy Tanovich had witnessed through the basement window. Unfortunately, that left quite a long period in which Joe had to avoid invitations to see the train set, to peer out the window for himself, to do what any other prosecutor would do. Anyone else would go down the stairs and into the basement to see what the witness could see.

The body parts and then eventually the tents would be removed from the crime scene, so he would have been in the way lurking behind the potting shed. So Joe found refuge inside it. Enright was consumed with charming and questioning every tech and cop in sight, so he didn't notice Joe slip away.

Once he was alone, Joe called his girlfriend, Kat. "Hey," he said. There was a woman in his life, despite Byron Enright's opinion, he reminded himself, she'd just never weighed in on his clothes.

"Hey yourself," she said.

"So, you gonna be home before ten tonight?"

"It could be arranged," she teased. "What's up?"

"Can you record the ten o'clock news?" Joe said. "My boss says I'll be on TV. I'd like to see it."

There was a long silence before she asked, "This is a 'good being on TV' or a 'bad being on TV?'"

"If it's on, it's good."

"Champagne good or white wine good?"

"A big kiss good."

"You always get that, good, bad or indifferent."

"That is always good and I'm never indifferent to it."

"Smooth talker."

"Is it working?" he asked.

"I'm trying to think of what to wear to the door."

"If you think of nothing, I'll love it."

"You wish."

"That I do," Joe said. "Listen, Kat, I don't know how late this is going to be. This new case is an awful mess."

"Come over when you can, but come over."

Left to his devices in the potting shed, he decided to inspect. There really was a potting table with hand gardening tools and even a few used pots plants had come in from the nursery. Had Sienna Tanovich come out here to get dirt under her polished fingernails? Joe wondered. Most of the huge 'shed' was actually a tool room and workshop.

There were a few signs of use. Some sawdust was scattered around, there were various pieces of wood and dozens of tools. But it seemed like Billy's toys to Joe, it was a display. Still, it meant Dusan Tanovich knew his way around tools. When he spotted a recip saw among the many power tools it occurred to Joe that nearly everything the killer had brought to the scene had been available right here, just feet from the crime scene.

If he got this to court, Joe knew the defense would point out how absurd it would be for Mr. Tanovich to bring all these tools when he had everything he needed at home. It would be an effective inroad to suggest there was another killer, that Tanovich was innocent, even a victim.

'Could there really be another killer?' Joe wondered.

"You're looking troubled, Counselor," Bittinger said as he peeked in on Joe in the potting shed.

"Wondering if it's possible Tanovich didn't do it."

Bittinger shook his head as they stepped out and watched techs fold up the tents and set numbered markers in place. The markers indicated all the grisly details.

"And forensics?" Joe asked hopefully.

"Not a print or useful fiber anywhere at the scene. Guy probably watched a lot of TV and learned."

"He planned well," Joe lamented.

"The kind of detailed planning that would make a guy capable of building two hundred houses at the same time."

Joe nodded and was relieved to spot a police tech setting up a computer screen near the huge trunk of the oak tree. It already had a live, wireless feed from a camera at the basement window. He'd be able to see what Billy saw and could still avoid the basement.

The day just kept getting better.

ONCE IT WAS DARK ENOUGH, the spotlight at the corner of the potting shed was turned on just as it had been when the police first arrived and saw the murder scene. The recreation of the crime and the moves of the killer to various locations around and behind the potting shed would be carried out by Bittinger who donned a bright orange road crew vest to give some sense of the killer's visibility in the ample light. Enright and Joe stood behind the computer monitor to view every step as it was recorded.

The tech split the screen between the basement camera view and crime scene photos which he could pull up so each step and position could be checked for accuracy.

It quickly became clear the boy could have seen anything which took place under the spot light. It sent a shiver down Joe's spine. The boy may have stood watching, knowing, seeing it all. Billy's place at the window gave him a clear view of the near end of the crime scene, all around where the duffle was presumed to have sat and where the boy said the 'man in orange' had taken off his face shield. It became equally clear, and a source of some solace to Joe and Enright, that the boy could not have seen the place behind the shed where his mother was actually stabbed and where it seemed most of the dismembering took place.

Billy Tanovich would not have to attest to what had been done to his mother, that was documented in horrible detail. He merely needed to place his father there wearing orange and taking off the face shield after the fact.

As LONG As he was with Enright and the techs, with the crime scene itself and Bittinger's accurate re-enactment of the murder and its aftermath, Joe was able to keep one element of those realities at bay. But when Enright dropped him off at the parking ramp where his rusty old Camry had sat all day, Joe was finally alone.

He found he had no way to keep the day's horrors from seeping into him as he sat in his car. He could not escape the flood of thoughts about his own life – whether they were memories, fabrications or nightmares mattered little – and it was half an hour before he could control himself enough to think about driving away. He'd seen blood before, lots of it. He'd seen brutality and watched the aftermath gnaw on frail psyches. Even so, he had damp eyes, realizing this was the first time he'd allowed himself to cry since he was eight. Those few reluctant tears hadn't been for poor Sienna Tanovich, as disturbing as her fate was. They were connected to his own past.

When he wiped his eyes, his hands shook and he realized his heart was thundering. He was in a panic about keeping this case from getting under his skin. But as he tried to get the key in the ignition, he realized it was already too late. The day's abundance of blood had made inroads through his armor and that scared him.

6

AT QUARTER TO ONE, KAT OPENED THE DOOR IN SLIGHTLY more than nothing and a whole lot less than she'd worn all day. "We will find the killer, we will indict the killer and we will convict the killer," she said with drunken enthusiasm. She'd already been toasting him with champagne.

"Guess I was on the news," Joe said as he entered.

Katherine Nolan poured champagne in crystal flutes, then Joe delighted in watching her traipse lightly across her spacious living room, her long dark hair contrasting with her short white nightie. His mind was already heading toward the bedroom to break free of the day of horrors, but first she had the DVR cued exactly right.

They clinked glasses and watched him speak like Winston Fucking Churchill. Kat gave him the big kiss he'd been waiting for and it calmed him more than he could have imagined given the fact he'd spent hours careening between Sienna Tanovich's blood and his own panicky and disturbingly vivid thoughts. With Kat, he believed escape was possible as he led her into the bedroom. Both were exhausted, but neither was willing to forego completing the celebration – naked, in bed, with champagne. Soon after making love, they fell asleep in each other's arms.

WEARING *a Twins baseball cap and grass-stained jersey, Young Joe tiptoed by the closed basement door in his family's shabby little house. He was about seven; skinny body but old and wary eyes. In the kitchen, he set his bat, glove and baseball on the counter, opened the refrigerator quietly and pulled out a pitcher of red Kool-Aid. As he reached for a glass, he saw the baseball rolling as if in slow motion.*

The counter grew taller and the baseball loomed larger as it escaped the glove's webbing. He grabbed desperately for it, but the battered old ball tumbled over the edge and plummeted to the linoleum with an unnaturally loud thump.

It seemed deafening.

He heard the distant squeak of couch springs, but it was drowned out by thundering steps from the basement. Each tread was louder than the last, reverberating around the ramshackle little house. Joe was petrified as the basement door flew open into the narrow hall from the front of the house.

An intensely bright light haloed George Felcher, Joe's father, who loomed in the doorway, filling it. His face was in shadow as his hulking shape stomped into the kitchen.

Joe lurched toward the back door, but George seemed to fly across the kitchen, his face red with rage as his enormous hands grasped the terrified boy.

There was a moment of stillness, of decision, of sheer malevolence – while a rising shriek seemed to fill the room. It was his mother, Aileen, struggling past the basement door. At the same moment George yanked Joe's skinny arm with such ferocious power, there was a horrifying, deafening snap.

Aileen leapt and clawed onto George's back, shrieking and

trying to tear his eyes out like a feral cat. Joe looked down in puzzlement at his hand flopping about backwards, then with growing horror he stared at the upper arm bone jutting right out of his skin.

His blood was pumping over him like jets as a terrified scream at last rose from his mouth.

JOE FOUND himself halfway out of bed, covered in sweat, heart racing and the end of the scream still on his lips. Kat rose beside him, shocked and confused. Before he could fully place himself back in the present and in her bed, she'd turned on the lamp and was staring at him strangely.

"Scared the shit out of me," she finally said, patting the place beside her, urging him back to her comforting arms. She leaned against him and kissed his bare shoulder.

"Yeah, me too. Sorry I woke you," Joe finally said as he willingly let himself be pulled back to her.

"Want to talk about it?" she asked.

He absolutely did not want to talk about it.

"Horrible crime scene today," he finally said, hoping that would assuage her and end the conversation. He wanted her to shut the lamp back off, but she was awake. He had the awful feeling she would insist they talk about it.

"Maybe I should have just thrown up when we were there like everyone else did," he offered.

She nodded and looked into his eyes. Damn that. This was what she did and she was not easy to detach once she'd gotten hold of a thread. Especially one of his threads.

Katherine Nolan was a psychological therapist for Ramsay County and she was working on her PhD at the U. She knew a lot, she felt and sensed a great deal, she was terrific at evaluating both behavior and perception. She helped people in trouble, she listened to them and watched them and tried to get ahead of them inside their own minds so she could guide them. Even so, she didn't know what she thought was going on with Joe. He was a tough case, but she was positive the dream that left them awake wasn't what he said it was. Once again. This was not the first time his nightmares had woken her from a deep sleep.

She clung to his naked body under the sheet and looked up into his eyes. He couldn't see condemnation, but he could tell she was trying to fathom him. That scared him more than if she'd just gotten angry and sent him home.

He tried to reach past her with the arm around her shoulders to turn out the light, but she adamantly wouldn't budge. He looked at his left arm in the air. It had a long, wide scar on his bicep with thick ugly marks from stitches on it. His 'Frankenstein scar' his teammates had called it.

Joe wondered how it really happened. He had so many doubts. Had it been about a dropped baseball? All he knew for certain was that Dad yanked hard, his arm snapped, Ma attacked, he howled. He sat out most of that season of Little League, then quit the next year for reasons that had nothing to do with his broken arm.

"I spent my afternoon and evening at a crime scene wading in blood," he said toward the ceiling.

"Was the nightmare about the crime scene?" she asked with far too much understanding.

"Provoked by the experience, I guess," he said. "Shall we call it a night? Big day tomorrow." He pointed toward the light, but she just sat up in bed, ready to work.

"Okay, I believe that," she said. "Who wouldn't be effected by such a thing? But what was the nightmare?"

"Not the crime scene, okay? Can we go back to sleep?"

"Why's it so hard to tell me? Please don't clam up like you do," she said with real passion. "It's not healthy."

"Told you I was fucked up."

Kat threw back the covers and leaped out of bed naked.

"I spent the day at a gruesome murder scene and I had a nightmare," he said. "Forgive me, but I just don't have the energy to be psychoanalyzed before dawn. Please don't take that as a denigration of what you do."

"I'm much more a behaviorist than a psychoanalyst and you know it, but that's not the point," she said. "Talk to me, don't talk to me, but talk to someone, Joe."

"I'm more of a pragmatist, I guess."

"No you're not, you're an escape artist," she said as she finally reached for her robe draped over a chair.

"Not the dreaded robe," he cried, jokingly.

She tossed the robe down and turned back to him, "If I stand here naked will you talk to me?"

"Interesting therapeutic strategy. You offer this to all your patients?" Joe asked.

"Clients. Will you?"

He shook his head. There was no way what she wanted would come out of his mouth. Not tonight. Not ever.

He watched her pull on the robe and cinch up the tie.

"I love you, Kat."

"I know you do," she said. "I love you too, despite how hard you make it to love you."

"I was thinking about the moving-in thing again."

"You're going to change the subject by sneaking your hand inside my robe and dragging me back to bed, right?"

"If at all possible," he admitted flirtatiously.

"How can a person be absolutely forthright and dishonest at the same time?"

He held out the left arm and its prominent scar. "I had a

nightmare about the bone sticking right through the skin and my hand dangling down backwards, spasming."

"How'd you break it again?"

"Baseball game when I was seven," he said as she nodded doubtfully. "One of those horrifying images planted in your brain. Freaks me out every time."

"I bet sixty percent of that's true."

"My nightmare was about my broken arm," he said. "I don't know if what I remember is a hundred percent true."

"It never is. Memory is subjective," she said.

"Never, ever, say that in court," he said with alarm. "Juries want black and white truth, not shades of gray. Qualifying a statement makes it suspect. A suspect statement can be made to look like a lie by a defense attorney and a lie means reasonable doubt. 'Not guilty.'"

"How can you stand such an imprecise profession?"

"Psychology is a paragon of quantifiable clarity."

"You got me there," she said with a little mischief in her eyes. "You want to entertain my brains out again?"

"See? I don't even have to talk, you read my mind."

"Promise me you'll think about talking to someone?"

"If you promise you'll quit thinking about me talking to someone," he said.

JOE WOKE up early and just watched Kat sleep. Since he could remember, his own sleep had been disturbed, but hers looked so comforting it amazed him. From the moment he first met her, he'd wanted to stay near that calm.

They met when Kat worked a domestic abuse case he was prosecuting. She'd finished her masters in counseling psychology and worked full time in Family Services while she went to the U nearly full time studying for a PhD. The last thing she had time for was a guy. Joe, who only knew how to swim upstream, didn't take 'I'm too busy with my life' to mean 'no.' He took it to mean 'work harder.'

At first she only let him part way into her life. When they started spending the night together, it was at his place. Not much would improve his apartment, but he started to buy wine with corks and invested in new sheets and towels. He thought she worked double time because she needed the money and the county helped pay her tuition. For months, she never invited him to her place. It was becoming an issue and he wondered if she lived with her mother. Or with a husband.

At last it couldn't be put off any longer, it was his birthday and she wanted to cook for him. He wheedled an invitation out of her, then didn't know what to think when he drove up to her building in its brick, nineteen-twenties grandeur. It faced the Mississippi on the very upscale, western-most side of St. Paul. Minneapolis was across the river. She lived on Mississippi River Parkway overlooking the dense forest park that lined both riverbanks. Maybe she worked as the building caretaker, he told himself.

She read his surprise when she opened the door and he got his first look at her truly beautiful apartment. "This is why it took me so long to invite you over, Joe," she said as she dragged him in. "I have some explaining to do."

"Family Services pays really really really well?"

"My dad owns the building."

"So you're like the caretaker for him?"

Shaking her head, she led him through the living room with its coved and carved ceiling, wood floors and fireplace. He glanced past it to the four season sun porch overlooking the river, then into the formal dining room with oak wainscoting. Fine china was laid out for them and the dinner looked gorgeous. Red wine was open and she offered to pour him a glass as he continued to stare around.

"I might need to go straight to bourbon."

"Jack or Jim?"

He looked confused until she gestured at the sidebar where all manner of whiskeys and brandies were lined up with a variety of glasses. She pointed at Jack Daniels and Jim Beam bottles. "Jack," he said. It had never occurred to him to own two bottles of liquor at the same time.

She poured two big ones, led him to the sumptuous couch and forced him to sit. She curled up at the other end to lean against the arm while she explained.

"I've been frightened you'd walk out on me when you saw..." she gestured around her home, then at herself.

"When have I ever given you reason to believe I would reject you for anything short of first degree murder? And then it would depend on who the victim was."

"Everything you ever got in life, you've struggled for."

"And you work at least as hard as I do," he said.

"That first night we spent at your place," she began. "I got so scared that if you came over here, you'd just go 'rich bitch' and not see me for who I try so hard to be."

"That could have happened except for one thing. I was already overwhelmingly in love with you," he said as she grinned. "I am pathologically incapable of rejecting you."

"Careful how you use psychological jargon," she joked.

Soon she gave him a brief tour, he glanced into the second bedroom, which was a lovely, lived-in office for her studies, and then headed for the bedroom where all the furniture matched. Yet another new concept to Joe.

AFTER HIS SHOWER in the morning, he found Kat waiting with a coffee. "I do believe you are perfect," he said.

"It scares me when you say things like that," she said. "Don't idealize me, Joe."

He gulped the coffee and said, "I promised Stacy I'd be in before court. I gotta get on the clock on Tanovich."

"You could get on the Tanovich clock right now."

"How's that?"

"I didn't want to mention it on the phone, but I had my first interview with Billy Tanovich and his aunt yesterday. We need to talk strategies," she said. "He's super closed down, but I don't think it's habit, it's circumstance."

"I've seen the house and his room and I know about the train, he can't be a normal nine-year-old," Joe said.

"I've heard his mother called a trophy wife, but I get the feeling she might have been a damn good mom."

"That's good for us, isn't it?"

"It's good for Billy. That makes it good for us."

"Could the boy talk yet?"

She shook her head sadly.

"How much do you think he knows?" Joe asked.

"His aunt told him his mom is out of town and she thinks he believes it," Kat said, "but until he talks, we don't know."

Joe was surprised when Kat said they didn't have to push Billy too hard or too fast for a statement. She said really big memories were deeply implanted. Encoded, she called it. A memory wasn't like a tape recording, it had to be modified by the person so it made some sense within their own context. "Key elements of what he saw will remain in tact, but he will sort of fictionalize the memory so it makes sense."

"Reasonable doubt will drive through that in a truck."

"It's the same for any witness, any age. What we store in memory combines the real event with our perspective. Memories aren't recorded, we custom-build them."

"I'm never putting you on the witness stand," Joe said.

"Any retrievable memory is ultimately subjective," she insisted. "That doesn't make it any less real."

Kat went on to tell him about encoding, storage and retrieval, the three stages of memory. If something impacts us strongly, we have no choice but to absorb it. Then we're stuck with it and have to keep it in some fashion – part fact, part fiction. The two factors can shift and be skewed by elements of our lives, at least temporarily, but memories that come through despite our best efforts to suppress them, those are unfortunately based on real experience.

'Like my nightmare about Dad and the arm,' Joe thought.

"A child isn't less reliable at this process than an adult," Kat said.

"So there's hope? What strategy did you have in mind?"

"Trust," she said. "That's what we have to build with Billy. If we barge in, either he won't be able to access the stored memory, even though it's still there, or he'll say whatever he thinks will stop the questioning."

"So I have to ask him without asking him?"

"You have to get him to unburden what he's seen when he's ready. You have to wait for him to talk," she said. "You have to build a relationship with him."

"Be like a big brother or something?"

"Be someone he trusts, someone who doesn't pressure him. Patient as a saint."

As he left, he wondered if she was actually describing the relationship between the two of them.

7

JOE MANAGED TO GET IN BEFORE ALMOST EVERYONE ELSE, made a coffee and peeked in on Stacy who was already there.

"I didn't hear you come in," he said, trying to bluff Stacy who was notorious for being first in everyday.

"Good one."

"So, I've done some research on memory retrieval and suggestibility among child witnesses."

"Those are big words for a first cup of coffee."

"Third," he said, being honest. He explained Billy believed his mother was out of town, then described the permanence of memory and its subjectivity, plus the need to take his time, to build trust to get the boy to open up.

"Patience is all well and good, but you still have to do it in a hurry," she said. "Grand jury, indictment, minor details like that. Drag this out and the press will haul you, me and Mike into a shit hole that swallows us whole."

"Patience on a deadline. Great."

"Marty Chesler has already entered a motion to suppress the 911 call," she said, handing him the motion.

"Before an indictment? On what grounds, wrong number?"

"It's a Hail Mary."

"First play of the game, he tries a Hail Mary?"

"He claims Tanovich is a protective father exercising parental rights to safeguard his son," Stacy said. "They want the 911 to be stricken from all records."

"That's like the old line about killing your parents and begging for leniency because you're an orphan."

"If Chesler can suppress the call, the boy loses a lot of value as a witness. That call is a helluva corroboration. Once he's indicted and we assign a guardian for his son, Tanovich loses any chance to suppress. So Chesler has to give it a shot now and he's got nothing to lose by trying."

Joe studied the motion unhappily.

"They're also offering a ten-million-dollar reward for the so-called 'real killer.' Chesler says we are all conspiring. He claims we're not trying to solve the crime, we just want to pin it on the rich guy."

"How many millions is Tanovich worth?"

"It starts with a B."

Joe thought somberly for a long time. "We should check on his contributions to the campaigns of district judges, see if he's built houses for any judges."

"You have a really nasty mind," she said, "I like that."

"Are our accountants as sophisticated as his?"

"Ours get ten cents on the dollar compared to his."

"Doesn't make his guys any smarter," he said.

"Look at us and Marty Chesler," Stacy laughed.

He headed for the door when she called after, "Let's let the police run with all the normal stuff and use Enright for all your cynical thoughts."

"I thought I was first chair."

"Sorry, force of habit. What do you want to do?"

"I think we should let the police run with all the normal stuff and use Enright for all my cynical thoughts."

"Good thinking," she said.

JOE SAT at the old metal desk in his tiny office poring over the motion to disallow the 911 call.

Marty Chesler was near the top of Mike's most hated list. He was known for his line, 'The case has been decided by the time the trial starts.' Everything was preparation, so Chesler's reasoning went. You go into the trial knowing who will win. Maybe he was right or maybe it was a sales pitch to clients who wanted to know everything that could be done, was being done, even if it had to be invented.

One of Joe's aberrant thoughts was discovering he actually felt anxious to meet the legendary Marty Chesler.

Enright stepped into the windowless office and said, "Bitt wonders if he could trade his no-good son for you."

"Like a prisoner-exchange sort of thing?"

"You scored with him, Joe. You gotta learn to accept when you're accepted, know what I mean?"

"Every team I was ever on didn't want me at first."

"Let me take a stab," Enright said looking him over. "You're built pretty solid. High school wrestling, 152-pound class. Got the scar in a match. Am I right?"

"Basketball."

Enright laughed. "C'mon, you can't be serious?"

"I'm taller than Mugsy Bogues," Joe said defensively.

"Who had, what, a forty-two-inch vertical jump?"

"That's Spud Webb," Joe said. "Mugsy Bogues played fourteen seasons in the NBA and he's only five three."

"So how far you get?" Enright asked.

"In high school? All-city. Second team all-state."

Enright slapped the desk and said with a grin, "I just figured out who you are. You're that shrimp kid from East St. Paul. What was it? 'Smallest man, biggest scorer.'"

"Helluva memory there, Byron."

"Didn't you go on to the U?" Joe nodded and Enright went on, "Did okay, if I remember?" Another nod. "Starter?" Joe smiled. "Highest scorer?" Joe grinned. "You gonna make me drag it out of you bit by bit?"

"Yeah." They shared a laugh, then Joe added, "You know how many guys in the NBA are under six foot right now?"

"Like you're even close to six," Enright said. "And don't tell me you went pro...I woulda remembered that."

"Law school seemed to offer more opportunities."

"Why in fuck would a guy your size, no offense, but why would you even think to go into basketball?

"At eight I didn't know I'd be too short for the game."

"Every coach underestimated you?" Enright guessed.

"In the first quarter, so did opposing teams."

"I hope Chesler underestimates you," Enright said.

"Already has," Joe said offering Chesler's motion. "Tanovich protecting his son. Parental rights."

"Won't work."

"Millions of dollars buys a lot of judges," Joe said.

Enright's smile dropped and he studied Joe a long time.

"Why does this make me believe you own a slingshot?"

"County permits will tell us if Tanovich Construction built any houses for judges, what was paid, what the tax records value the house at, all that."

"I actually like my job, Joe."

"Until he's indicted, we can't get Tanovich's parental rights severed. He's 'allowing' the boy to stay with his aunt. If he can use parental rights to squelch the 911, the boy won't be as viable as a witness. Tanovich murders his wife and then goes free to live with the only witness against him. Not much life expectancy for the boy, you think?"

"You want to go after judges right out of the block? Couldn't we start soft and attack drug lords first?"

"We're not going to ask the judges, we're going to check county records without telling our police friends."

Enright nodded unhappily.

"Campaign contributions too. Every dime Tanovich ever gave, at least what can be found," Joe said. "Let's also see if we can find any grounds to restrict Tanovich's ability to keep his son without having to make an indictment. Accidents, broken bones, hospital reports."

"Think Tanovich abuses the boy?"

"Been known to happen," Joe said.

"First time I ever found myself hoping a dad hit his kid," Enright said. "Then we could leave judges alone."

Joe left earlier than he needed for his ten o'clock summation. He had an unpleasant errand and since Liza hadn't stopped into the office to prepare with him, he had to take on the terrifying mission without assistance.

He dragged himself into Macy's menswear department. There were few places on earth Joe felt less at ease. Beyond looking at the price tags, he could make no distinctions in that sea of suits – which was a good one or a bad one. When he spotted a well-dressed clerk heading his way, he beat a hasty retreat. The suit would have to wait for another day.

Outside the courtroom, Joe waited for Liza who arrived looking fantastic. She knew about clothes and how to shop.

"They didn't even give me a chance to pitch you for second chair, Liza," Joe said.

"Yeah," she said and opened the door for him. "Now let's go put Mrs. Church in prison."

As they hurried to their seats, Joe smiled at Lydia and gave a little wave, then nodded to Mrs. Driscoll. Helena Church and Phil Thompkins were already seated as he and Liza sat at the prosecutors' table.

They all stood while the judge took her seat, went through the daily rituals and sooner than Joe expected said, "Mr. Brandt, is the state ready with its closing argument?"

He stood and said, "We are, Your Honor."

Liza whispered to herself, "God, I hope so."

"The real trial begins today," Joe told the jury, much to Liza's surprise and Thompkins' pleasure.

He brought a curled up yellow pad with him, changed his mind, flipped it closed and dropped it on the table before turning to the jury. "You've heard me speak thousands of words since you were sworn in. In that same time, you've heard my esteemed colleague Mr. Thompkins say tens of thousands of words." He got a polite laugh and realized he was essentially promising to keep it short. Not a problem.

Liza paged through the yellow pad to see what Joe had written and found the page empty. Staging.

"The real trial begins today because words have nothing to do with your job. In fact, words make your task more difficult. The defense has worked very hard to make your job more difficult."

Joe felt he'd stepped into a rhythm faster than he usually did and caught quiet approval from Liza. "You need to use your eyes and your head and your heart. Words only get in the way of each of these crucial elements."

Joe gestured into the gallery toward Lydia who wore a light blue dress which already had a drool stain on it. As instructed, Mrs. Driscoll did not hold Lydia's trembling hand as she so often did, today she let it quiver.

"I ask you to look at Lydia Church," Joe said and remained quiet so long Liza thought he was drifting. He was not going to let the jury glance and then focus on safer things, like words. "What you see is solely the result of a mother's brutal assault on her own daughter."

He stepped closer as the jury brought their attention back to him. He directed them toward Mrs. Church, who had not turned around to look at her daughter.

"Justice is in your hands, Ladies and Gentlemen. It's not in my hands or in the judge's or in Mr. Thompkins'. You are here to provide justice for an innocent girl."

JOE WRAPPED UP QUICKLY AND, just as he had predicted, Thompkins used ten times more words than he had. Before the morning was over, Thompkins had also finished, the judge gave instructions to the jury, they were led away and it left Joe and Liza free during the deliberations. They had to remain available for the verdict, so Liza suggested they find a café and clear Joe's calendar. She was anxious to take over their cases. He had another idea.

He raced through downtown toward the Juvenile and Family Services Building and ran up the stairs two at a time. Joe took a deep calming breath and let himself in to the reception area. "Is Ms. Nolan free?" he asked the reception-ist, who smiled broadly at the sight of him.

"She's just finishing up with a client, Mr. Brandt," she said with a smile. He wondered if she knew about them.

When a woman and two children emerged, the recep-tionist nodded and Joe hurried back. "Ms. Nolan, could I have a word with you?" he said quite formally.

Kat was just straightening up the child-size chairs and low table where a number of colorful drawings were laid out. "What can I do for you, Mr. Brandt?" she said just as formally as he closed the door.

"How about a kiss?"

"Do you deserve one, Mr. Brandt?" she asked and he nodded emphatically. "Very well," she said, stepped around her desk and pulled him into an embrace.

"Might I buy you lunch, Ms. Nolan?" he said. "We're awaiting verdict and we need to make a stop on the way."

She grabbed her purse. "What's the stop?"

The same clerk was working in Macy's menswear and instantly recognized Joe. He hurried over, looked hopefully at Kat as he said, "You brought reinforcements?"

"Rescue squad." He hoped they would leave him out of it and make all the decisions. He needn't have worried, they both knew enough not to trust him. Joe's only decision was to agree not to look at prices. He just hoped he had enough credit to cover their plans for him.

He dutifully allowed himself to be measured and have colors held against him. He obediently modeled and didn't even protest when four ties with something called 'tonal resonance' were selected. Kat secretly paid for expedited alterations – it was amazing what a tailor could accomplish in an hour when sufficiently motivated. Soon Joe was back in his old suit as Kat led him to lunch with a grin.

"This marks a new step in our relationship," she said.

"Spending my money?"

"Buying your clothes," she said, kissing his cheek. "It's a well-known fact that buying clothes together is a demarcation line as important as our first shower together."

"*Cosmo*?"

"*Sex in the City*."

"At least a trustworthy authority then," he said. "Is the

first shower together after first buying clothes together another important stage?"

"I hope so," she said with a smile that made him melt.

He knew he was in love and took that as proof of his wisdom and insight. He believed her when she said she was also in love – which made him question her judgment.

HE WAS ALREADY on his way back to court when the call came. A verdict in just under three hours. But when he walked toward Liza in the hallway, she looked right past him. She had no idea who the smiling young man was until he stopped and modeled for her. New suit, new shirt, new tie, new socks, new shoes. New Joe.

"Is *Queer Eye for the Straight Guy* shooting in town?"

"My body is a venue for others to express themselves."

"Well, keep it that way from now on," Liza said.

The bailiff told them Mr. Thompkins was en route, then he spotted Enright approaching and grinning.

"You did not choose that suit," Enright said. "How smart of you." Enright glanced at his feet. "No tassels?"

"Disallowed," Joe admitted.

"She cute?"

"Did you come here to critique my wardrobe?"

"If I'd known, hell ya," Enright said. "Coroner says there was enough sleeping agent in Sienna that she would have been sound asleep when she was carried to the potting shed."

"Proves he could also have carried her through the woods then, doesn't it?" Joe said. "Didn't need to chop her up."

"Proves there no struggle, no reason to have a broken lamp in the house or any kind of mess. Still, down the stairs with an unconscious woman is a lot easier than half a mile with dead weight. Especially at his age."

"Chesler will make a lot out of his age on this issue."

"That fucker could carry me down the stairs and I lost my girlish figure a couple years back."

"No doubt it was quite girlish."

"Envy of the sorority. So what are we thinking?"

"Sleeping pills? Daily or intermittent?"

"I'll check. Prescription for sure."

"If Tanovich knew she took them daily, that would be helpful," Joe said as he noticed the bailiff step out and indicate five minutes.

JOE ACCEPTED PHIL THOMPKINS' reluctant handshake as Helena Church was led away in handcuffs. It felt good. Really good. As Thompkins hurried away, Lydia came up to Joe with Mrs. Driscoll. He knelt to accept and return Lydia's hug and Liza knew she was going to cry. Maybe it was because justice actually prevailed and a jury rose up and did the right thing, but just as likely it was thinking about the future the poor girl faced. No father, jailed mother, assets to hire caretakers and therapists, but there was so little that would ever be put right for her.

When Joe stood up, his eyes looked damp. Wuss, Liza thought. "Ain't we a pair," she said.

"Maybe Stacy will relent. I need you in second chair."

"Hold on one goddamn minute there, Stretch," Liza said. "She promised me first chair on our remaining cases."

As he headed to his office, Joe turned his phone on and the display read, "Ma."

8

JOE HURRIED OUT OF RCGC WEST, TRYING TO ESCAPE BEFORE anyone saw him, but he failed. Enright insisted on joining him in the elevator on the way up to street level. As they rode, his face lit up. "I saw you play basketball," he said.

"I've been feeling a bit Googled all day," Joe said.

"That tingly feeling up the spine?" Enright laughed. "My nephew was a power forward for Mounds View."

"What'd I score? We played Mounds View every season."

Enright pulled some print-outs from his jacket pocket, "Nineteen. Five for five from the line, two for three at three pointers and four for four two pointers. Six rebounds, Joe. Six fucking rebounds. My nephew's six-four, scored twelve, only got three rebounds."

"I submarined," Joe said. "I lived below all the elbows. If the ball got down to waist level, I owned it."

"This gonna help us beat Tanovich?" Enright asked.

"If his team shoots as well as I do and they're six-four, I'm fucked, but when they miss and the ball gets low, I'm on top of it. Once I get the ball, I don't miss."

"This isn't high school anymore, Joe," Enright said as

they faced the thinning crowd of press hovering near the lobby. "Everyone's six-ten and a good shot."

"I should have asked for lifts in the new shoes."

Enright looked him over and said, "If she looks as good as the suit, you're a lucky sumbitch. Fuck the height."

They shook hands and Joe hurried down the block toward the parking ramp where his old Camry was parked.

As HE DROVE toward the grocery store, Joe pondered the two different food shopping routines he had – his own and his mother's. In this store he was known as the white bread, bologna, macaroni and cheese guy and the clerks thought he ate only preservative-rich foods. He had tried to change the routine for his mother, but there was no end to the suffering that caused.

He picked out the standard set of Kool-Aid packets and reverted to auto-pilot. He drove through the old neighborhood without looking at it and transformed himself into the son that only she would see. Like so many things with his mother, he had not been allowed to change in her eyes. The food in the grocery bags was just one manifestation. In his part of East St. Paul, time had stopped and his mother had not moved forward for so long, he'd given up hope there would be any improvement. She'd had one major leap toward a better life – when his dad ran out – and that would have to be enough.

The new suit was hung in the back of Joe's car in the zippered bag it had come in. He wore a polo shirt and khakis so she would recognize him. When he grabbed the groceries and turned to face his mother's house he saw the bars on the windows, a chain link fence that he was still paying off around the yellowish yard and, as always, no sign of life coming from inside. It was a one-story dump with fresh paint he'd put on a few summers ago when he started getting regular paychecks. He'd planned to get to the roof this summer, but now with the Tanovich case, that seemed doubtful.

He let himself in the gate, then walked around the side. The driveway was paved, but had long ago cracked. He had painted a free throw line and an arcing three-point line right over the fissures and had learned to dribble on an untrustworthy surface. The focus of all the lines was the only visible luxury, a relatively new basket and backboard bolted to the decrepit garage. As always, he approached the house through the back door into the kitchen.

As he was unlocking the door, he paused for a moment in surprise. The sturdy, extruded metal grating on the window in the kitchen door was badly bent. That was new and she certainly couldn't have done it. He so wished he could get her out of the neighborhood. 'But don't even start,' he told himself. Neither of them needed that futile distress.

He flipped on the light. "Ma, I got some groceries," he called out to the dark house. He heard shuffling from the living room as he started putting things away. He'd painted the kitchen back in college and the dishes in the rack had been a gift, Christmas before last. All the rest was the same. The same Formica table, the same chairs were in the same place, the same linoleum. His whole past, unchanged.

"How was school, Joey?" Aileen asked as she approached. She wore a shapeless housedress and walked with a permanent stoop. She had long ago resigned herself to yet another blow. Always.

"Work was good, Ma," he said as he kissed her on the cheek. There was a spark of light in her eyes as Aileen watched Joe unpack the food. But there was so much age and exhaustion in her, few people would believe she was just barely over fifty. She looked and felt decades older.

"I woulda made mac and cheese but we were out."

"Sorry about that," Joe said as he handed her a box from the bag. "Wanna get the bills as soon as that's on, Ma? It's end of the month."

"Already?" she said as she put a pan of water on high.

Aileen hummed to herself as she made what she believed was Joe's favorite dinner – mac and cheese with red Kool-Aid. It had been his favorite when he was eight. She granted him a cookie as he wrote checks from his account for her bills. Paying his own expenses plus hers didn't leave much for updating his car or buying new suits, even if he'd been inclined to do either.

She loved watching him eat, so he couldn't fake it, he had to chow down on the mac and cheese. The world was in perfect order in her mind. Joe had his homework, just the two of them lived in the house and he was eating a big dinner before going outside to shoot baskets. Life was good for her and he did what he could to keep it that way, even if it meant allowing her to maintain time warp delusions. There were times she knew he was adult, even that he was a lawyer, but those times just kept getting rarer.

While she did the dishes, he finished the bills, but the stack seemed too small. "This everything? Feels like something's missing," Joe said as he put stamps on the ones he'd finished. She went to the other room, passing the door to the basement which had a huge hasp and padlock on it. The door from the nightmare last night. Even now, so many years later, Joe didn't glance at the door. Looking at it always sent a shiver down his spine.

She returned with two more bills. Joe noticed

"URGENT" on one. "What's this?" he said as he tore open the envelope.

"They're trying to sell us something," she said. "We don't need anything new."

Joe scanned the official letter with rising alarm. "They could take the house away, Ma," Joe said.

"Of course they can't. Don't be silly, it's ours."

"The city can take property if it's put to public use."

Joe read through the letter with even more urgency. It was a notice of eminent domain proceedings against the house by the City of St. Paul. It said the city was building a community center which would take up two city blocks.

"Have you gotten any of these before, Ma?" Joe asked. "It says many notices have been sent."

"I throw out the advertisements. We don't need anything new," Aileen said. "Just throw it out."

"Eminent domain is a long and drawn-out legal process but this says it's been going on for months. Since last year, actually. Why didn't you show these to me sooner?"

"Throw them away and they quit sending them."

"No, you throw them away and they tear our house down."

"They can't do that, Joey," she said, now distressed. "I have to stay here. You know that."

"Have the neighbors been getting these too?"

"I don't know so many anymore. The Murchisons moved and the Acuffs..." she trailed off, absentmindedly.

"The Acuffs both died years ago, Ma," he said. Aileen had worked for their neighbors' medical billing operation, addressing and stuffing envelopes at this same Formica table. When he was a boy, he'd helped until the Acuffs got ill. After his mother couldn't work from home any longer, he'd gotten a job and taken over the monthly bills. Fortunately, the house she'd inherited was paid off and he'd always thought she would never move. But now, eminent domain?

Knowing there was no more he would get from her, Joe pocketed the letter and the bills. "I'll take care of it."

"'Course you will, Joey," she said with pride.

'Why shouldn't she believe it,' Joe asked himself. He had always taken care of things. Everything. Notes to teachers, his own doctor appointments, the special assessment when the tree in the boulevard had to come down. He'd forged her signature more than she'd signed it herself.

"I have a headache, Joey," Aileen said as she surveyed the clean kitchen. "Would you fix it for me?"

He kissed her on the cheek. "Glad to."

He watched her move through the little hall to the living room. As she passed the secured door to the basement she put a hand on it as if to confirm it was closed. She did this every time she passed the door. He listened until he heard the couch creak from her laying down, then let himself out, locked up, dropped the envelopes in the car and grabbed one of the basketballs from his trunk.

When he was eight, he and Mr. Acuff had installed a used basket he'd bought at a yard sale. She'd watched in terror from the kitchen as he'd climbed the ladder, but he was outdoors and there was nothing she could do but worry. She always worried except when she heard that sound.

Joe dribbled the basketball making the sound that fixed her headaches and reminded her why she was still alive.

He drove in for a lay up, fielded the ball, then did a high arching fade away jumper and swish. Then swish, another and another. He was comforted by the fact that his mother could hear her favorite sounds in the world.

As always, when he played basketball, two things

happened: Joe made nearly every shot and he found himself feeling happy. But his contentment only lasted until he took the ball back to the car. As he drove away, he took a good long look and noticed how many boarded up homes there were.

He should have seen the eminent domain coming.

BACK IN THE OFFICE, as others left for the day, Joe had law books open and was anxiously looking for precedents. None of it had to do with suppressing 911 calls to protect children. He felt guilty, but right now he had an urgent problem. He had to find a quick and permanent way to keep his mother in that house because there was no alternative for her. Unfortunately, he found nothing that limited the city's power to take over land for public use. A community center was unambiguously public use.

"Tanovich built a lot of houses," Enright announced as he strode in and plopped into the worn old chair.

"Any for judges?"

"Juries still out," Enright said as he shifted around uneasily. It was clear he was harboring bad news. "Transcript of the 911 call? Not so clear as we'd like."

"What do you mean? I read it," Joe said with alarm.

"Yeah, but our guys have been enhancing the hell out of the actual recording," Enright said. "The boy is whispering half the time, right? Toward the end, right when he says the man in orange comes back, the whisper goes even softer."

"I don't like where this is going."

"In the transcript it was written out as: 'it's Dad.'"

"Tell me that's what he said."

"That's what the 911 operator heard, that's what the transcript says. That's what I'm 99.9 percent sure he said, but...the tech guys can't make it sound like a clear and explicit 'Dad.' It was such a nervous whisper, muffled."

"It's strong enough that Marty Chesler wants to squelch the tape."

"He doesn't want the jury to hear the tape and decide for themselves if the boy is saying 'It's Dad'," Enright said.

Joe saw his case going south even if he managed to keep the one certain thing he had, the 911 call.

"Their tech whizzes and our tech whizzes will have opposite takes on what he says and the decision will end up going to the jury. That leaves them vulnerable. If they get the 911 call disallowed, it's off their plate," Enright said.

"First, try to suppress it completely. Second, make it sound like something it isn't." He understood Chesler's tactics. "But what the hell else could the boy have said?"

"'It's bad.'"

"You're telling me."

"That's what they'll say he said when he said 'Dad.'" Enright said. "Where's it leave us, counselor?"

"Urgently needing a statement from a boy who hasn't said one word since that night."

"You studied about this in law school, right?" Enright said, tapping the books. "Might want to reread that part."

AT A LOSS for how to resurrect the case he was losing just a day after getting it, Joe left shortly after Enright and went to the Project Management offices in City Hall. He'd never actually been there before, prosecutions and city building projects rarely crossed paths. He was shown in to see the project manager of the East St. Paul Community Center Project, Chip Bateman. He was a man after Joe's own tastes. He wore no suit or tie, just comfortable shoes, blue jeans and a polo shirt.

"What's the District Attorney's interest in our project?" Chip asked as they shook hands and exchanged cards.

"More of a personal issue, actually."

Chip showed Joe toward a large table and elaborate scale model. "That Forrestal and East Ninth?" Joe asked.

"You know your city," Chip said, looking strangely at him, then suddenly smiling. "You were on TV last night, weren't you?" Joe nodded. "Did he do it? He really did that to his wife with his kid at home?"

After no response, Chip's cheerful smile slowly returned and they looked at the model together. It showed a large community center building, a baseball diamond that doubled as a soccer field, tennis and basketball courts that doubled as skating and hockey rinks in winter and a sports and recreation building between the fields and courts. It took up two adjacent city blocks. No houses remained.

"Helluva project you got here, Chip. Fully funded?"

"Stimulus money, yeah," Chip said with pride. "About time that neighborhood got something to reverse the downward direction. You know the area?"

"Grew up there," Joe said, running his finger along the street labeled Forrestal as if measuring in from the corner. He touched a basketball court in the model and laughed to himself. "Don't think I'll recognize it after this."

"Good memories there?"

"What? No," he said. "So it's fully funded, it's a done deal? There's no stopping this project now?"

"Soon's all the residents are out, dozers come in and we build the future of East St. Paul. Want a front row seat?"

"I think I've got one," Joe said as he pointed to the basketball court. "My mother lives there."

"Mrs. Felcher? Man, am I glad to see you," Chip said excitedly. "We've been having a helluva time with her. Sorry, I mean, the city okayed all the buy-outs, the money is set, but we need a response. We've sent out people, police, registered letters and...well here you are at last."

"The thing is," Joe said. "My mother is agoraphobic."

"Can't go outside? Then how come she's never home when people knock? I've knocked on that door myself."

"She hides."

"She won't be able to hide from this project, Joe. It's going to happen," Chip said definitively. "She's going to have to leave that house."

"So it would seem," Joe said. "Any further notices you need to send her, could you cc me?" he said.

"You can take that to the bank, Joe," Chip said.

As soon as he was back in the hallway, Joe said, "Fuck!" loud enough to get a few nasty looks. But he ignored them as he drifted into an unwanted memory.

AILEEN, *with the greenish tinges of serious bruising lingering on her face, held the kitchen door open for young Joe. He was eight and it was first day of the school year.*

Heading down the cracked back stairs, he tripped and went flying. Aileen screamed and wanted to grab for him, but was unable to move. He got up and smiled back to her. "I'm okay, Ma," young Joe said. His upper lip was raw and still swollen from a recent wound that left his noticeable scar.

She never stepped outside as she watched him walk off.

9

KAT HAD CLASS UNTIL LATE IN THE EVENING, SO JOE WAS LEFT on his own to brood. He did that better alone anyway.

At the same time as he wallowed in the impossibility of getting his mother to budge, he desperately wanted Kat's help to figure out how to get a statement from Billy that completed the 911 call. He needed the boy to put his father at home murdering his mother without ambiguity.

The 911 call was the only thing that put Tanovich there committing the crime; everything else argued against that. What the boy had said on the call was the truth, Joe was certain. But Billy would have to start talking again, then he'd have to want to speak about his traumas and then he'd have to make a cogent statement, forcefully. Because a child was never considered a trustworthy witness, no matter what Kat said, he would be grilled repeatedly.

In the hands of Marty Chesler, the apparent uncertainty of the last word in the boy's 911 call would leave even his clear description of the events and his placement as an eyewitness subject to interpretation. Joe desperately needed Billy to say, 'Dad was there, Dad did it, I saw my dad.'

'Encoding,' Joe thought. Kat had said the essence of a memory was true, so there were horrific memories in Billy's mind. But could he be compelled to retrieve them? Joe knew he had no control over when his own memories and nightmares attacked him. All he knew for certain was that Billy was now in for a lifetime of unwanted and unbidden memories confronting him on their own schedule.

Kat had said Joe could get the statement only when Billy was ready to talk. If Joe was an example of the boy's future, that statement would never come. Joe had never chosen to unburden himself and, despite being haunted by unwelcome thoughts, he would never express them aloud.

Joe tried to return to Billy's plight, but serious work on the Tanovich case did not seem to be in the cards. His cell phone rang and the display read 'Ma.'

"You have to come home, Joey," Aileen said with great anxiety in her voice.

"It's nearly midnight, Ma," he said. "I'll come over after work tomorrow. No, wait, I have basketball practice tomorrow night. I'll come over right after practice."

"But Louie's been here again."

"Uncle Louie is in prison, Ma."

"He was just here."

"He's in Stillwater Prison. We're both safe, Ma."

"I coulda sworn it was Louie."

"I know. I'm sure it felt very real, but we're safe," Joe said. "It's not Louie."

ON HIS WAY in to the office in the morning, Joe bumped into Enright who said, "Damn you for being right."

"Tanovich?" Joe asked.

"That fuck built a house for a judge," Enright said.

"Bargain basement price?"

"What do I know about home construction? Looks like maybe another zero would have been in order."

"Which means I could lose the biggest case of my career in less than three days," Joe said. "Which judge?"

"Collier."

They peeked in Stacy's door and she beckoned them. "We have to argue Tanovich's assertion of parental rights over the boy's 911 call at four this afternoon," she said.

Joe and Enright exchanged a look. "Judge Collier?"

"Do not fucking tell me," Mike shouted across his desk at Stacy, Joe and Enright standing there in shame-faced silence. "I'm not going to impugn a judge. It's a fucking election year, Collier's been around longer than the courthouse building and his calcified body will still be at the bench when all four of us are in the ground."

"They suppress the 911 recording and our only eye witness is half useless," Stacy said.

"Byron, tell me we got Tanovich by the short hairs."

"Sorry Mike. This guy did his homework."

Mike stared out the window. "Gotta find another way around it. It's a crazy-ass petition anyway," he said.

"We could argue it's prior restraint," Joe suggested.

"A 911 call isn't free speech," Stacy said.

"And the kid isn't a publisher," Mike added.

"At least it wasn't released to the press," Stacy said.

"Damn well better not be or heads will roll," Mike said, then stared at them. "Or..." Mike let it hang.

"Ask forgiveness after the fact rather than permission ahead of time?" Stacy asked. "The teenager's mantra."

"It isn't a definitive statement anyway, with the 'Dad' muffled like that," Enright suggested.

"But it firmly establishes the boy as a witness which

forensics will back up and we can argue he says 'Dad' and leave it to the jury to decide," Joe said. "Without the recording, we got days of the boy on the stand and a hundred times the likelihood he'll crumble."

"So if it was accidentally leaked..." Enright started but stopped in mid-sentence when Mike shot him a nasty look.

They all looked uneasily to the others as Mike shook his head. He had implied a pre-emptive release of the tape which would make Tanovich's suppression plea moot. It was a dicey and illegal end-run and they all knew it.

Mike stood up to railroad them out and said, "You gotta find another way, because I am not punching a judge in the nose or lying that we didn't know about a leak."

"I got my first meeting with the boy at two," Joe said.

"Get a statement of him saying 'Dad' and we nail this."

"At the first meeting?"

"Wow me," Mike said and pushed them out the door.

On the way to the elevator, Stacy said, "Written directive from Family Services. Your meetings with the boy must be supervised by parent, guardian or representative."

"Tanovich is going to be there?" Joe asked with alarm.

"No, he wouldn't dare. The kid might point his finger on the spot," Stacy said. "But you're going to be watched."

"So I have to be patient, in a hurry, while watched and get a clear statement from a severely traumatized nine-year-old?"

"About it," Stacy said and stepped into her office.

ENRIGHT ACCOMPANIED Joe down to his small office. "Tanovich gave Mike's campaign a thousand bucks," he said. "Safety measure. Gave his last opponent a lot more through all the different entities he owns."

"So he's on the books as a backer no matter who wins?"

"Rich fucks are that way," Enright said. "But...look, Joe. Me and Mike and Stacy all like our jobs, so we aren't thinking of going on the attack. You look ready to punch noses. You independently wealthy?"

Joe laughed unhappily, shaking his head.

"Every case has a day you want to slit your wrists."

"Usually not in the first week."

"No," Enright conceded. "So you got any other perverted ideas? I got accounting geeks treasure hunting."

"Can we find out why he didn't have a pre-nup with Sienna?"

"I can tell you what I read in the papers back when," Enright said. "He wanted her to sign a pre-nup, but instead she just broke it off with him and started dating some guy on the Twins. That drove Tanovich absolutely crazy, losing out to some bum All-Pro ballplayer he could have bought and sold ten times over, so he finally came around panting like a dog. She took him back on one condition. Not sure if that's accurate, but I bought it at the time."

"You read gossip columns?"

"If it's got dirt on people, I read it, Joe. My job."

Joe smiled. "A liberal interpretation of your job," he said. "Let's corroborate. No pre-nup is a great motive."

"Got it. Anything else?"

"A plan this good, seems like a guy who builds houses for a living would have had someone to help him."

"Tanovich doesn't build houses, Joe. He kills other companies, he destroys the competition. He forces union guys onto their knees, he reams suppliers for fun, he bombs his way into hostile takeovers and he chops up the city's few remaining wildlife preserves to put up shitty houses."

"Sounds like a guy who would do his own killing too."

"Fucker built my house and it's falling apart," Enright said. "Golden Woods. Wife, kids, soccer field over the next block. It looked nice the day we moved in. Not no more."

"You suppose the same will happen to Judge Collier?"

"Somehow I think Tanovich wanted him in his pocket a lot longer than he cared if I was a happy customer."

"And Sienna, supposed bimbo and presumed trophy wife, outsmarted this captain of industry on the pre-nup?"

"Gotta love it, don'tcha?"

"She must have had some real balls. Playing that level of hardball with a guy like that," Joe said. "Turning down a billionaire rather than sign a pre-nup."

"Yeah, threw him over for a millionaire who was younger, better hung, better looking and didn't have a grown kid older than her. Life's full of tough choices."

"I wouldn't trade with her today."

"Good point," Enright said. "So I been working on how he could get from a hotel downtown to his house with his car overnight in the hotel parking ramp. Checked taxis, no dice. All the cars he owns are accounted for. Like I said, he had a good plan. Only loose end was the boy."

"Smart plan like that, you wouldn't think he'd leave the boy in the house at all that night."

"We've had no way of finding out about the boy."

"I guess that's my job. Any luck accessing his medical yet? Tanovich must have had something in place to make sure the boy slept through the whole thing. Drugged him maybe."

"Nobody thought to take a blood sample of the kid that night. Too late now," Enright said.

As Enright left the office, the receptionist came in with a thick packet. "This was hand delivered," she said.

The return address was Chip Bateman and it was legal

papers, the whole history of his mother ignoring eminent domain notices. Joe didn't need the distraction, the hole he was in on Tanovich just kept getting deeper.

KAT WAS SURPRISED to see him in the new suit until he explained he was meeting a judge later. When she ushered him into her office, the first thing he saw was a dour man in a charcoal suit watching them. He didn't bother to stand, extend a hand or even nod. Kat, usually the very essence of hospitality, didn't even acknowledge him as she gave Joe the papers which required the man's presence. Chesler's man was named Bayona the papers said.

Nicola Patterson was the sister of the victim, Sienna Tanovich. The lovely sister of a lovely woman, she was the screaming woman he'd seen at Paramount Hills. Several years younger than her sister, Nicola was just as curvaceous and naturally beautiful.

"Mrs. Patterson, this is Joseph Brandt, head of the District Attorney's legal team on your sister's case."

Nicola Patterson offered a hand hesitantly.

"Mrs. Patterson is taking care of Billy," Kat said.

"There are more people on the case, aren't there?" Nicola said, scrutinizing him doubtfully.

"I'm what is called first chair, meaning I lead the investigation and eventual prosecution for the District Attorney's office. Many others in our office are involved, along with the police. The full power of the District Attorney is behind the effort to find and convict the..." Joe stopped when he spotted Billy Tanovich at the kid's table.

"I saw you say that on television," she said. "Finding isn't the problem. Convicting him will be a whole different ball game," she said with a hateful rasp in her throat.

Joe could see Nicola hated Tanovich and had no shred of a doubt about his guilt, alibi or not. He wondered if that feeling predated the murder and knew he had to interview her alone, without the boy or Chesler's monitor around.

"Aren't there more, sorry to offend, let's say 'senior' people at the DA's office?" Nicola asked.

"You're right, Mrs. Patterson. Much of the office is more senior. My second chair, the woman with whom I will partner throughout the process, is Chief Prosecutor."

"Then why isn't she heading this investigation?"

In the best of times it was hard for him to toot his own horn, today it felt impossible, but Kat had no trouble.

"This case hinges on eyewitness testimony," Kat said looking at Billy who sat at the table drawing, apparently not listening. "Not every prosecutor is great with children. Most are not very good with kids at all in fact. Mr. Brandt has had quite a bit of success with children."

"These would be," Nicola said, "abused children?"

"For the most part, yes. Children are most often witnesses to crimes committed against them. Child witnesses to other crimes are more of a rarity, Mrs. Patterson."

"So you're sort of a specialist, then?" Nicola asked.

"You could say that, yes," Joe said.

"He convicted Helena Church yesterday," Kat added.

"That was you? Good," Nicola said, then turned to Kat. "You believe in him? Sorry to talk in front of you, but my job, as I see it, Mr. Brandt, is to look out for my sister."

"Mr. Brandt is the very best we have," Kat said. "The District Attorney hand picked him with good reason."

"My job, my first and perhaps most important job is to build rapport with your nephew, Mrs. Patterson."

"Then you better call me Nicola and let's get started,"

she said at last as she led him over to the small table. While she introduced Billy, Joe caught a smile from Kat.

Joe asked Billy if he could sit with him and the boy nodded, still maintaining his silence. Joe scrunched down onto one of the little chairs, his back to Bayona. He had his knees to his chin, his shins to the table, an aunt looking over one shoulder, a so-called supervisor looking over the other, his girl friend hovering nearby and a boy who could not make eye contact, much less speak.

Joe drew a picture in parallel play with Billy. He was a handsome boy with a thick swatch of hair that had been tamed into submission. Thin, as kids that age can be, and dressed in very expensive, designer clothes.

They sat drawing, faced off against each other when Kat realized Joe's discomfort. "Nicola, let's get a coffee."

Nicola hesitated but had already grown to trust Kat and followed her away, leaving just the three of them.

"Play any sports, Billy?" Joe asked.

Billy halfway looked up, then guardedly nodded.

"What? Let me guess, tennis?"

Billy nodded again.

After more questions, some shakes and some nods, it felt like an interrogation, so he changed modes. He talked about himself, how he played baseball but switched to basketball and how his favorite shot was the fade away jump shot.

Billy looked up and studied Joe for the first time. As he went back to drawing, he muttered, "You're not very tall."

"Don't I know it," Joe said, realizing Billy had spoken.

This was a huge move in the right direction, but he decided not to press his luck. Instead, he talked about the Timberwolves players in Billy's posters, about how many hours they must have shot baskets to become that good.

Finally, he hit on an idea, "Would you like to learn to shoot baskets? I'm a pretty good coach."

"Basket's too high," Billy said without looking up.

"They make adjustable baskets for guys like us."

Billy shrugged in a way Joe took to mean 'maybe.'

"How about if I ask your aunt if it's okay?"

Billy shrugged, but then more or less half nodded yes.

By the time Kat and Nicola returned, Joe had traded his drawing of a pirate ship for Billy's blue cubist roses.

Kat had worked on Nicola while they were out not getting coffee. Clearly Nicola had cried, but they'd dealt with the importance of Joe building rapport with Billy. So when Joe asked if it would be all right if Billy came and shot a few baskets with him this evening, Nicola was more than happy to accommodate.

Joe decided not to tell the aunt that Billy had actually spoken. He didn't want to build any resentments.

Bayona was not consulted, but was given the time and place of their basketball meeting. Billy was asked to wear sneakers and Nicola was thanked for being so open.

"Anything that helps put 'you know who you know where' is more than alright with me," Nicola said as they left with Bayona on their heels, still without saying a word.

Joe felt Kat's hand slide down his back.

"It looked like you two did okay," Kat said.

"Aunt Nicola wants someone better."

"She's willing to come around," Kat said. "Basketball sounds like a smart idea."

"I figured it was better than giving him legal lessons. The only two things I know anything about."

10

As he walked back to the County Courthouse for his meeting with the judge, Joe contemplated what failure would mean. If he couldn't convict Tanovich, the boy would eventually have to move back home. The sole loose end, the lone witness. A fall down the stairs. A disappearance.

One thing seemed clear as he rode the elevator in the courthouse building, it would be in Dusan Tanovich's best interest if his son were never able to swear under oath. This motion to suppress his 911 call was just the opening salvo in the war to make sure the boy never testified.

Stacy paced outside Judge Collier's office as Joe approached. "No statement yet. I got another meeting set."

"Get anywhere?"

"Maybe an inch."

"We need a mile, Joe," Stacy said. "Parental rights and child protection are phrases that are hard to fight against."

"Right is on our side, Stacy."

"Like that matters," she said as the door to the judge's chambers opened, his clerk beckoned and a group of men down the hall began to walk toward them.

Joe recognized Dusan Tanovich as he approached. He had paid good money to become a local public figure. Born in Yugoslavia but a child when his parents came to the U.S., he had displayed all the best of first generation Americans. He had ambition, drive, focus and sheer tenacity. Enright's report told Joe that Tanovich had worked as a carpenter putting himself through the U, where he got a business degree. He'd built a house with his own hands, sold that first house and started two more with the profit, then hired a bigger crew and built more houses. By the time he was twenty-four, he didn't use a hammer anymore, he used a pen. But to hear Enright tell it, he used a pen as if it were a hammer.

He looked as if he could still pound a sixteen penny nail into a two by four without much effort. Tall, broad shouldered, a thick head of graying hair and dark mustache – Tanovich would stand out even if he weren't wearing a suit that probably cost twice as much as Mike's best. At sixty-four Tanovich was a formidable presence, he certainly dominated the hallway as he approached. Tanovich didn't so much as glance at Joe and was almost ready to head into the judge's chambers ahead of everyone else, but he stopped abruptly, gestured for Stacy to go first and then followed her in.

"Must be a big day for you," Joe heard and turned to see a hand being extended, "Marty Chesler."

"Big day for you too," Joe said as they shook. Though he realized he was predisposed to dislike Chesler, he was surprised how instantaneous his loathing was. The handshake was so limp it was creepy. The blue eyes looked right through him as they lied, the smile was condescending.

The last two men were like Bayona, charcoal suits, no

introductions, hawk eyes looking for weakness as they sat in the back. Joe joined Stacy before an enormous oak desk.

THE HANDSOME OFFICE was one of the originals from 1932. Judge Nathan Collier was a bandy-legged little man, shrunken with old age. Somewhere near eighty, he was spry though he stood at an odd angle, with his neck seemingly bent permanently to the side. This was a man who pretended to no cordiality as he glanced about, sat and nodded to his clerk, who shut the door. Then everyone else took their seats.

Collier held reading glasses to look over the papers before him. "We have the welfare of a child at stake today," he said. He looked quizzically at Joe, but then turned to Chesler with half a smile and a nod. "Mr. Chesler?"

"Good to see you again, Your Honor. Martin Chesler representing the child's father, Dusan Tanovich."

The judge nodded, then to Stacy, "Ms. Whitcomb?"

"Good to see you again, Sir. But I'm second chair."

"A demotion? Have you been bad?"

"No, Your Honor," Stacy said without a hint of a smile.

"Then who are you?" Collier said to Joe coolly.

"Joseph Brandt for the state, Your Honor."

Without any real interest in Joe, the judge said, "Now let's get on with it."

While Chesler explained the need for his client to exercise his parental rights, Joe looked for the court stenographer but the group was simply: Tanovich, multiple lawyers on both sides and a judge. For Joe this confirmed the fix was in. This bogus motion was going to be railroaded through and he would have to go to trial without the 911 call, if an indictment could even be brought.

As Chesler elaborately explained why the son of a prominent and wealthy man was put in extraordinary jeopardy by having his unauthorized, unsupervised and perhaps unwarranted emergency call made public, Joe realized he may actually have been chosen for first chair for political cover. Maybe another kind of fix was also in.

He had no doubt Mike and Stacy wanted to convict Tanovich, but what if they needed a fall-guy in the event of failure? Who better than a so-called expert with too little experience? If someone had to be thrown under the bus, he would be it.

It was at that moment he stunned everyone by blurting out, "Shouldn't we wait for the court stenographer?"

Collier drilled Joe with a look of undisguised animosity. Now committed, Joe explained why any decision the judge made was potentially precedent setting – considering the generally accepted admissibility of 911 calls – and therefore they needed a transcript in case of appeal. Judge Collier's mood became increasingly hostile. He did not like his ruling presumed and seethed at Joe's implicit threat of appeal.

Chesler accepted the absence of a stenographer and Stacy sullenly turned the floor over to Joe. He was on his own. He realized this was no time to pull back so he went for it. "You feel an appeal is unlikely, Your Honor?"

"I do indeed."

"Yet it's impossible to predict what we might do. No one can see the future," Joe said. "Isn't it equally impossible to predict harm might possibly come to a well-protected boy from the use of a 911 tape, Your Honor?"

Collier stared daggers through Joe.

"Isn't predicting a potential harm essentially the same as preventive arrest, Your Honor?" Joe said, grasping at straws. "Preventive arrest is illegal in the United States."

"I am fairly well versed in what is legal and illegal."

Despite his obvious distaste, Judge Collier explored how a ruling to suppress the 911 call was analogous to arresting someone to prevent a future crime, which was clearly illegal. The law could only act on actual crimes that had been committed and unless an illegal act was believably threatened in advance, there should be no assumption that a crime 'might possibly happen.'

Collier abruptly dragged himself to standing. Everyone started to rise, but he shouted at them to sit, "Not one word." Then he shook an angry finger at Joe. "I don't like you Mr. Brandt," Collier said. "Smart guys have a way of being both stupid and sorry at the end of the day."

Joe nodded and waited for the scolding of a lifetime.

"Would it be safe to say that the state's interest is in presenting the 911 recording to the grand jury in the secrecy of the grand jury room?" Collier asked. Joe nodded.

"Is it also reasonable to assume grand jurors will not attack the sanctity of William Tanovich's person, home or privacy?" the judge said looking at Tanovich.

The judge went on to grill Chesler and Tanovich. They were both forced to admit a grand jury had to be trusted to maintain secrets. Then the judge summed up, "Given the secrecy of the grand jury room and absent proof that harm would inevitably result to the boy, I am bound by the law not to engage in any form of preventive arrest," Collier said. "It is out of my hands and I am compelled to allow the 911 tape to be played for the grand jury – and only the grand jury – is that clear, Mr. Brandt?"

Joe nodded.

"Mr. Chesler?"

Chesler was fuming but had to nod.

Tanovich was instantly on his feet and livid. Chesler could clearly feel the disdain coming from his client.

Stacy dragged Joe out the door and into the hallway. "Don't stick around and gloat," Stacy said as she pulled him toward the stairwell rather than wait for the elevator. "When you piss in the eye of a gorilla, it's a good idea to get away as fast as you can."

MIKE WESTERMANN LAUGHED. "You can gloat now, Joe."

Joe allowed a smile. "There were three gorillas," Joe said. "I'm still trying to figure out which one you meant."

"Only one is truly dangerous to you," Stacy said.

"Chesler?"

"You showed him up in front of his most important client and a judge he thought he had in his pocket," Mike said. "He is going to want to fuck you up."

"Collier loved you, by the way," Stacy added.

"Could have fooled me."

"You allowed the old goat to weasel out of the bind Tanovich had him in." Stacy said. "You and the judge conspired to make the man believe he had no power to suppress the 911 recording. You helped Collier prove he was helpless to rescue him, much as he wanted to. Together you two forced Chesler to agree to all of it."

"Judge Collier conspired with me?"

"Once it looked like it might work. That's why he said he didn't like you," Stacy said. "That man is a fox."

"So we're back to having a case," Mike said.

"He only gave permission to use the 911 for the grand jury. If we can't use it in the trial, the boy could still fold on the stand," Joe said. "He'll have to say a lot more than 'I made that call.'"

Mike and Stacy laughed. "Good Judge Collier will find his calendar impossible to reconcile," Mike said. "A new judge will have no reason to go against precedent and we'll have our 911 recording in court."

"We're certain Judge Collier won't be available?"

"He hasn't survived all these years without learning to manipulate the system, including his calendar," Stacy said.

"But Chesler will go for your jugular," Mike said as he escorted Joe to the door, patting his back. Joe decided he must have just been feeling paranoid earlier when he worried that he was soon to be thrown under the bus.

As Joe and Stacy left Mike's offices she said, "Listen, Joe, that was completely wacko with Collier today."

"Sorry. I didn't know I was going to do it until there was no stenographer."

"Someone court-smart like me and Mike would never have gotten into that battle in the first place," Stacy said.

"Sorry."

"As a result, you charged into an unwinnable fight and won big time for the good guys today. So good going."

"Thanks," he said with a smile.

"Don't go kamikaze ever again," Stacy said.

11

JOE HAD RARELY PAID ATTENTION TO THE NEIGHBORHOOD around Eastside Field where he held basketball practice, but as he parked, he noticed how run-down and dangerous it was. He'd asked Nicola to bring the richest nine-year-old boy in Minnesota to a place most parents would not venture at noon. It was dusk and the lights in the park courts hadn't come on yet as he pulled the string bag of basketballs out of his trunk, strung the whistle around his neck and headed to the courts. He prayed Nicola would show up.

"Hey Coach," Jamal yelled as Joe approached. He was always the first at practice, wanting a ball to work on his shot count. Jamal was eleven and Joe liked him. He bounced him a ball, Jamal drove toward the basket and put in a clean lay-up. "Seven thirteen, Coach," Jamal said.

Using the Parks and Recreation key on his lanyard, Joe unlocked the adjustable basket and lowered it from regulation ten feet to nine feet, then lowered the other basket to eight feet. He coached boys from eight to twelve years old and divided them up more by strength than age. It was important to Joe that they not expend all their effort just to get height on the ball. What they needed to learn was accuracy. They had to get the ball in the basket. Strength would come.

Len, Booker, Dobbs, Colby, Teddy and Altoona-Caroona, as he was called, came together and dug out more balls.

"Numbers guys," Joe said, then wrote on his clipboard the numbers they called out. Every boy on his team had a goal of making one thousand shots. They didn't have to count how many attempts. It was Joe's system and it had worked for him as a boy. The only way to win a game was put the ball through the hoop, no one subtracted points for missed shots. To Joe everything was secondary to shooting. Make shots, win games. The rest you can improve along the way.

At the eight-foot end, the boys weren't even expected to dribble most of the time, just pass and shoot. At the nine-foot end, he held them to loose standards of dribbling, not fouling each other too flagrantly and, as with anywhere on his court, the emphasis was on putting the ball in.

"Colby, get your hands in the right place. Make it an action you can repeat every time without having to think."

"What do we do when we've made a thousand?" Len asked.

"Then we set your goal at twenty-five hundred."

"That ain't fucking happening," Altoona-Caroona said.

"Mouth," Joe called sharply at him. The boy hesitated, but then relented and sprinted toward the other goal post, touched it and sprinted back to touch the nearer one. Joe's discipline was consistent and the boys found safety in that.

"Now, lay-up drills," Joe said. When the boys groused, he went on, "Lebron James and Steph Curry both make lay-ups when that's the best shot." Joe blew the whistle and the boys ran to the ends they were assigned and started lay-up drills.

That involved shooting, rebounding and passing to the next kid in a loop.

"Like Katherine says, you really are good with kids," Nicola said as she and Billy stepped out of the shadow.

"Been here long?"

"Long enough," she said.

"Welcome to the East Side Sinkers," Joe said, then spotted Bayona on the bench outside the fence.

Billy stared at the boys energetically doing the lay-up drills and Joe noticed his fancy new sneakers and crisp new Timberwolves 'away' jersey: mainly blue with green, white, silver and gray trim. He wore number 14, Pekovic's number. He or his aunt had picked the one Yugoslav on the team. Billy wouldn't exactly blend in, but then as a white kid, he was not alone, just in the minority.

"I didn't even think about the neighborhood when I suggested this. Glad you came," Joe said.

"We've got Quasimodo over there watching our back," Nicola said pointing toward Bayona. "We're safe."

"You ready to learn to shoot some baskets, Billy?"

Billy shrugged, but then looked without much hope at the boys using both baskets. Still, he followed when Joe led him to the tall chain-link fence with a series of circles spray painted in red at eight, nine and ten feet. "See those spots? Every boy on my team has spent a lot of time shooting at those." Joe shouted, "Hey, Jamal."

Jamal darted over and he introduced them. They eyed each other and Jamal said, "Sneaks are awe."

Billy seemed pretty uncertain what was even meant.

"I was admiring your shoes myself, Billy," Joe added. "So Jamal, wanna show Billy spot drill?"

"The shots I make count on my thousand?"

"What do you think?"

Jamal laughed and shot at the first eight-foot-high spot, got the ball bouncing back from the fence and shot at the next and the next as the spots got higher down the length of the fence. As soon as he got down to the end, Jamal dribbled back to them, quite proud of himself.

"You good, Jamal," Joe said and high fived.

"So we got a new guy, Coach?"

"Hope so," Joe said as he offered a ball to Billy.

Nicola watched Joe coach the silent boy, showing how to hold the ball, how to grab his own rebounds and how to take his shots with care, not speed. Billy was proud when he hit the circle and, it seemed to her, so was Joe.

Billy was shocked to learn he was expected to make a thousand baskets, but seemed to accept Joe's reasoning, all still without a word. Joe wondered if Billy would last, if he'd be at it long enough to make his first basket.

Half an hour later, the team was going through rapid-fire passing exercises across court and Billy still hadn't said anything. He was shooting baskets at the eight-foot end and then one of his shots went in. He shouted, "One, Coach," with great excitement. Joe ran over to high five him and Nicola began to cry. She was hopeful and scared.

Joe coached Billy, adjusting his hand placement and the boy made another basket. He shouted "Coach" again and actually seemed to be having a great time as he obsessively shot for his third, then fourth baskets.

Then Joe said it was time for Billy to join a team for a half court game at the eight-foot basket. Two other teams played half court at the nine. Billy appeared scared as he silently joined the others, but when he scored in an actual game and got high fives from the boys, he was thrilled.

So was Nicola standing at the side lines.

Joe hadn't tried to talk about anything but basketball

and now Billy was freely calling him 'Coach' like the rest of the team. He was also just as reactive to the whistle. Billy was sorry to see practice come to an end as he said good-night to the other boys in their slapping hands ritual.

As usual, Jamal was last to leave and helped bag the balls, but Billy kept the last ball trying to make his tenth basket. Nicola and Joe watched as Jamal rebounded for Billy and encouraged him until he made his tenth shot.

Nicola approached Joe. "I can't believe you got him to start talking," she said. "You make it look easy."

The park was empty now as they walked off the court following Jamal and Billy, who were carrying the bag of balls together to Joe's car and laughing. "This has been the best time he's had since..." Nicola couldn't finish.

"He's like me, I think," Joe said. "All my troubles go away as long as I'm on court and shooting."

"Do they come back with a vengeance when you leave the court?"

"There is that."

She watched Jamal teaching Billy an elaborate hand-shake. "Nice kids you work with, Joe."

"I love 'em."

"I can tell," she said and gave the whistle on a lanyard around his neck a flick. He unconsciously stepped back.

"So did your dad coach you? "

"My dad ran out on us when I was eight. "

"I'm sorry."

"Don't be. Only good thing he ever did for us."

She was on the verge of tears when she took hold of his arm, but he stiffened and she quickly let go. That's when her tears really started.

"We're going to put your brother-in-law away forever."

As she calmed, Joe walked Nicola and Billy to her Lexus and Bayona hovered nearby until they drove away.

JOE WAS TIRED AND SWEATY, but he'd promised his mother, so he headed farther east toward her house. As he drove through the old neighborhood, it seemed obvious the block was in the midst of being torn down and the final date was coming up fast. How had he missed all of this? No wonder Chip Bateman looked at him like he was a moron to think this whole thing could be stopped. It was all coming down. Soon.

"Ma, I'm here," he called from the back door and went automatically to the refrigerator where there was Kool-Aid waiting. He pulled things out to make a sandwich.

"Let me make something for you, Joey," Aileen said.

"That's okay, Ma. I'm big enough to do it myself."

"But I like making things for you," Aileen said as she nudged him aside with her hip and took over. He let her.

"Uncle Louie went to prison for twenty-five years to life," he said, "and that was less than twenty years ago, so he can't have been here. He's still in Stillwater."

"I coulda sworn it was him," she said as she put the sandwich on a plate and set it down on the table for him.

That's when he saw the bruise. "What happened to your cheek?" he asked in alarm.

"Louie doesn't hit so hard like he used to."

"It can't have been Louie, Ma," he practically shouted. "How did you hurt yourself?"

She uncertainly glanced at the barred back door window as Joe wrapped ice cubes in a dishtowel. He placed it to her cheek, then sat knee to knee with her.

"Tell me what happened. It can't have been Louie."

"Then I don't know what happened."

He finally sat back. "What do you think happened?"

"I coulda sworn Louie came to the back door. He said he'd tear the door off and then pounded so hard," she said. "I got afraid of living without a door, so I unlocked it."

Joe had no idea who she may have let into the house. A neighborhood being torn down attracted the worst people the city had to offer and now, somehow, she'd been hit for the first time in nearly two decades. Damn.

"I told him we still don't know where George went."

"Then he hit you?" Joe said. "Did he take anything?"

"He took the knife from me and threw it in the sink." She reached to a side drawer and pulled out a well-worn butcher knife. "The one I had when I unlocked the door."

Joe inspected the knife for blood, then put it back in the drawer. "Would you feel better if I went around outside and looked for him? Make sure Louie's not here?"

She nodded and he fetched a flashlight as she pulled the knife back out, but he refused to take it from her.

When he stepped out onto the back stairs, he found her standing in the doorway opening. She watched from there.

Joe made an elaborate show for her. He shined the light around the back yard, behind the garage, across the fence toward the Acuffs' house, into the yards on either side and even pretended to search for footprints. "No sign, Ma."

Searching for Louie – even though it was make believe – was unexpectedly disturbing. Louie was a frequent visitor to both his waking and sleeping nightmare memories.

YOUNG JOE, his arm and shoulder in a cast from the compound fracture, sat next to his mother in a courtroom. He had no scar on his lip. His father sat at one of the front tables while a doctor talked about the break in Joe's arm, about how his bone had been sticking through the flesh when he was brought into the emergency room by the Acuffs.

Joe clung to his mother until her name was called and she pried free. Uncle Louie said, "I'll take care of him while you do the right thing," then sat beside the boy.

He felt Louie's hand on his knee as his trembling mother went up to the front. She told the men she'd changed her mind and would not testify against her husband. It made all the men angry, but soon he was called, "Joseph Felcher."

Louie let go of Joe's leg and he stood, but as he was ushered to the stand, he could see that same big, powerful hand on his mother's knee. Louie was smiling right at him.

"Do you know why you're here, Joseph?" a man asked.

"Because of my broken arm," he said.

"How did your arm get broken, Joseph?"

Joe stared over at Louie sitting beside his mother. He thought about what his uncle told him over and over as they sat together and said, "I fell down the basement stairs."

The man in the suit got really mad at him and Joe saw his mother crying, but his uncle and father were smiling.

SHOW OVER, he went inside and sat her down. "There are things we have to talk about," he said. "I have thoughts – or maybe they're memories – and I don't know what they mean."

She looked toward the fridge, "Want some Kool-Aid?"

"I've been remembering things lately," he said. "I remember I used to play baseball and I had a mitt with a ball in the webbing. Where's my glove and bat and ball?"

"No, you always played basketball, Joey."

"Not always, Ma. I changed sports when I was eight."

"Shooting every night out there," she said defiantly. "I remember things too."

"You remember when Dad was on trial because of my arm and the Acuffs taking me to the emergency room?"

"No more emergency rooms, Joey," Aileen said angrily. "It just causes more problems, more of the same."

"Did they still beat us after we got Dad off?" he said. He couldn't recall much of anything after the trial. Until very recently, he hadn't even remembered the courtroom.

"You don't remember, Joey," she said soothingly. "You think you remember things but they never happened."

"I can picture the courtroom and Louie's hand on my knee, Ma," Joe said.

"You had lots of nightmares, that's all it ever was." Suddenly bright-eyed, she leapt up. "How about Kool-Aid? You must be thirsty after making all those baskets."

In her very limited world, he was always out at the garage shooting baskets. For so many years, it had been absolutely true, he couldn't stand to be inside that house. Now that the city was threatening to tear it down, he couldn't figure out why that idea would flood him with panic instead of relief. 'Why?' he wondered.

12

As he drove home, he called Kat, who was preparing for bed. He offered to tuck her in, but she said, "Didn't you tuck enough the other night?"

"I love how you can read my mind," he said playfully. "Can I buy you breakfast then? I've got more questions about memories. Especially storage and retrieval."

"Now who's a mind reader?"

They met for breakfast where they always did, Mickey's Dining Car. Built like a railroad dining car, Mickey's had opened its doors seventy years ago and never locked them. Tall buildings had gone up around it, but Mickey's stayed right where it was set down. It was still small, homey, comfortable and one of the few places Joe's mother might recognize. They had to wait, so they cuddled and he told her about basketball practice and Billy calling him "Coach." As always, he didn't mention visiting his mother.

After they got a table, Joe asked if memories could be consciously altered and manipulated. He knew she thought he was asking about Billy and wanted to keep it that way.

"If he had to go back to living with his father, could the

old man manipulate him into believing things happened different from what he actually saw?"

"Could he reprogram his son's memory?" she asked.

She explained that Billy was vulnerable, he was in a traumatized state and no doubt quite susceptible to manipulation. "He'd end up with big issues," she said, "if his father seriously tried to interfere with his memory."

"Which he'd do if we can't keep Billy away from him."

"For Billy to have a chance, we have to get him to a point where he eventually understands what happened, as horrible as that is," she said. "He's got to arrange it in his memory so he can deal with it. Not be surprised later."

"Like years from now?"

"You have to keep him away from his father so there isn't someone fighting against what he needs. My job will be hard enough keeping him from driving his experiences so far underground he has no idea what landmines are beneath him. I have to help him learn to live with what's happened to him and the memories created by it."

"Sounds like driving the memories underground doesn't really work anyway," Joe said.

"It can for finite periods of time."

"If he had his father manipulating him to believe his memories weren't real, pushing to drive all those memories underground for years, what would his chances be?"

"I don't know, maybe he'd find it difficult to tell his girl-friend about his nightmares."

As they walked toward Kat's office, she got a call from Nicola urgently asking for a meeting. Joe knew his afternoon was booked for another visit to Paramount Hills with

Enright, but he was free for the morning and thought he'd capitalize on his success the night before with Billy.

Nicola was surprised to see Joe at Kat's office and asked if he could spend some time with Billy so she could meet alone with Kat. He wasn't allowed to be unaccompanied with the boy, so he called Bayona and then raced to his car to get a basketball and his keys.

When he got back, he found Bayona and Billy waiting for him, but all the enthusiasm of last night had evaporated. Something had changed. Joe felt like an idiot with the ball on his lap in the waiting room between a hovering gray attorney and a dressed-up, angry boy.

"What's up?" he finally asked.

"My Mom died," Billy said angrily.

Joe now knew why Nicola asked for the emergency meeting with Kat.

"I'm so sorry."

"It's not your fault, Coach," Billy said.

'Coach.' Not all ground had been lost.

"I don't want to talk," Billy said. They sat in silence for a long minute as the boy stared at the ball.

"When I don't want to talk, I like to shoot baskets," he said. "We could go shoot. No talking." Billy nodded.

Joe left a note for Kat with the receptionist and led Billy and Bayona out. They walked silently toward a small old park on the edge of downtown. It had barely any green space, one meager swing set and cracked pavement on the disused basketball court. It was a daytime sleeping area for the homeless, but it had a basket with half its chain still attached. Joe's Parks and Recreation master key unlocked it so he could lower the rim from regulation to eight feet.

Billy made a shot, was about to shout, then stopped himself. Joe was beginning to think this might not have been such a good idea. But he rebounded and fed the ball to Billy, helped with his hand placement and his legs, his follow-through. He coached. Patience he told himself.

Billy's twentieth basket was a beautiful shot and the boy shrieked for joy, then caught himself and looked at Joe in horror. Then burst into tears.

Big, sobbing tears and Joe was paralyzed with fear of going near him. Bayona and the homeless guys were all staring, waiting for his reaction. Joe was so far out of his depth, but at last he ventured an arm around the boy's shoulders. If anything, the crying increased and he wanted desperately to flee. Instead he squatted down so they were eye to eye. Billy looked right at him through the sobs and Joe discovered he couldn't look away.

Billy pressed the basketball into Joe's hands and indicated he should shoot. So he made a shot, then another. Between shots, he looked over to Billy watching and crying, then kept on shooting. He was deadly that day. 'Go figure,' he thought, but after about two dozen baskets in a row, he noticed Billy drying his tears. He smiled bravely, but Joe could see there was incredible sadness.

Nicola was waiting nervously when they returned and saw instantly that Billy had been crying as she hugged him. She looked up to Joe with thanks and amazement as Billy let loose into her arms. She reminded Billy they were going to go buy him a train set this afternoon to help him get to sleep. Last night had been so difficult.

Joe told Billy he'd heard about the amazing train set he had at home and said he'd like to see it some time. He'd heard it had a whole circus and everything.

Billy wiped his eyes and nodded. "You should see it when the giraffe is heading for a tunnel and you think its going to hit but it just misses."

"I'd like to see that."

Billy stepped out of Nicola's hug and looked at Joe a long moment, then said, "You want to come see it?"

Joe did his best to hide his excitement. "Would this afternoon be all right if it's okay with Nicola?"

Nicola was beside herself trying to keep up with the emotional shifts, then spotted Joe silently begging her to say yes. "We're allowed back in there?" she asked.

"We can work it out," Joe assured her.

"Could we decide where to put up a basket?" Billy said.

"That's a good idea," Joe said.

Nicola dreaded the thought of taking Billy to Paramount Hills, back to the house itself, but she finally softened and they agreed to meet at the house later.

KAT RESISTED RESHUFFLING her afternoon after having just rearranged her morning until Joe told her Billy was going to show him the train in the basement where he'd made the 911 call. She feared Joe was pushing Billy too fast, but she was impressed with the rapport he had established. "We're walking on a razor's edge," she warned. "We push too hard and he could just shut down."

He had the same worry, but had sensed something with Billy, a desire, maybe even a need, to connect. He asked Kat if she'd been able to help Nicola and she said she couldn't discuss clients. He reminded her their first duty was to put Tanovich away and he needed the aunt to help him with Billy.

"Nicola's incredibly needy right now," Kat said. "A few months ago she had a husband, a sister she confided in daily, a nephew she liked to babysit and a life that made sense. Now she's got no sister, a nephew she can't talk to and a husband she kicked out of the house for being a garden variety shitty husband."

"She's not easy for me to talk with," Joe said. "There are things I have to ask her too, but she's so stressed."

"What kind of stuff?"

"I was hoping she'd be able to help me understand why Tanovich would do it when the boy was in the house."

"Sienna asked Nicola to come get Billy while she and Dusan were fighting. Billy was going to stay with her that night," Kat said. "But then Sienna called Nicola later, after Dusan left for the night, and asked her to bring Billy back. She didn't want to be alone in the big house."

This was great news. He wouldn't have to sell a jury on the idea that even a murderous father would choose to commit the crime with his son in the house. Tanovich thought the boy was with his aunt that night.

"So how did you get him to loosen up and finally cry?"

"We agreed not to talk and just shoot baskets."

"I'm starting to understand your basketball psychosis."

"I think of basketball as sanity."

"I'm leaning your direction," she said as she embraced him. "Last night...I wished you didn't have to call to see where you'd be sleeping," she said into his chest.

"There's something we could do about that," he said.

"I'm not moving into your place," she said.

"I wouldn't want you to. Well, I'd want you to but I wouldn't, that is, the mice and I have gotten used to each other and I'm not sure they want to share me."

"Is moving into your girlfriend's place emasculating?"

"I just don't think I can afford half the rent."

She pushed herself to arm's length and said, "You've dragged your feet because you think I pay a high rent?"

"Your dad cuts you a deal?"

"My dad doesn't own the building," she admitted, "I do. My grandmother gifted it to me over the years and I lied because I was afraid you'd walk out, the rich girl thing."

"This mean we actually decided?"

"The mice can't come," she said.

"That could be a deal-breaker."

She shut him up with a kiss.

13

WHEN JOE GOT TO HIS OFFICE, HE FOUND A NOTE FROM Enright reminding him of their site visit in an hour. There was also a packet of information, almost all of it bad news.

The guard booth at Paramount Hills logged Dusan Tanovich leaving four hours before the murder and never returning. His four cars and pickup truck were accounted for. Nicola arrived while Tanovich was still home and left with Billy, but then she brought the boy back after Tanovich left, more than three hours before the murder. At least the time logs suggested Tanovich didn't know his son was home and had reason to believe he was not.

Tanovich's fingerprints were found in expected places in the potting shed, the house and garden and in no places which would connect him in the least with the crime. None on the plastic sheeting or anything else from the crime scene.

Until he was indicted, serious forensic inspection of Tanovich's finances was out. This was Chesler's specialty, making information difficult to gather. Public records of the man's political contributions, his basic tax forms and so on all painted him as a phenomenally wealthy, generous and tax-paying citizen. His wife and son lacked for nothing. His daughter, who worked for Tanovich Construction, appeared to perform the work she was paid to do, plus she had a trust fund. On paper Tanovich looked very straight and narrow.

The absence of a pre-nuptial agreement now looked to be in Tanovich's favor. He so loved his wife, Chesler's story would go, he wasn't concerned about money. This was a man, Chesler would argue, devastated by this crime against his beloved wife, against himself and his son. While the absence of a pre-nup gave him motive, putting at stake hundreds of millions, even the most expensive divorce would still have left Tanovich extremely wealthy.

Interviews with household staff suggested no continuing quarrels between husband and wife, no serious fights. All the money in the world bought enough privacy that battles could be fought outside servants' hearing range.

There were no indications that Sienna Holville Tanovich had been having an affair. Her tennis coach, her masseuse, her hair and nails people, her friends, her sister, everyone Enright and Bittinger had found, had plausible alibis and knew of no lovers. She had no secret bank accounts, no stalkers though she had thousands of admirers. It seemed from the notes, Enright was among them. More photos of her were in the packet. Sienna had been a very beautiful woman. Joe's stomach turned to think that someone had not only killed her, but cut her into pieces.

"So how sick does it look?" Liza asked as she entered.

"The sickest part seems to be there is no reason."

"There's always a reason," Liza said, looking over his shoulder at the photos of Sienna. "The 'before' pictures are enough to make half the women in the world want to do her damage. How are the 'after' pictures?"

"You don't want to see the after pictures," Joe said.

"You're right. I'd rather resent her beauty than have images in my head that I can't get rid of."

Joe nodded. It was already too late for that.

"How's the boy's statement coming?"

"Billy has made twenty baskets."

"You're turning him into a freak?"

"What he witnessed did that. I'm just trying to find a channel for it and a way he can tell his whole story."

"Shooting baskets somehow leads to a statement?"

"That's the theory."

Liza hadn't been gone a minute when Joe's doorway was blocked by Ronald Sheldon, never a welcome sight. "I heard you messed up with Collier," he said.

"I kept the 911 call in play," Joe said defensively.

"For the grand jury, but you blew it where it counts."

"Thanks, Ronald," Joe said. "What do you want?"

"I want you off a case that's way bigger than you are. I want someone who's competent to prosecute."

"You?"

"You don't think I'm competent?" Ronald said testily.

"That's not for me to decide, Ronald, but it's my case."

"For the moment," Ronald said.

"Admirable team spirit," Joe said as Ronald left.

Joe stewed over the seeming dead-ends in the case plus the packet of unresolved eminent domain issues in his briefcase. He wished he could just go shoot baskets.

JOE DISCOVERED Tony McCullum accompanying them to the murder site. Tony was somewhere in his sixties and had been an ADA since before Joe was born. The prevailing wisdom was the DA office didn't need an archive, it had

Tony. "Tony's an encyclopedia of how murderers behave before, during and after they kill," Enright said.

"Everyone needs a hobby," Tony said. "Find something you love and get the world to pay you to do it."

"You love murderers' methods and madness?" Joe said.

"Nice book title, 'Murderers: Methods and Madness'."

"What do you love, Joe?" Enright asked.

"Putting abusive fucks in prison."

"Can't see that title selling," Tony said.

"I'd buy it," Enright said.

As they drove, Tony and Enright discussed the crime scene photos and the meaning of the reciprocating saw. It was about efficiency, Tony thought.

Enright wondered if the scene had been planned as a sick display of some kind.

"Disposal comes to mind, not presentation," Tony said. "The killer's problem was he couldn't take her body out in a car through the security gate. If he drove across the lawn in anything there'd be tracks and he'd still have to get her to a car on Valley Road, dragging her through dense forest. He was in a bind if he had to kill her there."

"What'd we decide she weighed, drained?" Enright said. "About one-oh-five? I couldn't carry that all that far."

"He's sixty-four," Joe added. "How's his heart?"

"From the looks of the crime scene, I'd say missing in action," Enright said. "But he is pretty big and strong."

"There's a thousand ways of disposing of a body. A lot depends on what you want," Tony said. "Do you want the body never found, ever? Do you want it just not found where you did the murder? Do you want the soul walking the afterlife?"

"I rule out the last one, Tony," Enright said.

"Burying the body in the woods is the most common

method," Tony said as they drove into Paramount Hills and he admired the beautiful forest. "But more rural than this is better. These woods must have walking paths. Burying in the basement, under your house or garage or tool shed, in your back garden, under your patio made with pavers. There's lots of places to stash a body if you have access and time."

Tony was just warming up, "All those methods leave identifiable parts if dogs or joggers or latrine diggers happen on the area. A found body leads to lots of problems."

Enright parked and Tony got his first view of the house and reacted with disbelief. "He built this for himself?"

"Probably not an extension of his ego," Enright said.

They walked past the 'Crime Scene' tape and back to the potting shed. Nearly every visible remnant of the crime had been removed. Enright went to talk with the caretaker and Joe followed Tony as he walked all around the shed, spending no more time on the killing side than he did on the others. Then he followed Tony inside the shed. He heard Enright return, but he continued to follow their murder expert.

Outside Enright had placed photos of the crime scene in their approximate places against the back wall of the potting shed. It was ghoulish and an unwelcome reminder.

Joe realized the first time at the site had been so over-whelming, he'd missed a few details. Sienna had worn unglamorous blue cotton knit pajamas when she was killed and he'd already forgotten that. She had been dismembered right through them; the killer had not undressed her.

"What kind of pervert wouldn't want to undress her before he killed her?" Enright asked.

"Our suspect had seen her naked before." Tony said.

Joe and Enright watched Tony walk beside the layers of

horrific photos. He seemed engrossed by the outline of the wrench, the crescent of the five-gallon pail, the images indicating the second power tool.

"This community have county sewer, its own service or do the owners all have septic systems?" Tony asked.

Enright went to talk to the caretaker while Tony mused about the killer not having a mine shaft to dump the body down or a river to toss it in. He commented that incinerating had long ago been banned anywhere near the city. Tony thought the sewer offered the killer permanent and untraceable body disposal. When he saw Joe's shock, he said, "Thinking like the killer."

"Everyone needs a hobby."

"What's your hobby, Joe?"

"Basketball."

"Throwing a ball through an arbitrary hole in space? A lot more constructive than thinking like a killer," Tony said with a laugh. "I like killers and their brains."

He sized up Joe. "As a boy you have fantasies of going pro?" When Joe nodded, Tony said, "Me too," and appeared serious. "You didn't have the size, I didn't have the cool nerves. Same thing," Tony said dismissively. "So you go with what you can do. Can't join 'em, catch 'em."

"Remind me to stay on your good side, Tony."

"Like you've ever been on it," Tony snapped back.

Joe hoped he saw the trace of a smile. A joke.

Enright returned to say Paramount Hills had joined the county eight years ago. The house was about six years old.

Tony concluded the reason the potting shed had been built was to cover up a sewage pump. While Enright searched inside the shed, Tony continued to elaborate on modes of body disposal. "We have all those idiots who try their garbage disposal and get a femur stuck. They call a repair man, then act surprised when they're arrested."

"He was going to flush the body down the drain?"

"He's probably last house on the sewer line so his shit literally has to be pumped to the mains," Tony said. "That means he's got a powerful pump."

"The potting shed is a pump house?" Joe asked.

"It sure is," Enright said as he came back. "The sewage pump has a direct in-put, like a six-inch pipe."

"Explains the wrench and the second power tool," Tony said. "He was going to chop her up into tiny bits, pour them down the drain, have it pumped into the city sewer never to be distinguished from the rest of the county's shit. Then he was going to pack up his things and leave nothing behind. Not a trace. There'd be no body. Ever."

"That fucker," Enright said with disgust.

"Might have worked if the police hadn't been called," Tony said. "If his wife just disappeared one day, there'd be no reason we'd send forensic teams out here to inspect the shed," he said with mounting enthusiasm. "I like it. The security cameras even work to his advantage."

"The security tapes would show nothing suspicious. We'd never see her leave, she just vanishes," Enright said.

"Wouldn't we still inspect the house?" Joe asked.

"A woman disappears, we send guys to look at the house, but they find no signs of violence inside or outside? No crime scene to send a full team to inspect?" Enright said. "We'd hand the case over to missing persons and not think twice."

"Would it be possible to leave the murder scene pristine enough that detectives would never suspect?"

"To the naked eye," Tony said, pointing around the crime scene. "What here besides the photos suggests anything at all? Police would check the house, walk through the grounds and see nothing suspicious. They'd think it was a kidnapping or that she ran off with her golf pro."

"It all depends on him being able to chop her up enough to pump her with the sewage," Enright said doubtfully. "What's he bring along, a Cuisinart? Wife-o-matic?"

"If we walked through the tool crib of a really big construction company, say like Tanovich Construction, what are the chances we'd find a portable, specialized tool that chops stuff up?" Tony asked. "Probably something that works inside a five-gallon bucket. He carved her up into pieces that fit inside those buckets."

"Jesus," Joe said, envisioning it all with disgust.

"Clean up doesn't even have to be perfect," Tony said, "We'd believe the story that she just disappeared. She's beautiful, he's old. I'd buy it in a heartbeat."

"We're sure of this plan?" Joe asked.

"Of course not," Tony said. "Find the chopper, figure out the funnel and the wrench for the sewer pump in-put, get Tanovich to confess and we're good to convict."

"I liked the sound of a confession," Joe said heavily.

"An eyewitness is good," Tony suggested.

"Even a nine-year-old one?" Joe asked.

WHEN KAT ARRIVED with Nicola and Billy, Enright quickly gathered the photos and Joe had to steer clear of Billy until Bayona arrived. The boy didn't like seeing so many people. He just wanted to show his train set to his coach.

Joe was just as apprehensive as Billy, but was suddenly distracted by the arrival of a shiny black Mercedes S65 AMG. Chesler drove the most expensive Mercedes makes.

Chesler's arrival drove Joe deeper into his funk. He'd

been so excited by the possibility of getting a statement from Billy, he'd ignored the fact it involved going into a basement. He couldn't actually imagine that happening.

After all the introductions, during which Billy hid behind Nicola, they were about to enter the house. "Could Billy and I go alone?" Joe asked. "He just wants to show me his train set."

"I'm sure he does," Chesler said with hypocritical sincerity. "You know that won't be possible, Mr. Brandt."

Joe now wished he'd never arranged this visit at all. The entourage was trimmed down to Kat, Nicola, Chesler, Enright, Joe and Billy. The thought of all of them witnessing his humiliation was bad enough, but then Stacy screeched up and dashed across the lawn.

Joe saw nothing of the house. He was focused solely on his thundering heart and sweaty palms. He kept hearing Kat whisper "Are you okay?" as he stumbled blindly ahead.

It was a well-lit service hallway where Nicola casually pulled the basement door open.

YOUNG JOE RACED across the living room and yanked the basement door open. He stared down into the blackness, the deepest abyss he'd ever seen, then felt blood dripping right through the dish towel he held to his lip.

"Go get yourself some more ice now, Joey," Aileen said.

KAT CAUGHT him as he stumbled backward. He saw her concerned look and tried his best to smile as he put a hand on the wall for stability. He forced himself to look down and it couldn't be more different from his mother's basement. But it was still a basement. He wanted to bolt.

Footsteps descending ahead of him seemed thunderous to Joe while Kat hovered behind him, sensing far too clearly just how difficult this was.

"Let's go see the giraffe, Coach" Billy said.

Joe couldn't move his feet. He took hold of the handrail, then he was holding it with both hands. But they were wet and slippery and he was dizzy, seeing white. Then he was sitting on the floor with thundering inside his head.

"Put your head between your knees, Joe," Kat whispered.

Joe glanced up, but the only face to come into focus was Billy's. It seemed to him that the boy understood.

14

"The train's not that big a deal," Billy said. "Some workmen put it together and it goes around and puffs smoke."

Billy looked at Joe for a long moment, then said, "You want to know what I saw that night, don't you, Coach?"

"I really think we should call an ambulance for Mr. Brandt right now," Chesler said in a panic.

Joe waved a hand to dismiss that idea. "I'm fine."

He kept his eyes on Billy. "Would that be all right?"

Billy nodded and took Joe's arm to help him up. "Will you still teach me basketball after I tell you?" Billy asked.

"Of course I will," Joe said with a jolt of energy that surprised himself. "You're a natural. You got moves."

"You're in no shape for this, Mr. Brandt," Chesler complained. "I really must protest." Joe ignored him.

Joe rose with enthusiasm as he looked to escape down the long hall. He took a step.

"This has to stop this minute," Chesler said again.

"You can observe," Stacy said, "but not interfere."

The closer to the door he got, the stronger Joe felt. By the time he and Billy were outside, his head was clear.

As they walked around the side of the house with Chesler just inches away, Joe pointed to a spot near the garage. "That would be a good place to put up a basket."

Billy nodded but kept on walking. "I don't think I'll be living here anymore," he said softly.

Joe heard a gasp and realized it was Nicola. She knew Billy was saying he understood more than he'd let on.

Joe sensed Billy really was ready. Chesler knew it too and was desperate to shut them down before that happened. So Chesler stood uncomfortably close to the boy, towering over him.

But Billy made demands, he just wanted to talk alone with Joe. This request sent Stacy and Chesler into private negotiation. Chesler insisted that Joe could not be unsupervised with the boy. Stacy tried to get Billy to allow both her and Chesler to join them, but Billy didn't like it. Joe felt his chance of getting a statement was evaporating as Chesler blustered about and tried to call the visit off.

Joe suggested Stacy and Chesler could stand behind Billy, out of his line of sight and just listen in, not say a word. Billy still didn't like it and it looked as if the whole day was going to be a bust. When the boy saw how important it was to Joe, he agreed to one person. Joe asked for Kat, but Chesler insisted it was him or no one.

ENRIGHT WAS COMING BACK from behind the shed and trying to make himself small when he slipped past the boy who led Joe and Chesler to the oak tree. Joe was struck by something odd about Enright and watched him join the others as Stacy ushered everyone out of earshot.

While Billy nervously paced around behind the house, Joe stepped toe to toe with Chesler and whispered, "You stay out of his line of sight or it's witness intimidation."

Chesler harrumphed but stayed out of Billy's sight as Joe positioned him near the basement window.

"Is this the view you had from the basement, Billy?"

Billy looked toward the potting shed and the yard, then turned back to Joe and nodded. He seemed scared.

"What were you doing down there? It was really late."

The boy glanced around and looked directly at Chesler.

"Just look at me, Billy," Joe said. "The last night you stayed here, why were you in the basement?"

Billy focused on Joe, "I woke up and couldn't get back to sleep. Sometimes when I have the train going around and around, the clickety-clack helps put me to sleep."

"Uh huh," Joe said. "But you didn't go to sleep?"

"At first I did, but then I heard a noise outside. It woke me up and I went to the window to look out," Billy said.

"What could you see from the window?" Joe asked though it pained him that he had to push Billy into all this.

"The noise was coming from behind the shed," Billy said, pointing exactly where the plastic had been laid out.

"Could you tell what was making the noise?"

Billy stared at Joe for too long and when he spoke, it was raspy. "A kind of saw that was long and it was all red."

"Was there enough light to see all that?"

"Yeah, the spotlights were on," Billy said softly.

Chesler was dying, but Billy now had forgotten him. So had Joe.

"Who did you see holding the saw?" Joe asked.

Billy looked down and kicked at the ground. He seemed unable to continue. Billy trembled inside, but he kept himself from stepping away. Instead, he took a deep breath and said, "The man in the plastic suit was using the saw." It was all rushed together and in a whisper.

"You're doing great," Joe said, his heart thumping.

For a moment it seemed that Billy would not be able to go on, though it looked like he was trying. He was very nervous and looking every direction but at Joe. Then, "He was wearing an orange plastic suit with a hood and everything was splattered in red," Billy whispered in a hurry.

Once he mentioned the man in orange, it was as if Billy couldn't stop from rushing ahead in an increasingly hoarse, yet diminishing whisper. He seemed frantic, but he kept speaking, telling details with astonishingly vivid recall. He said the man's face was covered by a clear plastic shield and he was cutting something that looked like a blue log. He watched the man go behind the shed, then come back to work under the spotlight and Billy didn't think there should be a man in their yard. But he knew his mother had taken her sleeping pill and he wouldn't be able to wake her. He knew his dad was not home so he decided to call 911 himself. The lady at 911 told him to hide, but he didn't hide, he stayed at the window talking into the phone as he watched the man in the back yard.

Billy's trembling hand pointed out where the man stood and it was exactly where Bittinger had said he was. Billy indicated where he saw a black carrier bag in the grass. He told about the man pulling an iPhone or something out of his pocket. Then the man started to move faster and put things away. The agitated boy demonstrated how the man took off booties and was accurate on every detail. Now without hesitation, he told everything he'd seen as if he were in a hurry to unload his memories.

To the panicky boy, it seemed as if those thoughts might

go away if he forced them out into the world through his tight and strained whisper.

Chesler was distraught, but could do nothing to stop it.

"You're doing incredibly well, Billy," Joe said, trying to contain his own excitement. "What happened next?"

"After he put some things in the big bag, he pulled off the hood with the face shield," Billy said ever so quietly. With that revelation, it seemed as if all the nervous energy was depleted. He was starting to shut down. Too soon.

"After the man in the orange plastic suit took off the face shield," Joe said as calmly as he could manage, "could you see the man's face?"

Billy opened his mouth, but nothing came out. Joe desperately needed him to push through, but Billy's eyes seemed as if they were seeking a far horizon, some place other than here, some time other than now.

Chesler started to move, trying to usher them away, but it was that motion which prompted Billy to unblock the dam.

"It was Dad," he croaked out.

Chesler froze in place.

Billy bolted across the grass right toward Joe who stood near where the carrier bag had been. "It was my dad," he moaned, softly but with real vehemence.

"You're positive it was your dad?"

"I know my dad!" Billy shouted as he flung himself at Joe in a torrent of tears. "Can we be done now, Coach?"

It felt like hours, but was only minutes later that they walked to the front of the house and Billy allowed Nicola to hug him. Nearby Chesler schemed with his assistants.

Joe couldn't begin to imagine how badly the boy needed

support, he was desperate for some himself. He knew Billy hadn't been told his mother was murdered, only that she was dead. Nevertheless, he wondered if the boy realized on some level what he had actually witnessed. Some day he would and those images he'd spoken about so vividly would flare up in his memory. He faced a lifetime of seeing them against his will.

Joe watched Stacy and Enright confer in whispers. He was pleased, relieved, scared and uncertain all at once. He was thrilled Billy had said it was his father, but when he looked at him, Joe realized the boy he'd befriended was now missing. Again. Billy was staring blankly, just the way he had the first time Joe had seen him, all dust-covered from the heating ducts. Had he pushed too hard? Had he done harm?

Billy didn't even seem to acknowledge Joe as Kat helped him inside her car. Then she said to Joe, "We have to talk," in a voice that projected worry but with eyes that enveloped him with love. But then Nicola stepped out from behind her and pulled Joe into a ferocious hug.

"Thank you, Joe," Nicola said into his ear. "Thank you. Now we can put that bastard away forever, right?"

"It's looking better," Joe said, freeing himself. "Billy needs a lot of help tonight. A lot."

"I know," she said as she let go.

"And we need to shoot baskets. No talk."

"Are you a saint?"

Joe shook his head and said. "He's got things stuck in his mind he's never going to get rid of. Baskets can help."

She kissed his cheek and Joe became aware that Chesler was watching. So was Stacy. And so was Kat.

"Let's shoot some hoops tomorrow," he said, stepping away. "Nine AM at Ms. Nolan's office?"

After they drove off, Joe turned to Chesler and said, "We're going to shoot more baskets tomorrow."

Chesler took Joe by the arm and walked him toward his expensive car. Joe's opponent was putting on the charm.

"When I was first starting out," Chesler said in an avuncular fashion, "a partner in the firm gave me advice I freely give it to you, as I do to all the associates who come to work for me." Chesler dusted off Joe's polo shirt in a fatherly way. "You may well wish to join my firm yourself when you want a better class of clothing on your back."

"I'm comfortable now, thanks," Joe said.

"I'm sure you think you are," Chesler said. "What he told me is that the case which seems all sewn up is the most dangerous case to have."

"That right?"

"Stitches have a way of coming undone."

"I'll keep that in mind."

As Chesler drove off, Stacy asked, "What did he want?"

"To make me feel twelve."

"Did it work?"

"I usually feel eight, so I'm feeling bolstered."

"You should," she said as she pointed toward her car.

AFTER THEY CLIMBED into Stacy's car, Joe gave her and Enright the short version. Billy had seen everything that happened near the spotlights but was spared the most gruesome details which occurred behind the shed. The boy remembered in distressing detail and everything he said supported Bittinger's read of the scene. Most important of all, he had definitively said it was his father.

There was plenty of time for the other shoe to drop so Stacy drove in silence letting Joe bask in the glow she expected him to have. He'd done what nearly everyone in the District Attorney's office had thought was impossible.

Unfortunately, Joe did not bask, he brooded. He had exposed a lot of dangerous personal territory for all to see. His primal fear of basements revealed secrets he had spent decades locking away.

"So, you ready to talk about it, Joe?" Stacy asked.

"Talk about what?"

"I was thinking about the new violinist at the Minnesota Orchestra," she chided.

"Billy's statement is all there," he said. "It does everything we could ask from a nine-year-old."

"Except it's uncorroborated," Stacy said.

"Even with two witnesses?" Enright asked.

Stacy nodded sadly and Joe already knew she was right. "There's no way we could compel Chesler to corroborate?"

"If he wasn't Billy's lawyer of record before the site visit," Enright said from the back seat, "he is by now."

"So Chesler says nothing and you're the lone witness to what the boy said he saw," Stacy said. "Inadmissible."

Though he'd known it was coming, Joe was disappointed. "So I have to get all of that out of Billy again?"

That kind of statement would be difficult for any witness, of any age, to go through again. But a child. On top of that, Joe realized, Billy could figure out at any moment what he'd seen was his dad butchering his mother. He could clam up even more permanently after that.

"Can we use this to sever parental rights?" Joe asked, without much hope. Stacy shrugged, it was doubtful. "But we can't let Tanovich take him home. We can't make him live with a killer."

"Go at the boy again, Joe," Enright said. "You had him in the palm of your hand."

"He'll have to do it in court anyway," Stacy said. "Tanovich has a strong alibi, he's willing and able to spend millions dollars to defeat us, and his counsel is half Iago, half Machiavelli. Did I miss anything?"

"Only that our case depends on tormenting a nice nine-year-old boy who will be fucked up the rest of his life."

"You a praying man, Joe?" Stacy asked.

"Not in the least."

"Thank god," she said. "Then I guess it's up to us."

"Any suggestions?"

"Keep Billy calling you 'Coach,'" Stacy said. "Marty will protest, making him come off like a prick. The jury will love you, the press will call you 'Coach' and it will be the title of the book you write about the case when you retire."

"I knew it was only the preliminary statement, but I'd convinced myself it bought us something of value," Joe said, now regretting the personal exposure it had cost him.

"There's no way to use what Billy said?" Enright asked.

"Let's see if Mike can think of an interim solution," Stacy said and put the DA on the speaker phone. She explained that Joe had gotten a terrific statement from the boy but Marty Chesler was the only witness. She described how that came about and told Mike that Joe's work had been a miracle. They told their boss they now knew exactly what the boy had seen and he reminded them that Chesler now knew it too.

"How soon can you get the boy to give the whole thing for a camera and witnesses?" Mike asked.

"He's nine years old, his mother's dead," Joe said, "and he hasn't figured out yet he saw Dad chopping up Mom. Once all of that hits home, who knows if he ever speaks again?"

Silence enveloped the car until Stacy asked, "Think we could indict with a deposition from Joe?"

"Joe swears to what the boy said?" Mike said pensively. "He can place Chesler there and I can explain to the grand jury why he can't be asked to corroborate. Might work, but the boy still has to step up to the plate sooner or later."

"If we can indict, we can sever parental rights and keep the boy away from his father. We get forensic accountants on his finances. We up the ante in the investigation and we buy time with the boy," Joe said. "We get a lot if we indict."

"How's your memory, Joe?"

"Verbatim," Enright said from the back seat. Joe was shocked to see a digital recorder and quickly shoved it down below seat level. He realized with alarm that Enright had hidden the recorder near the potting shed before the boy's statement. That was why he had looked so guilty.

"I like the word 'excellent' better," Mike said.

Stacy caught sight of the little digital recorder. "I think Joe has an excellent memory," she said to the speaker.

"Deposition today," Mike said and hung up.

"Good thing Mike was on the phone," Stacy said.

"Sorry about that," Enright said. "I just got over-excited by having the details from the boy. Nothing fuzzy."

Joe was terrified. That tape was not only inadmissible but it could put Enright in jail. Them too if they didn't reveal a secret tape had been made without legal consent. The consent had to come from the legal guardian, who happened to be the killer. All three of them sat in nervous silence, unsure what to do.

As they neared the office, Stacy off-handedly said, "Byron, will you help Joe prep for the deposition?"

"Jog his memory?" Enright said and nodded.

"I suggest he write notes to himself while the memory is

fresh, that sort of thing," she said. "That way there will also be a hand-written reference for later."

They all knew what was being said and left it at that. Joe couldn't even figure out how he felt about it. He trusted his memory, but it was not as good as a recording.

Behind Joe's locked office door, Enright wore an ear bud and had a hand on the recorder hidden in his pocket as Joe did his best to remember Billy's whole statement. Enright prompted, questioned and reminded him without ever showing the recorder so Joe could say he made his own notes from the conversation with the boy and had never listened to any tape of it. He even made a point of 'forgetting' a couple inconsequential parts. It would be more like real memory.

15

SOON JOE FACED MIKE, STACY, A COURT STENOGRAPHER AND A tape recorder as he swore to tell the truth, the whole truth and nothing but the truth. It was stated on the record that he had come back to his office after the interview with the boy and made notes for his own use during the deposition. Then he recalled Billy's statement with generally remarkable accuracy but something short of perfection. He gave nearly a question-by-question replay of the whole meeting at the site of the murder and offered detailed recollections of exactly how Billy answered most questions. 'I know my father,' was repeated for the tape several times, from a variety of different prompts which Mike and Stacy pursued in their own lines of questioning.

Joe wished he felt good, but his triumph was tainted and it wouldn't even be enough. He felt like the top scorer in a game they lost. He would have to torment Billy all over again at a time when it seemed like the boy was in emotional retreat. And why wouldn't he be? He was beginning to figure out the full meaning of what he witnessed and now the rules of evidence would require Joe to add to Billy's devastation.

Mike and Stacy were relatively optimistic an indictment might come through and that would sever Tanovich's parental rights. The aunt could become Billy's legal guardian and that would continue even after Tanovich made bail. Joe was alarmed the killer would not stay in jail and thought it meant Judge Collier was still in the man's pocket. Mike laughed as he said the judge had just announced he was having knee replacement surgery and would be out for a few months. The problem was that Tanovich had no priors, was an upstanding citizen and gave to every political campaign in the county.

"I'll consider it a triumph if we get an indictment," Mike said and stood to leave. "Now I gotta go sell Joe as the most honest man in St. Paul and Billy Tanovich as the poor little rich boy ready to crack."

"You'll be half right," Joe said as Mike left.

Stacy said, "I didn't think we'd ever have a statement. So good work, Joe, but be very careful about the aunt."

"She surprised the hell out of me with that hug."

"Don't let her sneak up on you again."

"Kat said Nicola is needy as hell right now."

"No kidding," Stacy agreed, then asked, "Who's Kat?"

"Katherine Nolan, from Family Services. She was there with them this afternoon," Joe said. "She's handling not only Billy, but Nicola as well. Got her hands full."

"She had her hands full at the stairs today too."

"Sorry about that."

Stacy studied him so intently he grew uncomfortable. "You read Edgar Allen Poe at an impressionable age?" He shook his head. "Do you have a shrink?" He shook again. "Thank god. Marty got hold of that and goodbye deposition, hello reasonable doubt. The thing with Marty is it's never about facts or truth It's about what can be manipulated, perverted, skewed and made to look like a lie."

JOE SAT in his office wanting to call Kat but he couldn't. He was scared of her response to his show at the stairs.

"You going down to Sheehans?" Enright asked as he beckoned from the office doorway.

"Hadn't planned on it."

"Plan on it. "

"Why?" Joe asked.

"You've never even been to Sheehans, have you?"

Joe stared and Enright knew that meant he was admitting he'd never gone for after-work drinks with the other ADAs, investigators, police liaisons and everyone else.

"Joe," Enright said as he overturned Joe's legal pad. "Have you ever let anyone pat you on the back except when you were wearing sneakers and a basketball uniform?"

"I don't think so."

"Then ain't it about fucking time?" Enright said.

"About fucking time," Joe said and got up to join him.

As they walked, Enright told Joe the indictment had come through, but the arrest had been negotiated for Monday. It pissed them off, but at least Tanovich had been indicted.

Sheehans was the sort of place with buckets of free peanuts, plus shells on the floor with the sawdust. "Two boilermakers," Enright said at the bar, then handed Joe his whiskey and short beer chaser. He guided Joe to a table where other investigators were already drinking.

News of the indictment had already spread, so Joe was man of the hour and everyone wanted to hear about the murder scene interview. He couldn't tell them details and he never mentioned the basement incident. Neither did Enright. They watched on television as Mike announced the indictment for the news and Joe was bought more rounds of boilermakers.

He always feared getting drunk, not just because his father was scary when he was plastered – which was often. And Joe might have that in him. He also worried what he might say if he had too much to drink.

On the other hand, it felt good to be patted on the back by people who had been around the block more than he had. He was filled with the feeling he'd always enjoyed on teams, 'it's us against them and we're glad you're with us.'

His first attempt to escape involved slipping out to the bathroom, but on the way he bumped into Ronald Sheldon.

"What kind of amateur doesn't have another witness for a crucial statement?" Ronald said. "You even go to law school?"

"Law review. You?" Joe said, knowing he hadn't.

"Didn't do you much good, did it?"

"I still got the case," Joe said, pushing his way past.

"Anything can change."

Joe stopped and turned back to Ronald. "This won't. The boy puts his father there. I got that, no one else did."

Ronald had left Sheehan's by the time Joe returned. He found a fresh whiskey and a fresh beer waiting for him.

He'd already decided by his second glass of whiskey, he'd wait until tomorrow to talk with Kat. He'd sleep on it, she'd sleep on it. He'd be at the top of his game in a neutral place. Mickey's Dining Car sounded perfect.

A lifetime of resistance to drinking kicked in and he finally escaped. He went to Court Café for their strongest coffee, then Patty's for a meatball sandwich. By the time the long summer twilight ended and night had settled over the city, Joe told himself he was ready to try to drive home.

As he walked through the deserted parking ramp, he heard footsteps behind him. Pretending he wasn't actually paranoid, he upped his pace and rushed into the car.

UNCLE LOUIE *ferociously tore apart Aileen's bedroom looking for something as she watched with her one open eye. The other was swollen shut. She had suffered one hell of a beating and fresh blood soaked her house dress.*

"George ran out and didn't leave nothing," she said.

Louie raised a hand at her, but just then saw Young Joe standing in the doorway, staring wide-eyed and holding a bloody towel to his split lip. Aileen saw Joe at the same instant, but Louie was bigger, faster and closer. He got hold of Joe's Minnesota Twins pajamas and screwed them up into a knot, strangling the boy. "Where's your old man?"

Joe tried to speak as Aileen pounded on Louie, but she was sent flying backwards.

"He ran out on us," Joe choked out.

Louie let out a scream so loud it rattled the house.

JOE JOLTED AWAKE, grasping at his throat.

He'd dozed off in his car in the empty parking ramp. Damn this case and damn his uncle. And father of course.

He felt sober enough to drive and was very careful as he pulled onto the road. It wouldn't pay to get a DUI.

He snaked through downtown St. Paul and realized it wasn't very late. There were people out and about, there was nighttime traffic as he drove under the interstate and alongside the Capitol. It was lit up and looked ancient, stately, gorgeous and perfect in its gold-domed splendor.

Just past the Capitol he turned onto University Avenue and it transformed from barely respectable near downtown to more and more seedy. Liquor stores, bodegas, used car lots and pawn shops lined both sides of the wide avenue which was scene of many incidents Joe's office prosecuted. Knife fights, shootings, domestic abuse, drug deals and overdoses all took place on the street Joe took to work. He'd left his mother's house, but in sensibility, he hadn't moved very far.

The newer apartment buildings had underground parking – basements – so he'd found an older building with garage units in the rear which kept the snow off his car in winter. He let himself in the back door to his building and made his way up the steps to the third floor, smelling dinners, hearing televisions and bickering. He checked the time and was surprised to see it wasn't even ten o'clock yet.

Kat sat cross-legged on the floor, leaning against his apartment door with her psychology books laid out across her lap. Probably reading up on his maladies, he thought. She'd refused the key he'd offered because she really didn't like coming over to his place. She did not look happy as she gathered up her things and he offered a hand to help her up.

She gave him a perfunctory kiss and, as he pushed the door open, said, "You drove smelling like that?"

"Been an unusual day," Joe said as he turned on the lights and looked at his apartment – it was orderly if not especially clean. "I didn't expect to see you tonight."

"So I gather," she said as she put her things down and followed him into the little kitchen where he started making coffee. He was going to be exhausted and wired at the same time. "Who'd you go celebrating with?"

"Half the DA's office by the end," Joe said. "Byron Enright dragged me down to Sheehans."

"You the local hero?"

"Something like that," he said, feeling her disapproval. "I spent most of the evening turning down drinks." When she only nodded, he went on, "That's why I didn't call to come over." She nodded silently again. "I'm sorry, Kat."

"Which part are you sorry about?"

He poured coffees for them both and they sat. For the first time, he really looked her in the eye.

"All of it."

"Could you be more specific?"

"Drinking." She nodded. "Not calling." She nodded. "The unexpected hug from Nicola which I did not return."

She nodded and they sat in silence. She was waiting for more and wasn't going to say another word.

"And the basement," he said out loud. 'There, I said it,' he admitted to himself.

"I love you, Joe."

That jolted him wide awake. "Scares the shit out of me when you start like that. It's what I stand to lose."

"You don't stand to lose my love, Joe," she said and put a hand on his. "I will still love you after we talk."

"But no chance of not talking?"

"No chance."

"Even though it's not fair because I've had more boiler-makers tonight than in the rest of my life combined?"

"Maybe that's what you needed."

"Really?"

"No, but that's what you wanted to hear, isn't it?"

"You're good."

"Not as good as you insist on believing," she said, perturbed. "I just want to talk."

"I know you do," he said. "But I can't."

"You think it was easy for Billy to tell you everything while suspecting the truth about what he saw?"

"No, but he didn't do anything wrong."

"Neither did you."

'Don't count on it,' Joe thought.

They sat in silence. "I'm not mad at you, Joe," she said. "You keep acting like I'm mad at you."

"And you're not going to stop until we talk?"

"You're good."

They both forced a laugh, trying to make a lighter tone to mask the impasse as they held hands. They looked at each other, lovingly, warily, uncertainly. She was hoping he would start, he was hoping she would call it off.

"You're scared."

"Yeah, that you're going to walk out that door."

"I saw your face at the top of the basement stairs, Joe. I know it's big and I know it's deep," she said. "Something horrible happened to you in a basement."

He couldn't look at her. She pushed up the shirt sleeve and revealed his ragged scar, then she touched his lip. "These healed but the inside didn't, did it?"

He unconsciously rubbed his finger over his lip.

"The dad you never talk about?" she probed.

He nodded and was genuinely surprised when she pulled him into a fervent embrace. She whispered, "In a basement?"

He felt like a complete shit letting her believe it.

"Did your mom catch him? That why he ran out?"

He shook his head.

Kat looked him in the eye. "When did she find out?"

"She still doesn't know," he said, then regretted it instantly.

"What do you mean 'still'?" she asked, stunned.

"Nothing."

Her eyes went cold. "You told me you had no family."

He nodded, unable to look at her.

"Then what do you mean that she still doesn't know about your dad and the basement?"

"I misspoke."

"A minute ago or when you said you had no living family or when you said your dad abused you or when?"

"I didn't break my own fucking arm," he said defiantly.

"Your father ran out on you?"

"Yes, when I was eight."

"And your mother?" she asked. "She didn't die?" He shook his head. "Where does she live, Joe?"

"In the house where I grew up."

"Which is where, East St. Paul somewhere, right?"

He nodded. Fuck. This wasn't what he wanted at all.

"Your mother lives, what, a mile or two from here?" He nodded. "And she lives there right now?" He nodded again. "Yet I've never met her."

Where this was going scared the shit out of him.

"You're not a fucking orphan, Joe!" she screamed.

"It's not as simple as you make it sound," he said then heard the door open. She had her books. "I love you, Kat."

"I love you too, but I can't be here tonight."

"But Kat," he protested.

"Now you want to talk?"

He couldn't talk, but he didn't want her to leave. He knew she wouldn't get the start of an explanation or an apology, just as he knew she believed the truth from him would fix them. And he knew it wouldn't.

16

THERE WAS NO INTIMATE BREAKFAST AT MICKEY'S DINER AND he did not see or hear from Kat before heading to Saturday practice with the kids. He just drove to Eastside Field early to shoot baskets by himself, but even that was not destined to happen. Jamal was waiting for him. He read Joe's mood, then wordlessly took a ball and went to the nine-foot basket. He watched Joe shoot relentlessly with deadly accuracy like a grim automaton and worked alone on his shot count. Jamal knew enough about the dark side of life to keep a solid distance from anyone with that look in his eye.

Fortunately, after enough basketball therapy, Joe lightened up just as the boys arrived and started their warm-up with shooting, shouting and shoving. The usual was comforting. He pulled out his phone and for half a second considered calling Kat, but wisely turned it off instead.

He had hoped Nicola and Billy would come, but after the statement the day before, wasn't surprised they didn't.

"The new guy going to come, Coach?" Colby asked.

"Maybe not today, but I hope he'll join the team. What do you guys think?"

"Yeah, I need a worse shot than me," shouted Dobbs. "Maybe if I had sneaks like Billy's I could shoot better."

"Ain't the shoes, it's the hands," Colby said.

"Actually it's the eyes," Joe said and began to talk about getting their hands out of their conscious thoughts so they could shoot the ball where their eyes guided it. He was soon aware of losing them in abstraction and understood his rumination was about Kat. He was as mystified by how to make it work with her as the boys were bewildered by shooting baskets without thinking about their hands.

BOTH KAT and Billy Tanovich were far from Joe's mind as he unloaded groceries at his mother's. Aileen refused to let him help as she cooked dinner and he'd already shot more than his quota of baskets for the day, so he went for a walk. There were signs of the city takeover everywhere and the signs said work would start next week.

He brooded during dinner and later throughout a marathon of *Golden Girls* reruns with his mother.

THE FAINT SOUNDS of the music of "Golden Girls" came through the door as Young Joe, wearing Twins pajamas, stood frozen, just inside his bedroom. When he heard a sharp ugly sound from the living room, it made him wince.

He pulled the door open and the music of "Golden Girls" became louder, but it was punctuated by another blow. It was stronger, harder, wetter. His fear surged into anger and he ran out of his room screaming, "Stop hitting her, Dad."

HE COULDN'T CALL Kat without a good story. Yet, in truth, he had no idea what, if anything, had happened in a basement or why that abyss terrified him. He couldn't tell her the unwanted images which plagued him and was equally at a loss for what they meant.

Back at home, he slept fitfully. When the phone rang in the morning, his hopes rocketed. Sadly, it was a man.

"Up for some hoops, Joey-boy?" Chuck Demby said.

"Who we beating?" Joe asked, covering his letdown.

"Huge guys from Frogtown who like to bet. Their court in an hour," Chuck said and hung up.

Chuck and Joe had been the two best players on the law school intramural basketball team. They were on radically different career trajectories, but liked each other anyway. Now Joe was something of a ringer Chuck liked to bring into games with money on the line. One look at him and the big guys increased their bets. A game was better than stewing.

Frogtown was a declining neighborhood in St. Paul that had once been swamp land filled with actual frogs. Home to an endless stream of immigrants since the 1880s, the area was nearly as tough as Joe's east side neighborhood and filled with a cultural hodgepodge that brought good, cheap restaurants and indefinable conflicts from block to block. A short white guy with a basketball was watched distrustfully.

The guys were all tall, some didn't even speak English as a second language and Joe started to feel guilty about betting with them.

Chuck was a good shot and a terrific playmaker. But at a head taller than Joe, good looking with a great smile and unrelenting success at everything, there was a lot for Joe to envy. And resent. Against the odds, they'd become friends.

Joe and Chuck played with a synchronicity that suggested they had been teammates since childhood. Chuck made plays and, if the other team didn't take him seriously, he'd put the ball in regularly. If they spared an extra man to guard him, he could always find Joe and the points were guaranteed before the ball left his hands. Usually.

After sixty minutes of non-refereed, elbow crunching play, Joe and Chuck and their team lost by a point.

Chuck paid Joe's share of the bet and accompanied him to the ATM afterwards so he could be repaid.

"You still seeing that same girl?" Chuck asked.

'Good question,' Joe thought. "Of course," he said.

"You know how many millionaire's widows I've slept with in the time you've spent with just one girl?" Chuck joked.

"Please don't tell me details."

"There must be some advantage to extended familiarity," Chuck mused over post-game Cokes. "I keep hearing about people who spend literally months, if not years, together."

"Like your parents?"

"If you can believe that," Chuck said with a laugh. That was why he liked Joe, they both had the same attitude toward Chuck's accomplishments. They both felt it was all undeserved.

SUNDAY WAS GONE so Joe spent the evening reading the Tanovich file and trying not to brood about Kat. He planned on hitting the ground running Monday. The arrest would make it a big day, but he was surprised when it started far earlier than he expected. When his cell rang, his mind again went to Kat, but the caller ID said Nicola.

"Is everything all right?" he asked with alarm.

"He's here and he's trying to take Billy," Nicola said.

Joe could hear pounding through the phone, loud and violent. "Call the police," he said.

"And tell them what, a boy's father wants to see his son?" Nicola said. "There's no restraining order."

"I'll make some calls and get the police to come out."

"You have to stop him, Joe," she cried into the phone.

In the background, he heard more pounding. "What if he..."

'What if Tanovich kills the one witness against him?' Joe thought as he ran out to his car.

Nicola gave him her address and it was in a 'Tanovich community.' She lived on the edge of White Bear in a planned village of cul-de-sacs. It had been a wedding present from her loving brother-in-law.

Joe woke Stacy up and explained the situation, gave her the address and kept driving out to confront Tanovich.

Billy held damning evidence and without him the murder case might disappear. But if Tanovich killed his son, he would just exchange one murder charge for another.

Unlike Paramount Hills, there was no guard booth, no expectation of exclusivity. The roads were public and if the houses had security, it came from a service. Joe had already told Nicola to turn her security service on. If Tanovich broke in, then the company would send someone out and Joe wanted all the back-up he could get.

Joe called Enright and said, "Midnight scumbag time."

"What rock are you messing with, Joe?" Enright said.

"Tanovich is trying to break into Nicola Patterson's house and get hold of his son," Joe said as he stopped in front of Nicola's house, saw a Bentley parked crooked in front of her driveway and could make out a big, broad shouldered man stomping about.

"Technically he still has guardianship of the boy until he's arrested in the morning, right?" Enright said.

"I can't let him near the only witness against him."

"Stacy on her way?"

"Yeah."

"I'll call Bittinger," Enright said and hung up.

Joe parked in front of the house. Tanovich saw him and stayed in the front lawn, staring at him. Joe stepped out of his car, but was prepared to leap back into it.

"Get the hell out of here," Tanovich yelled at him.

"You're not thinking straight, Mr. Tanovich," Joe said.

"He's my son."

Joe called Nicola. "Nicola, I'm outside."

The front lights came on and he could see Nicola looking out through the curtains. Tanovich just stood there, unarmed and, at first, not especially threatening looking. Then Joe noticed that a lawn lamp post along the sidewalk had been completely uprooted and was bent in half. This man was still damned powerful and damned excitable.

"You're the twerp from Collier's office," Tanovich said. "The one's got Billy shooting a basketball." Joe nodded.

"Why do you want to see him, Mr. Tanovich?"

"Because my chump lawyer can't do what he promised and you guys are arresting me in the morning."

"So you thought you'd stir up trouble tonight?"

"So I thought I'd visit my kid and see if he's all right and check if his Aunt Nicola is okay with him. She's such a bitch her husband up and left her and all."

"You're saying that's her fault?"

"'Course."

"She'd disagree."

"'Course," Tanovich said and sat down on a flagstone step and studied the damaged he'd done to one of the lamps. "You guys going to put me in jail early now?"

Joe ventured out from behind his car, "We need to?"

"Not on my account," Tanovich said, looking up the

empty street. "We waiting for something? SWAT team or something?"

"Do we need a SWAT team?"

"Don't answer questions with questions. I hate that."

"Fair enough. No SWAT team."

"Fair enough," Tanovich said, sizing him up. "Pretty young to have such a big case, Kid."

"I can't discuss it with you without Mr. Chesler here."

"We were talking about you."

"The District Attorney has confidence in me."

"Hope he's wrong," Tanovich said. "Brandt. German?"

"Couple generations ago."

"I'm first generation," Tanovich said, then looked at his watch and said, "Marty ought to be here by now."

"You called him?"

"When I tried to defend my parental rights, you stopped me in that judge's office. Thought I'd give Marty a second chance to impress me with something other than his fee."

Joe tried his damnedest to hide his smile. It didn't sound like Marty Chesler was doing well with his client.

"Your son's a really good kid," Joe said.

"So far, but he'll grow up to be a terrible mama's boy if he stays with her. He can't live with Nicola."

Tanovich was accustomed to sizing people up while small talking and most people were anxious to please him. That set-up usually gave him an advantage, but Joe was like him, holding back and sizing up. Small, solid, confident but, Tanovich sensed, something lingered under the surface. Other people's secrets were the best weapon to find and Tanovich was good at it.

Age hadn't softened this man who was so accustomed to being in charge. It had just leathered him, made him harder than nails. What unnerved Joe was the man's eyes, they were dark, deep set, like black holes. Joe felt this man was entirely capable of butchering his wife.

Stacy drove up and within half a minute, Chesler arrived to find the men staring across the yard.

"You two haven't been talking, have you?" Chesler said, but Tanovich just ignored him. As Chesler passed, Joe smelled cologne. He'd taken time to shave. Was he expecting news crews and a big scene? Was he relieved or disappointed?

Stacy joined Joe. "First person she calls is you?"

Joe didn't like the accusing look from Stacy. "I was at home minding my own business," he said defensively.

"He say anything helpful, irrational, threatening?" Stacy asked, looking at the torn-up lamp. But Tanovich was standing and now looked non-threatening.

"He was just sizing me up."

Chesler approached them. "My client would like to see his son before he remands himself to custody," Chesler said. "He is all right with it being supervised."

"It's two o'clock in the morning, Marty," Stacy said.

"The boy must be sound asleep."

"He'll watch him sleep then," Chesler said. "But there is no way I let the kid supervise," he said pointing at Joe.

"We can live with that," Stacy said. She stepped past Chesler and headed to the front door while Joe waited.

Nicola opened the door saying, "I want to talk to Joe."

Stacy beckoned Joe, "You okay? Where's Billy?"

"I bought a train set and he's trying to get to sleep." She pointed at the yard and said, "This is not helping."

She reached toward Joe, but he backed away. "I can't be unsupervised near Billy."

She watched Bittinger come up the walk, then glanced

at the lawyers looking at her. Her brother-in-law was waiting with what appeared to be complete passivity.

"I know you don't like it, but we have to let him see Billy," Joe told her. "You're not officially his guardian until the arrest."

"So you are arresting him?"

"We've agreed to a supervised visit. I'll supervise," Stacy said forcefully.

Nicola reluctantly nodded and stepped aside, gesturing Stacy inside. To Joe she said, "I'll put coffee on."

Stacy and Tanovich headed inside while outside Bittinger leaned close to Joe and said, "Man, braless."

"Huh?"

"Did you drive over here asleep, Joe?" Bittinger asked incredulous. "The little sister. Man, oh, man."

Joe looked through the still open door as Nicola reappeared and headed into the kitchen alone. She wore knit cotton pajamas similar to those Sienna had been wearing when she was killed. Braless indeed.

"I don't get to put cuffs on this fuck for hours yet," Bittinger said.

"How about we interview the sister together?"

"You'll go far throwing bones to us cops like that."

Joe stopped Bittinger from going inside and said, "Don't want Tanovich to overhear anything. Let's stay outside."

As he accompanied Bittinger to the patio on the side of the house, Joe watched Chesler use his cell phone. He wondered who he needed to call at 2:30.

17

IN THE SIDE PATIO, JOE TAPPED ON THE FRENCH DOORS UNTIL Nicola looked out from the kitchen to see where he was. He and Bitt took seats in the comfortable outdoor set.

"You ogle her and I give her my jacket," Joe said before Nicola came out with a coffee tray. She was surprised to see Bittinger there and instantly headed back inside.

"I swear, I didn't ogle," Bittinger protested.

Nicola hurried back with a third coffee cup. "He and Billy are lying on the floor with their heads on pillows and the train going around. Trying to go to sleep," she said.

"Sounds awfully domestic," Joe said.

"Tanovich wants a last image in the boy's mind of how great a dad he is," Bittinger commented cynically.

"Would he often put Billy to bed, Nicola?" Joe asked, then regretted the familiarity. Bittinger had noticed it.

"He's not as bad at being a father as he is at being a husband. He's terrible with women."

Joe and Bittinger shared a look and mental note. Joe asked, "Anything special jump to mind we should know?"

She snugged her legs under her. "He seems American

and he's been here longer than we've been alive, but he was born over there and he was raised by people from an old world village. So he appears American, but he's old world, old school, true Balkan style."

"What's that mean to you?" Joe asked.

"Traditional views of men and women, very old fashioned roles and expectations, rigid old world codes."

"Ethical codes?"

"Revenge codes. The Balkans balkanized for a reason."

"I'm just a cop. What's 'balkanize' mean?" Bitt said.

"To fragment into hostile groups, often having blood feuds, that sort of thing," Joe explained. "Like Bosnia and Serbia and Kosovo and Croatia and Albania."

"Hatfields and McCoys," Bittinger added.

"Right," Joe said, "you think it was revenge for him?"

"Personal revenge," she said. "What are all those animosities about, nations or people? Betrayal."

"He thought your sister betrayed him?" Joe asked.

"There's more than one kind of betrayal, Joe."

"You said before she wasn't having an affair."

"And she wasn't," Nicola insisted. "She wasn't involved in anything like that. If she were, I'd know it." She glanced inside and shook her head. "She was too scared of Dusan to do anything. Just like Billy."

She saw the alarm on their faces. "Billy's scared of his father but he's too afraid to show it. So they lie on the floor with the train."

"Billy told you he was afraid?" Bittinger asked.

"Everyone is afraid of Dusan. He intimidates the whole world as a daily part of life."

"So you and Sienna were pretty close?" Joe asked. "She confided about their daily life?"

"Some sisters hate each other," Nicola said. "But Sienna and I didn't compete. We told each other everything."

"Sounds nice."

"I don't know how I'll get along without her."

Joe couldn't imagine what she and her sister shared. The one sibling relationship he knew closely was utterly destructive. His father and Uncle Louie did nearly everything together, but they sure didn't trust each other.

"Is there something specific you're getting at?"

"Betrayal doesn't have to be real, just perceived."

"He saw infidelity when there wasn't any?" Joe asked.

"You two interviewed his business associates yet?" she asked back. "How'd he treat them?" she asked.

"Like they were all looking to cheat him," Bitt said.

"He wasn't any different with his wife and family."

"You don't have to be born in the Balkans to think like that," Joe said.

"But if you are and you're brought up to exult in all the ancient blood feuds, if you have a long tradition of making brutal vengeance seem honorable...it just becomes easier for someone like Dusan to rationalize his evil feelings."

"He was always projecting?" Joe asked and she nodded.

"What the hell are we talking about here?" Bitt said.

"The reason Tanovich treated business associates like they were trying to cheat him was he'd try to cheat them if he were in their position. He saw their behavior as being just like his own, even if it wasn't. Think Richard Nixon."

"They teach all this in law school?"

"Debate team," Joe said.

"And I'd just started to think you weren't a nerd."

Ignoring Bitt, Joe went on, "So when he felt betrayed, did he actually beat her?"

"Not so it would show. Not her face. That he adored," Nicola said bitterly.

"But he physically hurt her?" Joe said and looked at Bitt. "There should be medical records then."

"You won't find any," Nicola said. When he saw their surprise, she added. "Wealth can buy anything, including off-the-books medical care."

"Really?" Joe said.

"Not everyone is a boy scout," Bitt said. "Do you have any proof of beatings? Photos you took or anything?"

Nicola sadly shook her head.

"And she didn't try to get out?" Joe asked.

"Where would she go he couldn't reach her? He always had leverage on her. Billy. To say nothing of the lawyers and all the people he had watching her. Them."

Joe stewed in that for a moment. "He hit Billy too?"

"Of course."

"No medical records?"

"Of course."

Joe was ready to leap out of his chair, but Bitt pulled him back. "Any broken bones in the boy? Anything that would show up on an x-ray?"

Nicola shook her head.

"We can add beatings to the painful testimony we have to get out of Billy," Joe said.

"Sienna lived in constant fear he was going to take Billy away somehow," Nicola said. "It made her tolerate a lot."

Nicola told about a night Sienna and Dusan were going to a gala in his honor, thanking him for a huge gift. Nicola was babysitting Billy. Sienna looked fantastic in a low cut dress, jewels to draw your eyes, flattering fit, a little too much slit up the side. It was exactly what Dusan wanted. He wasn't jealous of other men looking at her, he wanted them to look so they'd envy him. But the looking had to be one way. Sienna couldn't even glance at another man.

"She had to gaze adoringly only at Dusan," Nicola said.

That night, one of the guests at the gala was a Twins player, not even the guy Sienna had dated, but she knew him. They'd been friends. Dusan ranted, accused her of deception in every way imaginable. Nicola and Billy cowered in the boy's room when they got home and she practically smothered him trying to keep him from hearing.

"Sienna was in serious pain for days."

"You couldn't call the cops?" Joe asked. She shook her head. They both understood the power Tanovich had.

"He'd been charming when they were dating," Nicola said. "Even I sort of liked him when he was on his good behavior. Bastard."

Joe finally asked the question he'd been wanting to ask, "Billy was here with you that last evening. Why did you take him back to the house?"

"I only had him because Dusan was on a rant. When he left, she called me. I was having my own troubles that night."

"What kind of troubles?"

"My divorce hasn't settled well with my ex," Nicola said. "I brought Billy over and we made a game of unplugging all the phones because my ex kept calling. I had a cell that only Sienna knew and she called to say that Dusan had stormed out and was going to spend the night at a hotel. She wanted Billy back with her," Nicola said, then started to break down. "If I'd just stayed over there that night."

"What happened was not your fault," Joe said.

Just then Chesler approached Bittinger and said, "Could we arrange for the arrest to take place here?"

Bittinger excused himself and followed Chesler.

Nicola watched Bittinger walk off, then glanced into Joe's eyes. "I don't quite know how to say this," she said with a sultry look.

"How to say what?"

"The other night when you were showing Billy how to shoot?" she said. "In my whole life I've never been around a man who was so gentle and giving and..." She put her hand on his and looked up into his eyes with invitation.

"Nicola," he said, pulling his hand away.

Flustered, she abruptly stood, then sat back down, accidentally spilling her cold coffee down her front. Her wet pajama top now clung to those breasts. Before Joe could move a muscle, she raced inside and he saw Bittinger coming back. 'Great,' he thought.

NICOLA DIDN'T RETURN and Joe knew the last thing he should do was go see if she was okay. Instead he set the alarm on his cell phone and went to lie down in his car.

At eight, Bittinger woke him up and led him to the kitchen, where Nicola, now conservatively dressed in jeans and a heavy sweater, was making a huge breakfast. She served everyone, even Tanovich, who watched as Nicola dished up toast and eggs for Joe and gave him an insecure look.

Joe looked around the sizable eat-in kitchen.

"One of our best designs," Tanovich said. "Twenty-three hundred square feet, four bedrooms, two and a half baths, Jacuzzi, eat-in-kitchen. Surprisingly affordable."

"Marty, I think your client is offering a bribe to our first chair," Stacy said over her eggs.

Chesler saw no humor in it and Joe almost agreed. This felt entirely too civilized and Joe asked himself how Nicola could stand it. Then he thought about all the times his mother served his father breakfast after a beating.

At nine, Bittinger arrested Dusan Tanovich while Billy still slept. The press had not been invited. Stacy called Mike and gave him an update on the visit. Neither father nor son mentioned the last time they had seen each other.

The cul-de-sac was clearing out and Joe did not want to be last to leave. He thanked Nicola and made arrangements to shoot baskets with Billy in the afternoon. While Stacy was still there, Joe drove away, but he wasn't even out the gate when his cell phone rang. It was Nicola.

"Please don't hang up," she said.

"Nicola," Joe said.

"Just let me apologize face to face."

He resisted, she insisted and then begged him to let her regain her dignity. Three minutes after he left, Joe parked in front of her house. Nicola opened the door and waited just inside the entryway. He stopped on the front step.

"I'm embarrassed," she said as he stopped.

"Nicola," he said. "You're going through a lot and it's sort of natural when someone's trying to help..."

"Can we be friends?" Nicola blurted out.

"I'd like that," he said and started to back away.

"Couldn't you at least have the decency to be a jerk about it?" she said with a smile. "You're making being a decent person very difficult here."

"Basketball and prosecution, okay?" he suggested.

"Okay," she said and held out a hand to shake.

He hesitated, then stepped closer to take her hand. While they shook, she leaned up close to kiss his cheek.

"Basketball and prosecution," she said as she stumbled back into the house and closed the door. He didn't mean to, but he grinned all the way back to his car.

18

Before he even made it out of White Bear, Joe got a call from Enright who told him Bittinger was going to interview Tanovich's adult daughter again while the old man was in custody. Did he want to be part of it? Did he ever.

He rushed home, showered, shaved and decided to wear the suit and a new tie. As he drove to the office, he stopped at a florist. He had plenty of sins to atone for so he ordered a big display of roses and had them delivered to Kat at work. Wasn't it time they announced their plan to move in together?

Enright just grinned at him looking unusually respectable, but that wasn't why. He said, "Cotton pajamas."

"Fuck off, Byron," Joe said, "I didn't do a thing."

"Touchy there, Stretch," Enright said as they walked to his car. "Bittinger says the aunt has her eyes on you," Enright said. "Care to comment?"

"Can we just talk about Tanovich's daughter?" Joe said.

"You're not as much fun as you could be," Enright said.

As they drove, Enright updated Joe. Tanovich had a

daughter from his first marriage and she worked for him. Senka, was mid-thirties and head of the company's design team. She worked with architects and interior decorators and consulted on everything from ceramic tiles to the layout of the cul-de-sacs, a Tanovich development hall-mark. There had been another daughter, Dejana, the first born, who disappeared twenty years ago when she was in her early twenties. Their father had hired private detectives and offered a big reward, but after years of searching no one had found any news of her.

"Dejana really didn't want to be found," Enright said.

"We're sure?"

"Police investigation, five years of searching, a big reward and a lot of clues to follow up. I glanced through the case books, but it looks like they did everything."

"Tanovich Construction digs a lot of holes every year."

"I'm with you, Joe. But Dejana salted away a few hundred grand, took her passport and some of her mother's jewelry when she disappeared. Sounds like a runner to me."

"And Tanovich's first wife, their mother?"

"Died fifteen years ago. Technically cancer ate up her insides and she died overseas, but to hear people tell it, she died of a broken heart after Dejana disappeared."

"Guess he didn't murder the first wife then?"

"Sent her to doctors in Switzerland," Enright said. "While she was gone, local celebrity babes on his arm until he met Sienna and started working out like a teenager."

"Senka have an alibi for the night Sienna died?"

"She was hosting at a Twins game, then home to bed."

"Alone?"

"You haven't seen her?" Enright laughed. "Definitely. And her home security alarm was turned on about eleven and not turned off until five the next morning. Daddy called her after he'd been contacted by police in the early morning and she went to support him. Or so they say."

"How's she like having a young step mother?"

"Senka is emotionless...imagine that in her family," Enright said. "You'll see."

As they approached Senka's house, they entered a world as close to Sussex as Minnesota offered. Her home was an oversized white 'cottage' with gables behind a magnificent English garden. It had stone walls, trimmed hedges, a fountain, and an abundance of elaborate bronze and stone statuary. Overstatement was apparently hereditary.

Bittinger was waiting out front for them. "This place is on the Christmas tour," he said.

"What Christmas tour?" Joe asked.

"Of the most decorated houses in the city. 'A thousand and one lights.' Or in this case, a million and one. These statues in her yard all go away so a life-sized Santa and elves can cavort with wise men and camels. Helluva show she puts on."

"You're a wealth of information, Bitt," Enright said.

"The wife leaves me alone during my football games, I take her out after dark to look at the lights. Fair trade."

"So Senka took today off because Dad's in jail?"

"Her assistant said she hosts a lot of their business associates in the evenings – last night at the Twins game – and usually doesn't go to the office in the mornings," Bittinger said as they wound their way through the garden.

"I hear," Enright said, "the beauty is only yard deep."

Joe's confusion lasted only until Senka opened the door. She was mid-thirties and severe. Rail thin with bluntly cropped short, black hair, an angular nose and even more angular jaw line. She had precise eyebrows over black and forbidding eyes. They were her father's eyes. She wore black, white and shades between.

There was a strange disconnect between the woman and her home, which was brimming over with white porcelain figurines of lively humans. Every surface held a group of astonishingly detailed little statues and the enormous living room looked like a museum. The statues were all idealized visions of life, like Norman Rockwell in three dimensions.

They were led down a porcelain-lined hallway dedicated to European culture and ushered into her home office. It was nearly as big as Mike Westermann's office. Here the mood changed, but clearly not the person behind it.

There was an enormous, cluttered and lived-in desk covered with samples of tile, drapery fabrics and paint color charts and there were shelves with models of their house designs. Yet every available surface sported bobble-head dolls of Twins and Timberwolves players while the walls were covered with pennants, posters, team photos and this year's schedules. She kept all the color in her life in one room. Joe wondered who she was, because nothing about her felt right.

"I already told you everything I know about that horrible day," Senka said.

"I'd like to ask about Mrs. Tanovich," Joe asked.

"You mean Sienna?" Senka asked.

"Do you think Sienna was happy in her marriage?" he asked, surprising the more experienced interrogators.

"Oh my, yes," Senka said. The words were meant to evoke enthusiasm, but they were said without animation.

"A husband thirty years her senior?"

"My father had more energy than men half his age."

"So she was happy? A wonderful son, a big house."

"She loved Billy with all her heart," Senka said.

"He is a great kid, Ms. Tanovich," Joe said. "Your father said he spent that night in a hotel because he'd had a spat with Sienna. Do you know anything about that?"

"I never saw them fight."

"And you didn't see either of them that night?"

"No, I was at a Twins game."

"Your father said she was jealous because he was looking at another woman," Bittinger added.

"My father loved looking at a lovely woman."

"So he had a roving eye?"

"Eye, yes," she said as if by rote. "But he was faithful. The looking was just aesthetics."

'Right,' Joe thought. "I see. And Sienna was perhaps a jealous woman?" he said.

"If they had a fight about it, she must have been."

"Yes, of course."

"My mother wasn't," she volunteered.

"Wasn't what?"

"A jealous woman," she said and mentioning her mother almost brought a light to her eyes. "She knew my father worshipped her and there was no reason to look at other women. She was the loveliest woman who ever lived."

Yet for Senka, all the hard angles and plainness seemed designed to make her disappear. In a way, she was like Joe's mother. Something had happened to her, he thought.

"Do you work closely with your father?"

"My father always says that men buy the basement and the roof while women buy all the rooms in between," she said. "I make decisions about the rooms in between."

"So your father really depends a lot on you?"

"I'm an integral part of the family business, yes."

"When did you last see your father?"

"Last night when he told me he'd be arrested today."

"Do you have any thoughts on whether your father could have done this?"

"He absolutely did not."

"How can you be so sure?"

"He couldn't do something so horrible. Sienna was so very lovely and Daddy just loved to look at her."

Joe had no more questions, but Senka didn't want to leave it sounding like that. She added, "They were far apart in age, but he loved her and I think she loved him."

'Like you would have a clue,' Joe thought. Enright had found no hint of a romantic relationship in her past, ever.

Bittinger wanted to look at the home security system, which seemed to bring some animation to her. It was defense of her precious collection. Joe asked to use the bathroom, then went to explore. In the hallway he found a wall of Tanovich family photos. There were a lot of pictures of Billy, many at Twins and Timberwolves games. There were a few of him with his father and with both his parents.

Down from the new family was a comparable display of the first family. His first wife was indeed lovely and bore more than a passing resemblance to Sienna. But there wasn't a single photo showing there had been two daughters. As a child and early teen, Senka had seemed lively enough, even pretty, but the photos of her stopped at that age. And time was just as frozen on that wall as it was in her museum of little statues. Senka surrounded herself with imitations of life.

Back on the street, Bittinger said, "The statues inside are worth more than the whole house."

"It's a multi-million-dollar house," Joe protested.

"Those things, they're called Lladrós and they're made in Spain. They cost a thousand to five thousand."

"Each?" Joe said with horror.

"Hundreds of 'em and you just know she's only got the summer ones out. She'll have 'em for every season."

"You know this how?" Enright said with amazement.

"My wife dreams about upgrading from what she's got," Bittinger said. "Lladrós are strictly her fantasy."

"You have things like that in your house?" Joe said.

"Says the unmarried guy," Bittinger said. "Just you wait. Starts with them changing how you dress... very nice suit, by the way."

JOE RODE with Enright to the ultra-modern offices of Tanovich Construction to meet the forensic accountants.

"Something happened to Senka Tanovich," Joe said.

"You think the old man?" Enright asked.

"In one fashion or another."

"Living with a domineering world-class prick has got to be hard on every woman in the house," Enright said. "Senka said something in the first interview that made me sit up... She said, 'Daddy waited a long time for my brother.' Some guys like Tanovich don't care about daughters, only sons."

"How old was Senka when Dejana disappeared?" Joe asked.

"I'll check it out. Musta been mid-teens, I'd say."

"Dejana took money, jewelry and her passport when she ran away? That's the story, right?"

Enright nodded, getting intrigued.

"Did Sienna have a household slush fund? A safe?"

"I'll check it out. You got a nasty way of thinking."

"Were Sienna's purse and jewelry and passport still in the house while she was being killed out back?"

"I'll go through inventory again, but I don't recall a passport and our dead lady owned about fifty purses."

"Look for her driver's license and wallet and frequent-massage card then. Figure out what she carried daily and see if it was there, if it's still around or if it's missing."

"You thinking he was going to disappear Sienna? That maybe he disappeared the daughter way back? He'd need to make it look like she was running."

They shared a look and a new direction of thought.

THEY WERE SHOWN through the Pritzker Prize winning building Dusan Tanovich had built as his corporate shrine to himself. They passed Henry Moore style sculptures, a state-of-the-art architectural studio, purchasing and legal affairs offices, a model-making studio and an in-house advertising division on their way to an enormous boardroom where they were to join the forensic accounting team.

Bitt and Enright both stopped outside the boardroom. "You go to Catholic school, Joe?"

"I escaped that fate,"

"Then mozel tov, but I didn't," Bitt said. "Just think of Alice as Sister Mary Margaret Magdalene of the Order of the Smacked Knuckles. She's got a ruler and she's not afraid to use it," Bitt said, then led the way into the big room.

Joe thought there was something suddenly quite pious looking about Bittinger as he approached the large woman. He glanced at Enright for a knowing look only to discover him in the same virtuous posture.

Alice Krevolin looked up with a pleasant, if somewhat suspicious, smile and stuck a hand out to shake with the men. She was large and wide and modestly dressed and did not make Joe think in the least about a nun, though he spotted an actual ruler in her hand. She was surrounded by stacks of financial documents on the table in neat rows. Most of those papers had rows and columns of tiny figures.

"Alice, meet Joe Brandt," Bitt said. "He's the ADA who put Tanovich in jail."

"For that whole hour?" she said with a look that allowed an inch of approval and yards in which to acknowledge his own failure. Joe was beginning to see what Bitt had meant.

Alice led them down the table with a history of Tanovich finances. "Ten million in bail, frozen assets, had to give up his passport," Alice said. "Wrote a check in court," she said. "Who keeps that much in their checking account?"

Joe laughed thinking it was meant as a joke, then discovered he'd just lowered himself a notch with Alice.

Alice pointed at a couple of seated men bending over reams of financial papers with less heavy-duty rulers. They looked like monks working on illuminated manuscripts.

"Alice has probably put more crooks in prison than Byron and me combined," Bitt said to flatter her. "What failures in his accounting have you found for us, Alice?"

"Once I saw how many escorts this man has hired, I thought we'd have him no matter what else he did."

"He hired hookers while married to Sienna?" Joe asked.

Even before he'd finished the question, Joe spotted both Bitt and Enright signaling him to stop.

"It is not the fault of women who find themselves in unfortunate circumstances and there is no justification for calling them names, Mr. Brandt," Alice said sternly.

"Sorry, I just meant that he was married to one of the loveliest women in the state and..."

"I know what you meant and I share your sentiment, not

that the beauty of the wife should be a factor in a married man's fidelity," she said turning to the papers. "In any event, a man as prodigiously unfaithful as this one usually makes a misstep we can use to collar him."

"Not true with Tanovich?" Bitt said.

"When they spend six figures a year on such activities, the desire to hide it in the books is almost overwhelming," Alice said, "Usually they call it 'entertainment.' Then end of fiscal year, they write their entertainment expenses off on their taxes and we put them in prison for their dalliances with unfortunate young women."

"So he doesn't write off these...women?" Joe said.

Alice assessed him grimly to see if he was making fun of her, then said, "Smarter than most. He does hisn't try to write off entertainment expenses. He dutifully pays his full share of taxes on his infidelities.

"Didn't he watch a movie in his room that night in the hotel?" Joe said. "Why not hire a woman?"

"Maybe Capitol Suites has fantastic movies," Bitt said.

"I know very well what kind of movie he watched in his room, gentlemen," Alice said. "He didn't watch that kind of filth in the other hotels we've looked into."

"He usually dallied," Bitt said.

"He stayed at Capitol Suites?" Joe said. "Isn't it a bit lowly for him?"

One of the monks looked up and said, "Capitol Suites is a four star and he paid six hundred fifty-two for the suite."

"That's how much hotel rooms cost?" Joe said.

"Not ones I sleep in," Enright said. "So, did he usually stay in four star?"

The monk shuffled through the papers and shook his head. "Five star, five star, five star...here's a four-star in... some town overseas. Bet they don't have a five star."

"He ever stay at any other hotel in the Twin Cities?"

"Stayed at The Grand in Minneapolis a few times. Five star. Never at the Capitol Suites before that night."

"What's our thinking?" Enright said excitedly.

"Let's check out security at both hotels," Joe said.

"Sure, what are we looking for?" Enright asked.

"Maybe The Grand has fewer cameras, more discretion for their rich clients," Joe said.

"Making The Grand easier to sneak out of," Bitt said.

"Leaving a less verifiable record of not leaving. More cameras at the Capitol means a better alibi," Joe suggested.

Bitt and Enright exchanged a look, impressed.

"So, ma'am, you got anything else for us?" Joe asked.

"Let's talk jet airplane."

"What's wrong with his jet airplane?" Joe asked.

"He builds houses in Minnesota," Alice said. "He's not going to Paris on business. Doesn't need a corporate jet."

"Something illegal in it?" Bitt asked.

"Not that I can tell so far, but a lot of trips begin and end here in St. Paul, go up, fly around, land. Why?"

"He could be taking an escort up, show her around? Mile high her, so to speak."

"Good thought. I'll cross reference," she said. "If he writes those circle flights off on his taxes, that's the kind of oversight I can sink my teeth into."

"He doesn't use the jet except for that?" Enright asked.

"Sure, he visits suppliers, conventions, goes to, where is it, Albania of all places, once in a while," she said. "It would be cheaper to charter than own his own plane."

"Could just be ego," Enright said. "Just to show off."

"And he's got the money?" Joe said. "Right? Is he as rich as he makes it look?"

"One thing he hasn't been faking is the amount of

money he makes from his many enterprises," Alice said and slapped the ruler down meaningfully on a stack. "But what will it profit him? Prison and the ultimate judgment."

The three men saw themselves out as Alice turned back to the papers looking like a grand inquisitor.

19

As they were leaving, Joe's cell phone rang. It was Stacy, "Mike wants to see you in three minutes."

"I'm all the way over at Tanovich Construction."

"Then make it five," she said. "He's ready to explode."

It was impossible to drive from Tanovich's office to RCGC West in under twenty minutes, but Bittinger shut off his siren fourteen minutes later as he dropped Joe at the door.

Mike, who manned his two phones as usual, registered the suit and tie with a sense of relief as Joe entered. He didn't know the man sitting by Mike's desk who stood up.

"Don Ward, Pioneer Press," he said as they shook and Mike held up a hand to tell them he'd be right with them.

"Joe Brandt," Joe said. He knew the name. Ward was a local columnist for the St. Paul daily paper, his column was 'Don Ward and Upward.' Joe seldom found it interesting enough to read. Ward's stock in trade was poking holes in city government. He wasn't always wrong, but he was never generous, forgiving or understanding. His underlying assumption was, 'They're cheating us.' Given the nature of government and people in general, plus the perpetual scarcity of money, he was kept pretty busy digging up dirt.

When Mike hung up his calls, Joe said, "Sorry, Mike, I was at Tanovich Construction looking at the books."

Ward set a digital recorder on Mike's desk and said, "I'm giving you a chance to comment on tomorrow's column."

Joe found Mike making a gesture to wait, to listen.

"You are the son of George Felcher," Ward said, glancing at his notes. "He is a two-time felon, an ex-convict and his whereabouts are presently unknown."

"Mike, I..." One look from Mike stopped him.

"That also makes you nephew of convicted murderer, Louis Felcher who was recently paroled from Stillwater Prison."

"Louie's not in Stillwater?" Joe blurted out in alarm.

"So you admit it, Mr. Brandt?" Don Ward asked. "Then you also admit that Joseph Felcher is your real name?"

"My real name is Joseph Brandt," Joe insisted. "I had it legally changed to my mother's maiden name."

"That doesn't make it your real name," Ward said.

"A legally changed name is a real name," Mike said. "Is your mother calling herself Mrs. Ward just an alias?"

Ward made a dismissive gesture.

"So who else is running with this, Don?" Mike asked.

"I'm pretty sure it's an exclusive, but don't ask me to stomp all over it, Mike," Ward said. "I won't."

"Did I ask you that?" Mike said. "How would you feel if Tanovich walked? That help your reputation in town?"

"It wouldn't be my fault," Ward said defensively.

"You sucker punch one of my best people with irrelevant accusations, then want a statement while he's seeing stars."

"He's been covering up his past for a long time, Mike."

"So you say," Mike said. "Allow us time to comment. We can have something..." he looked to Joe questioningly.

"This afternoon," Joe said.

"We lock the print run at six," Ward said.

"Like hell you do, but you'll have our statement by five," Mike said as he stood to usher Ward out. Joe refused the offer of a handshake and just fumed in his seat.

This was how Chesler was going to play it, Joe realized. Just as Stacy said, anything that got him an edge. If it knocked the other side off balance, it was worth doing.

Joe was reeling from the news Louie was out of prison. Uncle Louie really could have given his mother that bruise.

"This means Marty Chesler is scared of you," Mike said. "If you get that same statement from the boy in court – you already got it once – Marty's big bucks client goes to prison, fires him and hires someone else for appeal. Marty's fucked double time. He gets trounced in a big, front page case and he loses his rich client very publicly."

Joe nodded but his mind had stopped working at 'If...'

"We need to figure out how to play this," Mike said. "Get back here at one," Mike said. "We got a shitstorm to contain and only a few hours to do it."

As Joe headed toward the door, Mike called after him, "Don't talk to anyone or even leave the building."

Joe desperately needed to see his mother. Louie's arrest for murder shortly after his father's disappearance had been a godsend that had allowed them two decades of peace. Now history was coming back with a vengeance.

YOUNG JOE FOLLOWED noise out of his bedroom toward his parent's room. He peeked through the open door and saw Uncle

Louie tearing the furniture apart with a primal rage as he shouted, "Where in fuck is it?"

JOE ATE TAKE out at his desk while sequestered behind a locked door and an unanswered telephone. He didn't dare call Kat or his mother. He just sat and stewed.

He tightened his tie back up as he was let into Mike's office at one and found Stacy at the conference table. She had a couple thick, old police files spread out in front of her. They were labeled George Felcher and Louis Felcher.

She looked up as Joe sat across from her. "You are making me a believer in nurture over nature, Joe."

"Thanks, I think."

"Can't see you inherited much from these two."

Joe wasn't sure he hadn't inherited a few things from them which was why he'd hidden his family his whole life. But that was over. He felt his family was now poised to take him down all over again.

"How are you holding up?" Stacy asked. "You look pretty good, considering the long night and having met Don Ward."

"Soap and coffee do wonders."

She glanced over at Mike, who was still on his phones, then she leaned across the table at Joe.

"Whatever gets decided, Joe," she said, "you did amazing work and we couldn't have indicted without it."

"But?"

"Byron told me about your basketball hero. Did this Bugsy Mogues guy ever catch an elbow right in the face from one of those NBA giants and get taken out on a stretcher bleeding like a butchered hog?"

"Mugsy? Yeah, I kinda think so," Joe said, then added, "He also played fourteen seasons."

"Then let's keep that in mind," she said.

Mike joined them and looked Joe over. "So where am I going to put you?"

"I'm moving, I take it?"

"Can you give me a way to keep you?"

"Let's get everyone in and hash out the alternatives," Stacy said. Ronald and Bruce led the way, but Joe was happy to see Enright and Tony following them. He needed allies. He thought Stacy was on his side, but the others would probably just as soon take over the case. Ronald clearly hoped to see him taken off the case right away.

Stacy gave a good summation of the lives of Joe's father and uncle. George had been arrested a dozen times for fights, drunkenness, drunken assault, petty theft and twice for burglary. Once he and his brother had burrowed into a sporting goods store from the empty shop next door and had stolen guns and ammunition. They'd been caught selling weapons out of the back of a car and both did serious time for it.

George's other major felony conviction was when he and Louie had tried to blast into the safe of a jewelry store. They used homemade explosives and they didn't know what they were doing. The detonation knocked them out cold and they were lucky it didn't kill them. When they woke up, they were in custody. There were domestic abuse reports against George, some called in by neighbors reacting to screams and some reported by emergency rooms. George had been tried for a domestic abuse charge, but had been acquitted because of insufficient evidence.

Louie went to prison for beating a man to death with his bare hands. The victim was a some-time associate of theirs.

Louie had laid-in-wait, making it first degree murder and he'd been sentenced to twenty-five to life. Given the crowding of the prisons, Louie had been released several weeks ago after almost twenty years.

Joe had not known half the details Stacy was telling. And the things he did know, he'd never revealed to a soul. In a matter of half an hour, a great deal of what Joe had kept under wraps his entire life was laid bare and the rest of the world would know it all within the day.

Joe was dumbfounded. No wonder Dad and Louie were so touchy about noises in the house, they were making explosives in the basement. His father's convictions were just the times they'd been caught and he had been acquitted of assault only because Joe and his mother had been intimidated by Uncle Louie into lying in court.

Joe found everyone staring at him as Mike said, "Joe?"

"Yes, Mike?"

"Have you seen your father since Burton Covey died?"

"Who?"

"The man your uncle killed," Stacy said.

"My dad ran out on us when I was eight."

"Not a single word from him since then?" Mike asked.

"We never looked. Good riddance, Ma said."

"I'll second that motion," Enright said.

"Then you were raised by a single mom?" Stacy said.

"Sins of the father aren't the sins of the son," Enright said. It might be true, but every face suggested otherwise.

"Want me to run the alternatives, Mike?" Tony asked.

Mike absently nodded. Joe figured he knew the alternatives and couldn't think of one he liked.

"Sorry, Joe," Tony began. "This is what we do when prosecutors are called into question for any reason."

Joe tried to listen as Tony told about prosecutors who

were removed for cause, shifted to second chair or replaced between preliminaries and the trial. Joe quit listening as the list of dishonest behavior grew longer.

"What's our thinking?" Mike asked.

Everyone was mum until Enright said, "As the only non-lawyer here, can I speak?"

Mike nodded and Enright said, "Joe's interview and deposition got us the indictment. He's the one who got the son putting his old man there doing it."

"We only got his word for it," Ronald said. "He made a gigantic error having Chesler as witness to the statement."

"May I finish?" Enright said testily. "Stacy and Tony and I were there. Give Joe enough time with the boy and it will all be on record. Take him off this case and I don't see us getting there. Without Joe, Tanovich goes free."

"We're agreed we want Joe to prosecute, but how do we weather the storm?" Mike said. "Can Joe stay in the boat? You just know the press are going to hound him."

Bruce, who had prosecuted a lot of murders, said, "We got our Chief of Prosecution in second chair. Let's put Stacy in first chair and move Joe to second to work with the boy. If the storm subsides, keep it that way. If not, Ronald or I could slip into second."

Lip service was given to the idea Joe was not on trial, but discussion was dominated by self-nominations for second chair and unanimity for Stacy in first. Tony was consulted on the efficacy of shifting Joe to second chair before easing him out completely. Discussion shifted to the embarrass-ment the DA's office would suffer and the points Chesler would score in the expected battering from the press. Joe was numb and quiet and his absence allowed the others to talk more freely. There seemed to be no support for keeping him in first chair or even on the case.

Joe began thinking about his high school debate team. In one state tournament, he'd been assigned to support the massive dumping of carcinogens into Lake Superior based on a real case which had taken place in Minnesota. In debate, each team's stance was assigned, so a debater had to learn to argue the best of the position given. Debate was good practice for law and one lesson he learned was to turn being on the wrong side to your advantage. That was what Chesler was now doing and it was exactly what Joe needed to do too.

"Were any of you on the debate team in high school?" Joe asked. They all seemed to have forgotten he was there.

"Don't think it will help you," Ronald said.

"What's our biggest disadvantage here?" he asked. "I come from the scum of the earth."

"I wouldn't put it that way," Stacy said.

"But that's the essence of the argument. They paint my family as criminal degenerates and they're not wrong," Joe said. "Until Dusan Tanovich, I thought my father had to be the worst human being ever to walk this earth. Jury's still out as far as I'm concerned."

"What are you saying, Joe?" Mike asked.

"They aren't accusing me of any crime, just guilt by association as Byron says," Joe said, gaining their interest. "My forced association with sleazy criminals formed me."

"How to write their article for them, Joe," Ronald said.

Mike shut Ronald up with a scowl.

"I've never spoken about my father or uncle or how I was brought up. I was ashamed, but it also came from hating them, distancing myself from them," Joe said as he stood and took his suit jacket off, then loosened his tie. "The only advantage we have is what incredible degenerate abusers my father and uncle really were. Trust me, they were far worse than anything Stacy found in those files."

Joe threw his jacket and tie onto his chair, then started unbuttoning his shirt. "When anyone asks about this scar on my lip, I've always said I was hit by a line drive in Little League. It's actually courtesy of my father when I was eight. It was not an accident." He tossed his dress shirt onto his chair and revealed his Frankenstein scar. "With his bare hands, my father broke my arm. A compound fracture when I was seven. It was no accident."

"Jesus, Joe," Stacy said.

"What are you suggesting?" Mike asked.

"Is Don Ward the only journalist we know?"

"Not by a mile," Mike said, liking where this was going.

"I never wanted to do this, it's against every instinct in me, but I do an interview. I show scars, I paint a realistic portrait of growing up with the kinds of criminals we put away every day. I tell about the daily life of a victim. I tell everything I never wanted to tell," Joe said, but didn't mean it. He couldn't tell everything. Ever.

"'Victim of domestic abuse prosecutes abusers'" Mike said, envisioning the headline.

"They tar me with the sins of my father," Joe said.

"But that tar don't stick," Enright practically shouted.

"Could backfire," Stacy worried. "Tony?"

"Halfway measures might backfire," Tony said. "How'd you do in debate?"

"State champion," Joe said. Mike and Enright smiled.

Tony thought for a while and finally said, "Can't think of anyone who ever tried to dump more shit on himself."

"They want to make Joe look bad because of his father and uncle," Mike said and went over to Joe's chair. "We make him look like a fucking saint because he not only survived them, he locks up dirtbags just like them."

Mike handed Joe his shirt. "Get dressed. I don't want any of the rest of you thinking it's okay to undress in my office." Everyone laughed.

"Tony, get hold of Sid and his photographer. Stacy, get Joe through this like it's a deposition. Joe, matter-of-fact will end up being more dramatic than hyperbole."

"I gotta start carrying a dictionary," Enright said.

"I will release a statement that Joe is our first chair and has my full and complete backing," Mike said.

Everyone except Ronald patted Joe on the back as they filed out. Mike held Joe and Stacy back.

As he pulled his suit jacket on, Joe realized he'd untied his tie completely and fumbled trying to knot it. Without even being asked, Stacy took over.

"You okay with all this, Joe?" Mike asked.

"No."

Stacy cinched up the tie and looked him in the eye, "So you okay with all this?" she repeated.

"I'll get there."

20

JOE HAD AN HOUR AND HOPED IT WOULD BE ENOUGH TIME. HE raced out of the office heading to Juvenile and Family Services. He prayed Kat was in and would speak with him.

He was welcomed with a giant smile from the receptionist who eyed a huge spray of roses. She knew he was the source.

"Miss Nolan is meeting with lawyers," she told him. "They didn't say how long it would be."

'Lawyers?' Joe thought. He wondered what that could possibly be about as he glanced at his watch and took a seat. He couldn't believe he was about to tell all his secrets voluntarily. A lot of his memories were vague, just nightmares. Despite what Kat said about memory retrieval, he and his mother had severely restricted his recall.

"Mr. Brandt?" Marty Chesler said, surprising the hell out of Joe. He was leading a parade of his assistants from Kat's office. She was behind the crowd and seemingly relieved to see him. For his part, Chesler seemed confused.

"It is now the role of the district attorney's office to counsel social workers during questioning," Chesler said.

"Questioning?" Joe said, looking past them to Kat.

"Miss Nolan works with an important witness in our case, Mr. Brandt," Chesler said, looking from Joe to Kat. "Is counseling Miss Nolan not why you're here?"

"I'm here because Miss Nolan works with an important witness in our case, Mr. Chesler," Joe said.

Chesler nodded as an assistant opened the door for him. When he stepped out, he smiled a Cheshire Cat grin, leaving Joe frozen. Finally, he followed Kat to her office.

Kat did not offer a kiss and simply plopped down behind her desk looking exhausted and stressed.

"So what did Marty Chesler want?"

"Help in undermining Billy Tanovich."

"What did Marty Chesler get?"

"'I'm not allowed to discuss that aspect of a client'" she said. "I can't tell you how many times I said it."

"Good," Joe said. "Could you do me a big favor and write down all the questions he asked. It will tell me something about what he's thinking."

"I can't do it for a while, I have a full afternoon."

It felt so good to see her, he said, "I've missed you."

"We need to talk, Joe," she said solemnly.

"That's why I'm here."

"You come when my schedule's full and I have five minutes...so you can weasel out of having a serious talk."

"I've come to beg you to reschedule the afternoon."

"Not going to happen," she said definitively.

"It has to. I can't say everything twice. I need you."

"Say what twice?"

"Marty Chesler has dug up dirt on my family."

"What are you talking about?"

'Here goes,' he thought, then said, "Tomorrow's paper

will say my father is a felon, ex-con and domestic abuse suspect and my uncle is a vicious murderer."

She stared at him for the longest time.

"I've never said any of that out loud in my life."

Kat picked up the phone and pressed a number with shaky hands. "I have an emergency. See if you can give my next client to Celia and cancel the others," she said. "I don't care, it's an emergency." When she hung up, there was some sympathy in her eyes. And a whole lot of fear.

He glanced at his watch and said, "I have to meet a reporter and tell everything. Please come with me."

She stared, still trying to comprehend as he stood up.

"If I had any choice, I would take it to my grave."

She grew frigid. "What do you want from me then?"

"You can hear it from me directly when I speak to the reporter or you can read about it in the paper tomorrow."

"I don't understand."

"Chesler planted a nasty story. I have to tell my story."

SID MENDELL and Stacy were waiting in her office with a photographer and two tape recorders when Kat and Joe arrived. Introductions were made and soon they sat at the small table Stacy used for strategy meetings. Joe was quaking inside.

Sid and Stacy reached for recorders, but Joe stopped them. "Before we record," he said, "I need to explain why Kat is here. It's not part of the article, okay?"

Sid nodded. He was an old-time reporter, a real journalist who had survived all the cuts at the newspaper. He and Ward were a world apart. Ward's underlying assumption was that everyone cheated. Sid felt that, despite their faults, people tried to do as well as they could. Joe wasn't sure either of them was right, but it gave the paper balance.

"Kat should already know what I'm about to tell, but I have never been able to force myself to reveal it, to her or anyone else," Joe said. "I know I can't do this twice and Kat deserves more than to read about it tomorrow."

"Okay by me," Sid said.

Stacy looked from Joe to Kat. "Are you comfortable with this," she asked.

"Comfortable, no," Kat said. "Resigned to it, yeah."

The recorders were turned on and Joe launched into a brief introduction to his childhood in East St. Paul, to the tough neighborhood, what life had been like in that area back then. He told about his parents' marriage and the ages and birthplaces of his parents and uncle. Stacy helped with exact dates and details that were in the police files.

"I have no memory of a time when my father did not beat my mother," he said and heard Kat gasp.

"*STOP IT, DAD,*" *Young Joe screamed as his father leaned over his mother sprawled out on the floor. George's giant hand was dripping blood and rising above him, as if in slow motion. Joe grabbed the fist with both hands and was lifted off the floor by the punch George was in the middle of throwing.*

JOE SHOOK off the image that had flashed through his head. "One time he ran out on us for several months and that was great. It might have been when he was in jail, I don't know. My mother started to relax after he'd been gone a while, but the moment he came back, the whole atmosphere of the house turned instantly back into fear and dread."

Joe glanced over at Kat, she was quietly crying.

"I really couldn't tell you the first time Dad hit me," he went on. Joe tried to recount the constant abuse, what it took to leave his bedroom, what it was like to drop a baseball on the kitchen floor, the beatings he had been spared because his mother inserted herself between them and took the whipping for him. He recalled the beatings she got he could do nothing to stop, how he remembered his mother, bruised and swollen, trying to soothe him.

He told about his mother packing bags to escape. When they were caught, Dad beat them until he was exhausted, then Louie took over. They were prisoners.

Joe reported on the stacks of VCRs and cases of liquor in his dad's car. It was the way his father and uncle made a living. Whatever they had been caught doing was just a small portion of the crimes they committed.

Joe disclosed how often his father and uncle would come home with cuts, bruises and swollen eyes from bar fights, street fights, fights with each other. Over the years his mother had gained a lot of experience at mending wounds, an expertise born of need.

He had to stop briefly while Stacy deflected an urgent call. It was enough time for haunting images to flood him.

AILEEN PLACED *Louie's hands in a shiny enamel basin of water. The big man had his back to Young Joe, but the boy could tell she was cleaning out wounds to his hands.*

"Go someplace else next time, Louie," she said. "George is gone for good this time."

"He'll be back."

"I don't want him back and I don't want you to set foot in this

house ever again, Louie," Aileen said with a degree of force that surprised Joe.

Louie raised a fist at Aileen and Joe saw his hand was a bloody, torn-up mess. It was damaged enough that he didn't follow through and hit her already swollen and bruised face.

JOE EXPLAINED his obsession with Little League, saying it took him out of the house. It was his daily escape.

He described how his father would twist his shirt into a knot, the times he had passed out from it, the time his mother hit his father with a frying pan to make him stop. When he woke up, she was unconscious in a pool of blood, the door was open and his father was gone, so he ran to the Acuffs' and they called an ambulance.

He said his uncle was as bad as his father. Joe knew nothing about the man Louie had killed with his bare hands. Stacy revealed from the files that Louie had been turned in by a snitch, presumably someone who witnessed the beating.

"When did you last see your father?" Sid asked.

Joe realized he had been talking a long time and that once the flood gates had opened, he had spoken nonstop without prompts or questions. Once he'd tapped into his early childhood, he'd just spread his life open for them. Sid's question brought him back to the present.

He tried to conjure a picture of his father leaving.

YOUNG JOE STARED at his mother. One eye was swollen shut, the other was a slit, her neck was purple and Joe could see the imprint of his father's thumbs on it.

"Go get yourself some more ice now, Joey," she said.

In the kitchen he tossed out the pink ice in the dish towel he'd held to his badly split lip. When he heard a thump, it sounded like his father stomping up from downstairs. He froze in fear, then he heard another thump.

Terrified that Dad had come back to beat them more, he stood dripping blood into the sink until the sounds stopped.

It seemed like hours later when he went to the living room with ice in towels for himself and his mother. By then they had the house to themselves and at last it was quiet.

HE LOOKED AT KAT, then consciously touched the scar on his lip and said, "The last time I saw my father was the night he gave me this."

Disturbed, Kat studied him, but he couldn't look at her.

"He was beating my mother in the living room. *Golden Girls* was on television. I tried to get him to stop and that's when he split my lip."

"What finally made him stop?" Sid asked.

"I'm not sure."

"Jesus."

"This was the last time you saw him?" Sid asked.

"He ran out on us that night."

"Could you elaborate, Joe?" Sid asked.

"That's all I remember."

"How was your mother?"

"We sat with ice on our faces and hoped he was gone. Then some time later that night, she sewed up my lip."

"She sewed up your lip? " Sid said. "Like stitches?"

"Yeah, she'd had a lot of practice."

Joe saw Sid involuntarily shudder at the thought.

"Dad stole a lot of supplies from an ER during a visit," he said. "She bandaged her own cuts and we were glad he ran out on us. We never wanted him to come back."

The room was deathly silent. "My mother has never really recovered," Joe said with a wary glance toward Kat. "There's only so many times a person can be hit that hard without it...doing things inside." Joe was suddenly alarmed. "Can we leave that out? This is about my father, not about her. Please don't put that in. "

"I won't. I've got enough to do a week."

"Please don't. I just want it to go away."

"I don't think that's possible, Joe," Stacy said.

"How the hell did you come out normal?" Sid asked.

Joe looked at Kat. "Kat might say I didn't."

"You're assistant district attorney with the biggest case in the state," Sid said. "You're doing something right."

"I think so," Kat said.

"Never another word from your father?" Sid said.

"Ma told me he must have known he'd go to jail for beating us that badly, so he just disappeared," Joe said.

"You were eight when he ran out?"

"Yeah."

"What was the date of that?"

"I have no idea."

"Was it around the same time your uncle beat Burton Covey to death?" Stacy asked, consulting the files.

"Maybe, but it's pretty fuzzy. I seem to remember my uncle coming around looking for him."

"You've got enough, Sid," Stacy said. "Can I see a draft before you go to print?"

THE PHOTOGRAPHER RECOVERED his senses as Sid and Stacy stepped into the hall. Joe didn't really want any pictures taken, but then there was a flash and he'd been photographed. He showed his scarred lip, the scar on his arm and then, at long last, he was alone with Kat as the photographer left. The moment they were alone, she dove in for a ferocious hug.

"I'm sorry, Kat."

"Me too."

"What are you sorry for?"

"I'm sorry all that happened to you. I'm sorry I was so hard on you for not telling me things I couldn't even begin to imagine. I'm sorry I've been so mad at you."

"Still mad at me?"

She squeezed him. "No. So is it a relief to have it out?" He shook his head no and she said, "Really?"

"Yeah," he said. "I've just replaced one dread with another. All of that is going to be revealed and everyone will say 'Oh poor Joey Felcher' and people are going to want to 'talk.' It was a lot easier when it was a line drive in a Little League game when I was eight."

"Is easier better?"

"In my world it is. After Dad left, life was easier."

When they opened the door, they discovered an unprecedented number of his colleagues in the hallway. It was clear they had been the object of much discussion.

"Everyone," Joe said, surprising himself and Kat, "I'd like you to meet my girlfriend, Katherine Nolan. Kat. Some of you may have worked with her over in Family Services."

Bruce and Tony and others stepped up to greet her and give Joe not-so-secret high signs of approval. Liza sidled up real close and tugged on his tie.

"Explains the sudden advent of taste in your sartorial

choices, Joe," Liza said. "Good going on all fronts." There was distinct disappointment in her, but Joe never noticed.

"Thanks," he said and watched his friends and colleagues gather around Kat more than him. Just the way he liked it.

21

KAT WAS WRAPPED AROUND JOE'S ARM AS THEY WALKED TO HIS car to get his lanyard and a basketball. He had changed out of the suit and was going to meet Billy to shoot some baskets. It would be their first time together since the boy had told his story. From a strictly evidentiary viewpoint, he should ask Billy to tell him everything all over again.

'Not going to happen,' he told himself. Both he and the boy had changed since that afternoon a few days ago in the back yard under the oak tree. He didn't know what it would take to get to that moment again. If it was even possible.

Kat had cancelled her afternoon and was determined not to let Joe out of her sight. He kept saying he was fine, but this was the same guy who'd made her believe he had no family. Why should she believe him when he said he was okay? She'd seen clients struggle with similar revelations, but few who had driven the secrets so deep and remained sane. 'Apparently sane,' she thought. Disturbed, certainly. Her life-long project, she hoped. Sane, probably. Healthy, maybe someday.

Joe was really looking forward to shooting baskets with

Billy again. He really liked the boy and thought he might actually be good for him, a fellow sufferer. Two wounded souls shooting baskets.

What he hadn't anticipated was Marty Chesler. Why no Bayona today? Didn't he have more important things to do than to chaperone Joe and Billy working on the boy's shot count? Then it struck him, this was the most important thing Chesler had to work on. The case hinged on Billy Tanovich and Chesler needed to build rapport with him just as Joe had done, with comparable oversight from the DA's side. Until now he had not attempted to get close to the boy.

Fortunately, Chesler was fending off panhandlers in the park as they walked up so he didn't see them. Joe peeled Kat from his arm and announced their presence by dribbling the ball right past Chesler, making a nice lay-up.

"What a pleasure, Miss Nolan," Chesler said extending a hand. "I hadn't expected to see you again so soon."

"Nor I," Kat said coolly as they both watched Joe. "I've come to see how Billy is doing with play therapy."

"That's what this has been?" Chesler said as he watched Joe sink a beautiful fade away jump shot. "He's a man of many dimensions."

"So I'm learning."

Joe joined them and offered the ball to Chesler, but it was graciously refused. "Not among my talents, I'm afraid."

"Excellence at pool, shooting baskets and pinball are all hallmarks of a misspent youth," Joe said and dropped another perfect shot through the basket. "Or so I'm told."

"I don't believe you misspent your youth," Chesler said with his most charming smile. "Mike has given you what must be the most prized case in the office."

"Most challenging for sure."

"I suspect you value challenge above all other

things."They smiled awkwardly. Joe knew Chesler was behind the Don Ward ambush. Now he had a surprise coming.

Joe found it nearly impossible to resist shooting to clear his mind, even though it left Kat alone with Chesler.

Chesler watched him shoot with apparent admiration and said, "I was last chosen for any athletic team."

"So was Joe, I think. I mean, Mr. Brandt," Kat said.

"I believe he counts on being underestimated," Chesler said as Joe worked up quite a sweat shooting.

Kat hoped Nicola and Billy would arrive soon, she was finding it difficult to maintain civility with this man. With children, she had a patience of astonishing durability. With smug, hypocritical adults, she had no patience at all.

"Apparently there's considerable division within the district attorney's office about Mr. Brandt's position in this case," Chesler said casually.

She tried to hide her surprise. "I didn't know that."

"Hey Coach," Billy cried as he came racing onto the court. Joe fed him a pass and ignored his complete failure to dribble as he went in for a lay up and almost made it.

"Good try, Billy," Joe said as he got the ball and passed it back to the boy. He waved hello to Nicola who was just now arriving, but stopped when she saw Chesler with Kat.

Kat was relieved as she headed to Nicola with an outstretched hand. Nicola was equally thankful. Billy had been looking forward to shooting and it was the healthiest part of their daily life now, anticipating basketball.

Joe shrugged off his disquiet at seeing Kat and Nicola together and grabbed the rebound when Billy made his first shot of the day. "Way to go, what are we up to now?"

"Fifty-three, Coach," Billy said with pride. "I shot over the weekend and practiced already this afternoon."

Joe watched Kat and Nicola walk away to talk and that left him with Billy, Chesler and the homeless. Joe felt surprisingly relaxed, bordering on euphoric, as he coached Billy, corrected hand placement, suggested dribbling was a crucial element. They seemed like boys in the backyard. Even the homeless guys cheered when Billy made baskets.

Chesler stood awkwardly to the side with a fixed smile.

By the time Kat and Nicola returned, engrossed in an emotional discussion, Billy's tally had risen to sixty-eight and he was desperate to get it to seventy, but Nicola insisted on leaving. Joe was surprised when he got a hug from Billy and not even a look from Nicola. He put the basket back up to regulation height and gave a few bucks to the homeless guys for the invasion of their territory.

"Thank you for the instruction, Mr. Brandt," Chesler said, shaking with each of them.

"Wear sneakers and come to shoot next time," Joe said.

Chesler politely shook his head and went to his car. Behind him, Joe had taken over the Cheshire Cat grin.

"Has there been controversy about you on this case?"

Joe's grin evaporated. "What'd he say?"

"He said the DA's office was divided about you."

Joe was upset as he watched the Mercedes drive past. "Chesler knows what goes on in our office?" Joe said.

"So there is controversy about you?"

"Yeah, but how does he know about it a few hours later?" Joe asked. "He's got a mole inside our office."

"A spy? You make it sound like war."

"A billionaire indicted for murder?" Joe said sullenly. "That's the definition of war."

Kat pulled him into a kiss. "Only happy subjects."

"I'm happy. So what'd you and Nicola talk about?"

"I gave her a heads up on what to expect in the paper tomorrow," Kat said. "She couldn't believe it."

"Yeah, me too."

"You lived it."

"I can't believe it'll be in the paper tomorrow."

"Nicola thinks you're a saint."

"You set her straight, I assume?"

"Now why would I do that?" Kat joked.

THEY AGREED to meet later at her place and agreed expressly not to talk about either the case or Joe's family.

As he drove from downtown toward the west side, passing the mansions along Summit Avenue, including the place where F. Scott Fitzgerald had once lived, he stopped to pick up a bottle of wine utilizing the meager skills he had developed under her guidance. Buy French and the more specific the words between 'Appellation' and 'Contrôlée' the better. This from a guy whose previous variety was in the color of his Kool-Aid.

Joe let himself in and she called, "What took so long?"

She inspected the bottle and said, "Good choice, I'm going to be able to take you out in public pretty soon."

While she opened the wine, Joe shut off his cell phone and took his turn in the shower. Kat came in with two glasses and wanted to chat through the shower curtain. "Why do you suppose Marty Chesler came to the park?"

"He's looking for weakness. Anything that will help him drive a wedge between me and Billy," Joe said.

"I don't think I like your business. You suppose he discovered anything while you were shooting baskets?"

"He went away knowing he can't compete with me in

getting close to Billy and gaining his trust," Joe said. "That's why he didn't even try to approach him."

Joe shut off the water, yanked aside the curtain and found Kat wearing just a smile.

AT DAWN, Joe left Kat sound asleep. He was still wearing the clothes he'd played basketball in, but a smile unlike he'd worn in some time. He planned to make a quick visit home, but stopped for much-needed coffee on the way. When the barista wouldn't let him pay and gave him the weirdest look, he should have guessed. When he turned off University Avenue toward his apartment, the dime finally dropped. For half a second he thought there might have been a shooting or drug bust on his street when he saw the news vans with their satellite dishes. Then he saw the TV reporters standing directly in front of his building.

His luck lasted for one more minute as he turned down an alley behind his building, but good fortune was short-lived. He was accosted at the parking ramp near RCGC West.

"Mr. Felcher," the news jerk said as he shoved a microphone and camera practically through the window as Joe used his parking card to enter the ramp. "How many men do you think your father and uncle killed?"

"My name is Brandt," Joe said as the gate rose and he was able to drive slowly past the assault. He bulldozed past more news crews between parking the car and the building, but the throng at RCGC West was too dense to push through.

"How many scars do you have? Have you seen your uncle since he got out of prison?" The questions came like a mortar barrage. Just as he was about to explode, a big hand took hold of him and he heard the voice of Byron Enright say, "This way." Enright ran interference and did not let news people get in his way as they entered the building lobby where police were holding the press at bay.

"What the hell's wrong with those people?" Joe said.

"They think that has something to do with democracy."

In the elevator Enright said, "Mike and Stacy want to confab a.s.a.p.." Then he looked at Joe strangely. "You got balls of titanium just surviving this long, Joe." Enright kept studying him and finally added, "You're going to get this a lot today, I couldn't even begin to imagine."

"Yeah."

On the eighth floor, Joe was surprised to find a lot of his colleagues nodding to him. He realized his relationship with every person he knew had changed in one day. He was half leper and half saint now. Not one person he worked with would ever be indifferent to him again.

Just outside Mike's office, Joe stopped Enright. "Could you do me one more favor, Byron?"

"Name it."

"My mother," Joe said. "If this is happening to me, something must be going on at her house. She's still named Felcher. She must be terrified."

"I'll have our police friends escort her out of there."

"She won't leave the house."

"Man, she shoulda left there so long ago."

"Tell me about it," Joe said. "There's a fence. Could we have them held back to that until this shit storm passes?"

"Done," Enright said as he pulled out his cell phone.

Joe went ahead into Mike's office and found Stacy and Mike together with Tony at the conference table.

"Seen the papers yet, Joe?" Stacy asked as Tony turned two news sections to face him. In the far left column on the front page was the headline, "We Never Wanted Him to Come Back." That was Sid's story and below the fold was a photo of Joe at the window, the scar on his lip very pronounced. In the 'Community' section, on its front page, was the 'Don Ward and Upward' column with the headline, "Can We Trust Those Who Work for Us?"

"Don Ward types with a hatchet," Tony said.

"And Sid?" Joe asked.

"A few actual journalists remain in journalism. You're still first chair thanks to Sid and near as we can gauge, we won another round with a knock down," Stacy said.

They all turned to Mike. "Just one question," Mike said. "After all that, can you be impartial?"

Joe thought he knew what he was supposed to say. He also knew he couldn't honestly say it. "No," he said as Enright let himself in and joined the eerily quiet group.

"If I've ever appeared to be impartial," Joe said, "then I'll be able to continue to give that impression, Mike. But I've never been impartial to abusive fucks a day in my life."

"Just what I wanted to hear. If you lived through that and said you were impartial, I'd know you were a liar."

'I am a liar,' Joe thought, 'just not about that.'

"We got a man on your mom's house," Enright said. "How long we expect the feeding frenzy to last, Mike?"

"Until the next major natural disaster or a baby falls down a mine shaft," Mike said. "The press will feed as long as there's scraps," Mike said. "If we cut off their food supply, they move on."

"How do we cut off the food supply?" Joe asked.

"You've watched idiot jocks and senators who keep changing their story?" Mike said. "First they admit just a bit while still denying most of it, then they change and admit more. What they're saying is, 'There's more to come.'"

"So we stick to exactly what has been said? We don't give them any reason to believe there's more?" Joe asked

"Bore them to death and they go away," Mike said.

AS THEY LEFT Mike's office, Joe stayed with Enright and asked, "What'd they say about my mother's place?"

"Handful, but our guy's got them outside the fence."

"She's got to be in a panic," Joe said as he discovered his cell phone had been off since the night before. He had nearly forty calls – the press and a dozen from his mother.

"How can I get to my mother's house?"

"Not a good idea. That's not very boring."

"Not going is not an option."

Enright nodded and escorted Joe back to the elevator, then pressed the button for the basement level. Joe immediately panicked. "I can't go in the basement, Byron."

Enright studied him. "Wasn't an act for the boy, huh?" Joe shook his head. "The tunnel over to the courthouse?"

"Might as well be a basement," Joe said.

Enright was at a loss for an escape route and started making calls as Joe went to his office and called his mother. "The policeman is there to protect you, Ma. He'll keep them from getting in the yard." She didn't really hear him.

He called Kat but the receptionist couldn't put him through, Kat was trying to catch up with her backlog from yesterday. He asked if there had been any press around and was relieved to discover Kat seemed to be off the radar.

Enright peeked in, "How are you at cross-dressing?"

"Lousy," Joe said.

"Okay, just checking," Enright said and again was gone.

When there was a noise at the door seconds later, Joe

didn't even look up. "No dresses, Byron," he said, then discovered Ronald Sheldon standing there, smirking.

"Gotta give you credit," Ronald said and Joe just looked at him warily. "I knew you were off balance, but now I see you're as whacko as the rest of your killer family."

"I'll be sure to give my uncle your address."

"Murder runs in families," Ronald said with a grin.

Ronald slipped away and Joe fumed, but just then Chip Bateman stepped into his office looking very sympathetic.

"Our team has been talking," Chip said.

"I'm getting a lot of that today," Joe said.

"Anything we can do, you got it, Joe," Chip said.

"Short of canceling the project or building around her?"

"Short of that, yes," Chip admitted.

"I really appreciate it, but that's the only thing that would really help her," Joe said.

"We can access any agency, counseling, help packing, just ask," Chip said. "All city resources are yours."

"I appreciate it," Joe said. "But not only does she not leave the house, I'm the only one she lets inside. But if I go there now, it'll just lead press to her and make it worse."

Chip stared, thinking. "Think the press would follow a city truck?"

Joe brightened up. "Think it would work?"

"We could put crews out there a little early and block access to her street. Tear-down starts in a few days anyway."

Tear-down was starting that soon?

22

Less than an hour later a city work truck pushed aside the reporters as it parked at the doors of RCGC West. Four workers in coveralls, orange vests and hardhats walked inside and went to the third floor where Joe and Enright waited. Chip Bateman gave his gear and hardhat to Joe and soon a slightly changed foursome climbed into the city truck and drove off. Chip Bateman walked out without causing a media stir.

Angry news crews had been pushed outside a barrier at the corner of Forrestal and East Ninth by city workers. The barricade was pulled aside for the truck which parked and four workmen headed to the backs of four different houses. Joe used his key to let himself in the back door of his mother's house without being identified by the press.

As he closed and locked the door behind him, he heard an ominous click, then Aileen said, "I got a gun."

He turned and took the hard hat off. "It's me, Ma."

It took Aileen a second to recognize him, but finally she lowered the shotgun to her lap. She sat on a kitchen chair propped under the basement door knob.

Joe took off the work clothes and edged close to take the shotgun away. He tried to make certain not to hold it where it could be seen through any window as he uncocked it.

"You can't shoot anyone, Ma," Joe said.

"I will if I have to, Joey."

"That will only make it worse," he said. "If they see a gun, they won't go away. More of them will come."

"Then you make them go away."

"I'm working on it, but it might take a day, okay?" Joe said as he went to the living room and pulled the shades down, then the shade in his old bedroom. He came back to find his mother with the shotgun back in her lap.

"I still got Louie to worry about," Aileen said.

Joe let her keep the shotgun and sat down knee to knee with her. "I was wrong. It was Louie, he's out on parole."

"Can you get him put back in?"

"I can try, but as long as cops and work crews are around, Louie isn't going to show his ugly face," Joe said as he seriously inspected the shotgun. "That was Dad's?"

"He forgot to take it when he ran out," she said.

"Can I see it?"

She reluctantly handed it over and he realized he'd never held a gun before today. He had to search to find the lever that let it open and discovered shotgun shells in both barrels. "Jesus, Ma, it's loaded."

"Wouldn't stop Louie or them otherwise."

He pulled the shells out and they just crumbled in his hand. "It would have just blown up in your face."

"There's more shells downstairs."

"There are guns and ammo downstairs?" he said. "That's why you made me so afraid of basements."

"Your nightmares made you scared."

"I remember when you put up that lock and told me

never go down there," he said as he looked at the door, wincing.

"I put the lock on cuz you were so afraid, Joey."

He discovered he could detach the barrel end from the trigger and butt end. He carried both parts as he went to his bedroom and stepped into his past. Anything he hadn't taken with him when he moved to college was where he left it. Boy's books and trophies on the shelves, Timberwolves posters on the walls. He opened the closet to have a look through his former life. He found basketball jerseys, tattered and over-used sneakers, Goodwill sweaters he'd worn to debates in lieu of a suit and tie. He spied an old gym bag.

With the shotgun in two pieces, each half fit inside the gym bag. He stuffed sports socks and sneakers in to try to mask the shape and hoped it looked like a bag of junk. Mike had said not to give the press anything more to feed on and he was now planning to leave the house carrying a shotgun. Great.

When he went back out, the basement door was unlocked and open. He froze as panic surged through him.

He stumbled back and felt lightheaded when he heard footsteps coming upstairs. It sounded like stomping, that old awful sound. His heart thundered and he was instantly eight again. Utterly terrified. Aileen came through the door with a box of shotgun shells, set it on the kitchen table, then closed and locked the door. The key to the lock was on a chain she strung back around her neck, tucked it inside her house dress and said, "Red or blue?"

While she started a pitcher of Kool-Aid, Joe stared at the door he had feared since the night his dad ran out.

Aileen set a glass down and reached for the box of shells, but he was faster. "I'm going to take those too."

"I'd rather you left them and took all those people."

"I'm going to try to talk them into going away."

JOE CALLED Enright and asked if he could pick him up on the barricaded corner, then let himself out the back door with the gym bag. He went through the Acuffs' back yard so he could walk around behind the news crowd. He saw there were already demolition workers taking down a house on the far corner. It was all happening way too fast.

Nobody noticed Joe behind the crowd at the barricade.

"It's no longer an open street, it's a construction zone and it will be closed until further notice," Chip yelled.

The reporters saw no reason they couldn't harangue Joe's mother to their hearts' content except that Chip said they weren't allowed. A policeman beside him backed Chip up. Joe knew the cop would have to leave some time, the workmen would eventually quit for the night and his mother would again be vulnerable.

"There's nothing you want over there," Joe shouted. At first they ignored him, but soon the newsmen gathered. "There will never be anything you want at that house."

Cameras and reporters surged at Joe and a fusillade of questions were shot at him, all screamed over the others.

"You will get only one statement here, so if you're not quiet, you won't be able to broadcast it."

One of the reporters was about to shout a question, but Joe shot a finger out and shut him up.

"You are terrifying a woman who will tell you nothing. I will say absolutely nothing so long as any of you are near that house," he said.

Protests began, but he held his hands up to stop them.

"If all of you leave right now and no one comes back to frighten my mother," Joe said, "I will make a statement tomorrow at 9am at RCGC West. If I hear of anyone coming back, there will never be another statement. Ever."

Gym bag in hand, Joe hurried to join Enright in the SUV. Together they surveyed the news crews.

"How is she?"

"Ready to offer them the lead story of the day."

They watched the first news truck pull away and Enright began to laugh. "You might be onto something here."

"What are my chances that no one will sneak back?"

Enright flipped open his cell phone and called. The cop at the barricade answered his private cell. "We got coverage into the evening, Earl?" The cop nodded and Joe watched as other news trucks drove off. "I owe you a case of Heineken."

"How many times you saved my life today?" Joe said. "Thanks,"

"I figure I'll be able to get free drinks at Sheehans off this day alone for a couple years."

"I buy the first round."

"Don't get too thirsty just yet, I got the bad news now," Enright said, jerking his thumb over the backseat at Joe's suit hanging on a hanger. "You've been summoned."

"To Mike's?"

"Worse. Judge Woodward," Enright said, then added, "Tanovich never built her a house. Already checked."

Joe blanched. Whatever it was was not good news.

Joe asked him to stop beside the cop and promised him a second case of Heineken for his help.

"Mike's gotta start worrying about you, Joe," Enright said. "You won votes from half the city population today."

"And the other half?"

"Fuck 'em."

As they drove, Joe started to change in the car. "So what statement are you going to make tomorrow?"

"Haven't a clue," Joe said.

ENRIGHT WAS on the cell phone as he drove past the reporters at the County Courthouse and went around the side where there was a fire exit. It was a permanently locked door without even a handle on the outside. The door opened, a policeman stepped out and waved to them.

"Have I joined a vast conspiratorial organization?"

"I'll teach you the secret handshake later."

As he was about to get out of the car, Joe's foot hit the dense gym bag on the floor.

"Could you hang onto the bag for me?" Joe said as casually as he could manage.

"I'll put it in your office."

23

JOE FOLLOWED THE COP INSIDE AND FOUND STACY UPSTAIRS.

"Good news and awful," Stacy said as she paced. "Good news is it looks like your massive revelation was colossally successful. Even Don Ward is embarrassed and saying, 'I didn't know,'" Stacy said with a grin.

"And awful news," Joe said. "What's Marty doing now?"

"Accusing you of misconduct," she said. "He says you charmed your way into the pants of the person assigned to protect the only witness against his client." Joe stared. "The girlfriend you introduced to everyone yesterday."

"We've been together quite a while," he said.

"Since before you met Billy?"

Joe nodded, but saw Stacy looking at the door, which read: 'The Right Honorable Maureen Woodward."

Maureen Woodward was generally a fair and impartial judge, the sort you hoped to have if you were ever falsely accused. Unless you were accused of predatory abuse of women. Men in Judge Woodward's court for crimes against women were shown no mercy, no impartiality and it was all done without appealable violations.

Joe was being accused of predatory behavior and using the power of his position against a woman who worked for the county in the protection of a vulnerable child with the intention of subverting justice. That would be Chesler's argument and it just might find a sympathetic ear.

Stacy and Joe saw Kat walking toward them, beaming.

"I don't think I'm ever going to catch up with my case load," Kat said. "I've got clients in the waiting room."

"Chesler is trying to get me taken off the case," Joe said. Kat looked genuinely shocked, but before he could tell her what it was all about, Judge Woodward's clerk beckoned them just as the Tanovich team approached.

Judge Woodward's office had a feminine touch without undermining its judicial solemnity. The upholstery on the easy chairs and the flowering plants. There was no doubt this office belonged to a powerful woman.

Judge Maureen Woodward was a handsome woman in a tailored suit, elegant shoes, well controlled hair and make-up, but she made no effort to deny the realities of time.

"First, Mr. Brandt, I am well aware of the articles in the paper this morning and the courage it took to bring forward your most unfortunate childhood," the judge said.

"Thank you, Your Honor," Joe said.

"Second, nothing in this matter today has anything to do directly with Mr. Tanovich, is that clear?" she said.

Joe found himself wondering what kind of balls it took for Chesler to bring this case – the murder and dismemberment of a woman – this close to Judge Woodward.

"We will ask Mr. Tanovich to step out," the judge said.

As Tanovich left, Joe noticed a court stenographer had entered and was keeping record of the proceedings. Either

Chesler had learned his lesson or it was to his advantage to have all of this in the record.

"These are serious charges, Mr. Brandt," the judge said.

"I will represent us, with your permission," Stacy said.

"So granted," the judge said.

"We stipulate a relationship has existed between Joseph Brandt and Katherine Nolan for some time."

"Is that right, Ms. Nolan?" the judge asked Kat. "Have you been in a relationship with Mr. Brandt?"

"Yes, Your Honor," Kat said, puzzled by it all.

"Mr. Chesler it seems your detective work is mistaken."

"We continue to assert that Mr. Brandt has used his power of persuasion over Ms. Nolan, the social worker assigned to help and protect the boy."

"Psychological therapist," Kat said angrily.

"Ms. Nolan," Judge Woodward said. "I realize you are not a lawyer, but you do not talk unless addressed."

"Yes, Your Honor. Sorry."

"You are not a social worker, I take it?"

"No, Your Honor."

"Mr. Chesler, I suggest you amend your thinking."

"Thank you, Your Honor, I will indeed," Chesler said. "However, as psychological therapist she is in the same support position with a vulnerable boy while she also is in the sway of the man leading the case against my client."

"What exactly are you alleging as misconduct?"

Chesler presented a sheaf of photographs to the judge, who looked them over and handed them to Stacy. Joe fumed and Kat could barely contain her anger as they looked through the telephoto shots. They showed a variety of shots, them at breakfast, them holding hands, photos of Joe and Billy shooting baskets and then Joe and Kat kissing under the same basket. There were pictures of Kat entering her building and then Joe entering at night with a wine bottle.

"Their relationship has been stipulated, Mr. Chesler."

"It has, Your Honor," Chesler said. "However the commingling of their private relationship with the delicate work of helping an impressionable boy amounts to misconduct."

"In what way?" the judge asked.

"It's clear how enamored Ms. Nolan is and he flaunts that relationship in front of the boy. He is in a position to manipulate the protector and the boy she protects."

Joe signaled he wanted to speak. He explained that he and Kat had dated since long before this case, that the boy had not been present when they kissed and that all contact he had with Billy was monitored by either Mr. Chesler or his representative. Chesler protested that they had not been allowed to monitor contact between the boy and Kat.

"Nor will you," the judge said, growing impatient. Joe was heartened, but it was too soon. "Mr. Chesler, I fail to see any evidence this relationship impacts the care and protection of the boy."

"Your Honor, if I may," Chesler said, pulling out more photos. "We assert there is a more disturbing reason Mr. Brandt kept his relationship with Ms. Nolan hidden." He presented new photos to the judge, who looked through them, then handed them to Stacy.

Joe and Kat looked over her shoulder at another set of telephoto pictures. These included Joe and Nicola on her patio. She was wearing pajamas and looking at him with demonstrable affection. Others showed Nicola handing him a coffee and touching his arm, then wearing other clothes and talking with him at her front door. The grand finale included her kissing Joe's cheek and Joe leaving her house apparently quite pleased.

Kat leaned forward, clearly hurt and confused.

Joe realized the accusation with Kat had simply been a ruse to blindside him with this. He found Stacy glaring at him and realized the two sets of photos made him appear like some predator. In the last photo with that smile on his face, he looked like a man who'd just gotten laid.

"It is our contention, Your Honor," Chesler insinuated smoothly, "that this establishes a pattern of manipulative behavior. He has seduced both Ms. Nolan and Mrs. Patterson to gain domination over the boy in order to subvert this case."

The judge seemed to be buying it. "Ms. Whitcomb?"

Stacy unhappily handed the floor to Joe.

"Not a bit of it is true, Your Honor," Joe said.

"You contend these are doctored photographs?" she asked.

"I don't know if they're doctored, but they do not tell the story they purport to tell."

"Enlighten us," the judge said.

"The night before his arrest Mr. Tanovich went to Mrs. Patterson's house and she called me to make him go away."

"Why did she call you?"

"I don't know, Your Honor. I urged her to call the police and only on her insistence did I go to her house," Joe said. "I immediately called Ms. Whitcomb and the police, plus Mr. Chesler was there that evening."

"And these other photos?" the judge asked.

"On the patio I was with Mrs. Patterson and police detective Ed Bittinger. I was not alone with Mrs. Patterson. The pictures have been cropped to give a false impression."

"You were never alone with her?"

"Mr. Chesler called the detective away at one point, but that's when I went to my car and slept in the back seat."

"And the front door? Who else was there?"

"No one, Your Honor," Joe said sheepishly.

"It is clear," Chesler said, "once the crowd at Mrs. Patterson's had dispersed, Mr. Brandt returned for a tryst."

"That never happened," Joe shouted, losing his cool.

"Mr. Brandt," the judge said coldly.

"I'm sorry, Your Honor," Joe said, reining himself in. "Ask Mrs. Patterson, she'll tell you it never happened."

"I believe we must do just that," Judge Woodward said and gave orders for Nicola and Bitt to be summoned, then they were all dismissed. Joe chased after Kat, but she wouldn't look at him and found Stacy only marginally more sympathetic.

JOE SLUMPED down the hallway toward Enright who waited.

"What'd you do?" Enright said.

"I need Bittinger to tell them I never seduced Nicola."

Even Enright didn't entirely believe him.

"Let's see if Bitt can meet us at Home Depot."

Joe followed Enright downstairs and tried calling Kat's cell. It was shut off, but he left a message. As they snuck out the fire exit door Joe asked, "Why Home Depot?"

"Recip saws and wood chippers."

Joe brooded as they drove, then abruptly returned to the present with alarm. "Did you put the gym bag in my office?"

"Sometimes I do the klutziest things," Enright said as Joe grew concerned. "I was on Shepherd Road below downtown where it's next to the river and the water's fast."

"What did you do, Byron?"

"I accidentally kicked the gym bag in the water," Enright said and waited as Joe began to understand.

Was there ever going to be an end to the debts he owed this man, Joe wondered. "Thank you all over again."

"Don't get too thankful, you haven't seen the secrets Home Depot holds in store."

Wood chippers and reciprocating saws delivered mixed news. The saws were quiet enough that they wouldn't rouse the neighbors who were all a considerable distance from the murder scene. Wood chippers were loud enough to raise the dead a mile away. Bittinger, Enright and Joe all agreed there was no way a wood chipper could have been used to grind up the body.

"Tony's theory won't fly?" Joe asked.

"Gotta keep looking," Bittinger said as he left.

"Think his plan would have worked, Joe?" Enright asked.

"Maybe Tanovich already tested it twenty some years ago and found something quieter than a wood chipper."

"They looked everywhere for his daughter back then."

"If you knew there was no body to be found, you could dispatch a hundred investigators to look for it," Joe said.

On the drive back, Enright asked, "Can you convict without having to sell the whole chop and drain scenario?"

"Tanovich killed her and cut her up. In the end, that's what he did and it's all we gotta prove," Joe said.

JOE WAS LET BACK in by the side door and waited for the crowd to return to the judge's chambers. Even when the others arrived, he was alone. Kat and Stacy were aloof, Nicola was uneasy. Bittinger was his only ally.

After introductions and greetings, the judge asked Chesler to lay out the photos and the accusations.

"That's outrageous," Nicola said, unconsciously covering her breasts with her arms. "What's going on?"

"Mr. Chesler," Judge Woodward said.

"We have reason to suspect counsel of attempting to manipulate testimony"

"So you had paparazzi stalk me at my home?"

"Mrs. Patterson," the judge said. "I share your outrage at the intrusion into your privacy. However, now that it has taken place, we have serious issues to consider."

"You were not the object of our concern or surveillance, Mrs. Patterson, Mr. Brandt was," Chesler went on. "It is our belief that he has attempted to influence both you and Ms. Nolan seeking to sway the boy's statement."

"Bullshit," Nicola exclaimed. "Sorry, ma'am. Joe never did anything to me," she said indignantly.

"Perhaps it didn't feel like manipulation," the judge said, trying to gauge the dynamic between Nicola and Joe.

"He was there," Nicola said, pointing at Bittinger. "I was, Your Honor," Bittinger said. "The pictures are cropped to cut me out, but I was there next to Joe."

"But you left with Mr. Chesler?"

"Yes, for about five minutes, Your Honor. And when I came back, they were both gone and I saw Mr. Brandt sleeping in his car. It was middle of the night."

"At what time did you leave in the morning?"

"I arrested Mr. Tanovich at nine and left then."

"Mr. Brandt was still at the house when you left?"

Bittinger looked at the photos and said, "Yes, Your Honor. So was Ms. Whitcomb, I believe."

"Thank you," the judge said and dismissed him.

Bittinger let himself out without looking at Joe.

"Were other people still there when these photos were taken, Mrs. Patterson?" the judge asked, indicating the kiss.

"No."

"Why is that?"

"After everyone left, I begged Joe to come back."

The judge looked from Joe to Nicola. "Had something happened?"

"I made a pass at Joe. Okay?" Nicola said angrily. "He turned me down in the nicest possible way but I didn't get a chance to really apologize and I begged him to come back so I could tell him I was sorry. Okay? Have you all humiliated me enough yet?"

That hung heavily in the room until the judge said, "Just so we're clear, Mrs. Patterson. He turned you down and when he returned, it wasn't to, that is to say, accept?"

"He turned me down twice, okay?"

"This is hard to believe, Your Honor," Chesler said.

Joe asked if the photos were digital and available. Chesler didn't like it, but the judge made him produce the photos on one of his assistant's laptops. Joe demonstrated that the pictures on the patio had been cropped to exclude Bittinger. Then he found the time codes on the photos of him going to Nicola's front door in the morning and then walking to his car with that incriminating smile on his face. They were taken just over a minute apart. Everything at the front door had happened in a few brief seconds.

The judge scanned the photos, then turned to Chesler.

"There are judges who would believe that there has been deception here, Mr. Chesler," she said, then looked from Joe to Stacy to Nicola and last to Kat. "I might be one of those judges. You have entered photos as part of your case and therefore they are subject to the rules of discovery."

Chesler grew alarmed.

"A complete set of these photographs, will be given to opposing counsel," she said. "Right now," she added.

Chesler unhappily nodded to the assistant, who started making copies from the laptop onto a memory stick.

"You will cease all surveillance of Mr. Brandt, up to and including the trial. Am I quite clear, Mr. Chesler?"

Chesler nodded and handed Joe the memory stick.

"Mrs. Patterson, the court would like to apologize to you for this intrusion into your private life and any embarrassment this unfortunate incident has caused."

"Thank you, Your Honor," Nicola grudgingly said.

The judge dismissed Chesler, his assistants and the court stenographer, but had the others stay. "Ms. Nolan, the court wishes to apologize to you as well and it is the order of this court that Mr. Brandt follow suit, tonight, over the best dinner he can afford."

Nicola looked from Joe to Kat and back, then said to Kat, "I didn't know. I am so sorry. Oh my god, I..."

STACY USHERED them all into the empty hallway. Joe found himself surrounded by grim and unhappy women.

"Listen, all three of you," she said solemnly. "The big picture is that you three are the keys to bringing in Billy's testimony to convict his father. You have to find a way to get through this. Am I clear?"

Nicola nodded tearfully and rushed off.

"This was meant to throw Joe off balance," Stacy said.

"It worked," Joe said. He turned to Kat and thought of putting an arm around her, but pulled back. "We okay?"

Kat whispered "Yes" under her breath, but then hurried away. When they were alone Stacy turned to Joe. "You can't let Marty get you so distracted."

Joe nodded but still felt uncertain of his relationship with any of them. Chesler was damn good at his job.

24

LIZA WAS THE PERFECT PERSON TO ASK WHAT RESTAURANT WAS expensive and good. Just from the question, she knew Joe was in deep trouble with Kat. Then when he admitted he'd been seeing her a long time and kept it secret, he could add Liza to the long list of women mad at him. But curiosity overcame her anger and she pried the story out of him, including the pictures.

After hearing all the incriminating looking photos, the hurt looks and Kat rushing away in pain, Liza said, "I'd suggest Luigi's Ristorante."

"I don't think I can sell my car that fast."

"This is the woman so important you kept her secret. That means you are head over fucking heels in love."

"Still friends?" he called after her as she rushed off.

"Hell no," Liza said, peeking back in with a grin.

Joe's cell rang and, hoping it was Kat, he answered. It was Sid Mendell. "Sid, I hear it's a great article."

"So what's this about another statement tomorrow?" Sid said. "You hold something back on me?"

"I told you more than I'd told the woman I love."

"I love you too, Joe, but how's about letting me have it first? I hit one out of the park for you."

"I doubt they'll call my bluff, so I'm not expecting to make a statement," Joe said. "I just want this to end."

"Your story has about run its course," Sid admitted after Joe assured him there was nothing new to add.

After he hung up, Joe called his credit card company and was amazed he could negotiate to raise his credit limit. Then he made a reservation for eight at Luigi's and called Kat, but got voice mail. He left her a message about the time and place.

"I heard how noisy wood chippers are," Tony said. "My theory's still good, we just gotta keep problem solving."

Tony explained that the speed of the motor made wood chippers noisy. A slower motor might make it whisper quiet. "It'd still grind bone just fine," Tony said. "Tanovich probably swapped out the motor himself on a portable wood chipper in his workshop. He geared it slow and quiet. He could have used a motor from a winch, they go nice and slow and the speed can be adjusted."

"It just seems so complicated," Joe said.

"I'll keep thinking about it," Tony said, then grew conspiratorial. "Want to know the best way to get rid of a body? The way I'd get rid of my wife if I killed her?"

"If you want to think of it that way."

"Always."

"You worry me, Tony."

"About time," Tony said. "I've studied thousands of cases and what I've come up with is home construction sites."

"So Tanovich is in the right business?"

"No. Too big. Commercial construction has all kinds of security. But a single house built by a small, independent contractor has a secure place for their tools, but they usually only have a half-assed fence to keep vandals out."

"Okay, so what do you do with the fictitious corpse?"

"It's much more fun if we think of it as my wife."

"Really?"

"Not a day goes by."

"You're a real beacon for all us single guys, Tony."

"So, I've killed her," Tony said. "Gloves and plastic sheeting, all the things they teach you on TV. Where do I put her so she'll never be found?" Tony went on excitedly. "A single house site just when they get everything done in the basement, but before they start to put in the joists for the first floor. So, I have to kill her on a Thursday."

"Why Thursday?"

"They pour cement on Friday," Tony said. "When they build a house, they dig the hole for the basement, build cinderblock basement walls on a footing and only when they're done with the plumbing and electric rough-in do they pour the cement for the basement floor."

"And they pour that on Friday?"

"So it can set up over the weekend," Tony said.

"What if they don't pour cement?"

"City building code has required cement for decades. Some older houses still have dirt floors, but not so many," Tony said. "So I kill her on Thursday, take her to a site that's ready to pour cement the next morning and it's still dirt down there. A little disturbance in the earth won't be noticed. The ground's been dug up and smoothed over repeatedly during construction. I find a disturbed area, put her in a shallow grave a few hours before they pour cement. Her body is then buried under someone else's house. No connection to me even if it's found later."

"That's brilliant, Tony," Joe said. "So who did this?"

"What do you mean? It's my plan."

"Your plan?"

"She's my wife," Tony said. "Now that I told you, she's safe for another thirty-eight years."

ENRIGHT LOOKED up as Joe entered and studied the timeline chart on his office wall. It included last sightings of Sienna and Dusan, the time of death and police arrival, the time during which Tanovich watched porn in his hotel room. There was also a map covering the area from the hotel to the house and the drive time between them. The files on his desk were reports from half a dozen detective agencies which had attempted over many years to locate Dejana Tanovich.

"Tony's been thinking about the slice and dice theory."

"Of course he has," Enright said, closing up his folder."It's about speed, a slow motor would be a lot quieter."

"Bitt and I will look into it."

"What do you know about Tony's wife?"

"Adores her. They're a really cute couple together."

"He has a strange way of getting there."

"Whatever keeps your life raft from sinking."

"What's our thinking on Dejana?" Joe asked.

"They spent a shitload on the search. Lots of false sightings, but no verifiable signs of her."

"Almost like she got swallowed up by the earth, huh?"

"The year she disappeared, Tanovich construction broke ground for three hundred and forty-one houses," Enright said. "But we got no reason to believe we could get three hundred forty-one search warrants and that many jackhammers."

Joe looked over the charts on the wall.

"So you made up with her yet?" Enright asked. "You don't have the look of make-up sex, so I'm betting it's no."

"Luigi's at eight tonight."

Enright whistled and said, "Man, I've never been in that much trouble. We're more Bob's Big Boy and hit the hay."

Joe laughed and Enright went on, "His hotel stay has us stumped. I liked your idea he wanted more cameras."

Enright said The Grand's cameras would not have shown Tanovich's presence very well, but the cameras in Capitol Suites Hotel covered the lobby, elevator and parking ramp, but not hallways or stairwells. Tanovich arrived before ten, ordered room service, turned on porn and nothing indicates he left the room until the police arrived at three thirty. His car never left the garage, he didn't use the elevator or go through the lobby, but Enright said it was possible to exit by a fire door, just like Joe had done at the Court House.

"How would he come back in except the lobby or garage?"

"Watergate," Enright said, but Joe looked puzzled. "Tape over the latch. If the tape doesn't get discovered, he can slip back in, open it from outside. But tape leaves residue," he said, shaking his head, "and there's no residue there."

Enright thought Tanovich could have carved a piece of wood to put in the door mechanism. The door would close, but wouldn't really latch so it could be opened from outside. He throws away the wood piece on his way back in. Plus, Enright figured, a timer could shut off the hotel television and that would record the moment the pay-per-view porn was shut off.

"Making him appear active inside the room?" Joe said.

"He gets proof he's in his hotel room while he's actually leaving by the fire door," Enright said. "Once he's outside, our big problem starts. You can't walk to his mansion and back in the time he had, much less kill and get to the river with the duffel bag, which he didn't have when he checked in to the hotel or when police came at three."

"An accomplice?" Joe said. "That leaves loose ends and defeats Tony's do-it-yourself murder theory."

"From Billy we know he did it, Joe," Enright said. "We just haven't figured out how he made it work. Plus, Bitt and me were asking ourselves, if you're making elaborate plans to kill the missus," Enright said, "why have your alibi include that you had a fight?"

"I can answer that one," Joe said. "A lie that makes you out to be guilt-free just looks self-serving. A lie that makes you look guilty of something else is more believable."

"Why does that sound like the voice of experience?"

"I'D TELL you but it wouldn't make me look good."

"See what you mean."

ON HIS WAY down from Enright's office, Joe received a text from Kat agreeing to meet him at Luigi's at eight.

As he entered the third floor from the stairwell into the back hallway, he was startled by Dusan Tanovich waiting for him. Alone. The big man was unescorted and roaming about the Government Center. He'd gotten past news people, the police in the lobby and the pass-key locked doors to the District Attorney's offices.

Tanovich came bounding toward him, looking ready to kill. "You little prick."

"I can't talk to you without your lawyer," Joe said.

"You're going to need a doctor not a lawyer."

"That's a threat, Mr. Tanovich," Joe said.

Tanovich looked up and down the empty hallway, then shook his head and smiled. "No, it's not."

They were alone and Tanovich was right. No witnesses meant it could not be proven.

"I still can't talk to you. Let me past."

Tanovich leaned heavily against Joe, pinning him to the wall, an arm across his throat and his full weight behind it. Joe could barely breathe as he pushed with all his might against that enormous arm. He couldn't make him budge. He knew if this man was willing to live with the consequences, he could kill him right here and right now.

"You took my boy away, you asshole," Tanovich said in a deep, hoarse whisper.

"You were indicted for murder."

Having proven his dominance, Tanovich stepped back. He dusted down Joe's shoulders. "Only got the one cheap suit?"

Joe stepped farther away and said, "You lost Billy when you killed his mother."

"You ain't proved shit," Tanovich said, still blocking the way. "I want my son back."

"That will never happen. I'll make sure of it."

"A guy with a business the size of mine, it's like a country. Takes real strength to handle it. Iron control."

"You lost that when you decided to kill."

"What the fuck do you know?" Tanovich said impatiently. "I'm talking about the long haul. The future. I built an empire, something that's permanent."

Tanovich sighed like someone dealing with a child, then leaned close and whispered, "So what's it gonna take?"

"Sorry?" Joe said.

Tanovich rose back up, his size seeming to double. "Just tell me what it will take. Let's settle this like serious people."

"We are not having this conversation," Joe said.

"My boy has to live with Senka, not that Nicola bitch...you can make that happen."

"Not going to happen," Joe said and tried to move past.

"Your life can change. I have the power...there are ways that can't be traced. You got the discipline it takes not to go buy a Maserati, just live free and easy."

"All I want is for you to leave."

"Okay, I'll double it."

"Double what?"

"Whatever figure you got floating in your head and don't tell me you don't. Everyone has a figure. You still get to be the crusading prosecutor. Whatever happens in the trial happens in the trial, but the boy is with his sister..."

Joe stepped backward to the stairwell door and pushed it open. "I want you to leave."

"I always get what I want. If it's not with you, then it's right straight through you."

As Tanovich brusquely pushed past Joe into the stairwell, he said, "You're always gonna be small."

"JUST YOUR WORD AGAINST HIS," Mike said. "No way we can swear out another indictment, we'd look like idiots."

"What color Maserati?" Enright whispered aside to Joe who still couldn't really control the shaking of his hands.

"He wasn't asking me to throw the trial, just get Billy away from Nicola, get the boy into the hands of his daughter to raise him as a Tanovich," Joe said.

"The ice princess," Enright said. "She could probably turn anyone into a psychopath like their old man."

"What's this tell us?" Mike asked.

"Marty's client is not in Marty's control," Stacy said.

"I like the sound of that," Mike said. "What else?"

"He's over sixty," Joe said. "He figures he can run the empire another, what, fifteen years until his boy is mid-twenties and ready to take over. Mrs. Patterson told me he only appears to be American, he's old world all the way."

"Nineteenth century old world," Stacy added.

"Could be. It's his parents' world," Joe said. "He wants the boy, an heir to carry on his name and to be like him. Ruthless. He believes Senka can turn the boy into that kind of man, Nicola can't. She wouldn't."

"You think the daughter is like him?" Stacy asked.

"Makes me wonder if we shouldn't indict them both."

"Let's just make sure we keep him in our sights. I want you putting your heads together and figuring out how to leverage this," Mike said as he led them out.

As they left together, Enright asked, "What number?"

"I didn't have a number in mind," Joe said defensively.

"Seventeen and a half million," Enright said and hurried away sporting a grin.

JOE HAD enough time to go back to his office and change his shirt and tie. He wore his best clothes with an attitude approaching pride and told himself, 'It's not a cheap suit.'

He drove down along the river and turned onto the road that led to Luigi's which was built on the Mississippi River bank. He had no business going into this world of Mercedes and people who knew what to do with all that silverware.

Then he was surprised by recognition and a genuine smile from the maître d' who graciously showed him through the wealthy diners in the main room. They kept going all the way to the windows. Kat was waiting at a table for two with the most spectacular view up and down the river. She looked fantastic and he couldn't take his eyes off her.

"It's an incredible view," she said.

"I'll say."

"You haven't looked out the window," she said.

"I don't have to."

She studied him for a long time before starting to smile. "This sort of repartee usually work for you?"

"Have I been talking?"

"You're good."

"You're great."

She just pointed out the window until he looked. It was indeed an incredible view. Above them was Fort Snelling, the birthplace of the city, standing watch over the bend in the Mississippi right where it was joined by the Minnesota River. Across from them was Pike's Island and the wide expanse of water seemed bathed in twinkling light from the city above. Everything looked storybook pretty.

They were interrupted by the maître d' with a bottle of French wine with a name Joe couldn't pronounce. It was a gift from an old couple who had recognized Joe. They nodded thanks and, embarrassed, Joe stumbled through the ritual of smelling the cork and tasting the first drops. Once their glasses were poured and the maître d' disappeared once again, they raised glasses to their benefactors and silently toasted.

Then Kat toasted to Joe, "Here's to my celebrity."

"I'm yours?" he asked after clinking glasses.

"How much trouble do you think you're in?" she asked.

"I don't know, I haven't looked at the prices yet."

She laughed and reached across the table to him. She

said she knew they were both victims of Chesler and Tanovich. While she spoke, he admired her sexy, tight-fitting white dress with a shimmer to it, more cleavage than she generally showed, a necklace that looked more expensive than he could imagine and her elegant shawl. He was luckiest guy there.

"I still don't like the look on your face when you walked to your car," she said, "but...you walked to your car."

Joe realized he was being forgiven and relaxed.

After dinner, while he was still reeling from the bill, his cell phone vibrated in his pocket. He glanced at the display, it said, 'Ma' so he apologized to Kat and answered.

"Hey, Ma."

"Louie's been around again," she said.

Panic raced through him and Kat immediately saw it.

"I'll be over right away," he said.

"What is it? What's the matter?" Kat asked with alarm.

"My mother says my uncle is there right now."

"I'll go with you," she said, grabbing her shawl.

He was still trying to figure out how to say no when she stood and reached a hand down to drag him with her. "It's about time I met the mother of the man I love."

"Let's hope she's the only member of my family we see."

25

THE FARTHER INTO HIS EAST SIDE NEIGHBORHOOD THEY drove, the more fearful Joe became about Kat following him in her car. Most of the houses on his block were empty and the impoverished desperation screamed this was not the place for a woman alone. Joe found the barricades still blocking the street, but no police and no news crews. It was quiet and peaceful, but that wasn't at all reassuring.

Kat and Joe parked on the street and he found himself marveling at just how awful the house looked.

"It's not too late to drive home," he said.

"No way," she said, looking hopefully at the house.

"I'm not sure how to do this."

"How did you do it last time?"

"I've never brought someone to my house before."

"We open the gate, go up the steps, knock and she lets us in, you introduce us. It'll come to you," she said.

"Several problems. I don't enter through the front door and it would totally freak her out if she heard footsteps on the front stairs. She won't invite you in, that much I can promise. It's not my choice, but that's the reality."

In the end Kat waited inside the fence while he let himself in the back. He explained who was with him and tried to get her to the door. After a couple false starts, Joe dragged Aileen to the front door and turned the porch light on. Outside, Kat pulled her shawl around her shoulders and smiled tentatively as Joe pushed open the screen.

Aileen spun on her heel and disappeared back into the house. Before Joe could apologize, she returned with two kitchen chairs and handed one through the door to Kat. She put her chair inside and held the screen open with her foot. She and Kat faced each other across the threshold.

Joe watched in astonishment. "Shut the TV off," Aileen said, then turned to Kat. "Do you go to school with Joey?"

"We know each other from work," Kat said.

Joe shut off the TV, got a flashlight and headed out the back as he marveled – the two women in his life were talking. As he stepped outside, he felt like he was just going through the motions again. It had probably been a news crew which upset his mother.

But then, what he found was quite disturbing.

Behind the garage there was fresh digging near the foundation. There was demolition up the block, but no sign of work nearby, yet here was freshly dug dirt. His light clearly showed a rectangular box had been in the hole, but was now gone. Louie had been here. Fuck.

Overcome with fright and his light trembling, he inched around the garage and found the rickety side door had been kicked in. The garage had been left untouched for over two decades because he'd never ventured into his dad's world. Until now.

Very large and very fresh footsteps led through twenty years of dust that had settled atop the packed and grease-stained dirt floor. The footprints went straight to a corner where garden tools stood. Louie must have come for a shovel to dig up the box, Joe figured.

The garage was packed with remnants of his father's and uncle's sordid history, stacks of all kinds of things they had stolen. They had broken into trucks, warehouses and storage rooms to take anything they could carry.

Joe noticed a large, fresh footprint in the dust on the floor near the tools. His heart raced as his flashlight played erratically about the musty garage, then it flashed across eyes staring right at him from the shadows.

In an instant Joe was sent crashing onto the dirt floor.

The flashlight skittered away as massive hands grabbed him by the suit jacket. Joe heard a rip as a fist slammed into his head again and sent him hurtling back down.

"Where in fuck you hiding it?" Louie shouted.

Louie took hold of Joe's new tie and twisted it around in his hand, strangling him with it. An altogether too familiar movement. And he kept asking the same question as he pounded Joe's head and face.

Then as suddenly as it began, the beating stopped.

Joe staggered out the side door, yanking blindly at the tie until he had it stripped off completely.

He headed to the light from the front porch and heard Kat say, "I didn't go to high school here, I went to private school, St. Paul Academy."

When he got to the front steps Kat screamed, "Joe!"

Together she and Aileen helped him inside, led him into the kitchen and he collapsed onto a chair. Kat started to clean up his bloody face and Aileen went to get her first aid supplies. Joe stared in amazement to see Kat in the house.

Feeling his thundering adrenaline, the throbbing head wound and dish towels on his wounds Joe drifted into memories of his childhood. Cuts, bruises and blood. His mother administering first aid was distressingly familiar.

Kat eased his jacket off while Aileen cleaned out the cut at his temple and he told them about the hole behind the garage. About going inside. About finding Louie.

"Louie kept asking where we're hiding it," Joe said.

"Do you know what he wants?" Kat asked.

Joe shook his head and said, "Ma, do you know?"

Aileen shook her head and inspected the cut near his hair line. "Told you it was Louie," she said.

"I wanted Kat to meet my whole family," Joe said.

"Louie is not family," Aileen flared, suddenly angry.

"It's a joke, Ma," Joe said and gave a knowing look to Kat. While Aileen made an ice compress, he realized Kat's lovely white dress was stained with his blood.

"Any chance that will come out?" Joe asked.

"I know a dry cleaner who's a miracle worker," she said with a sympathetic pat to his face. "How about you?"

"I heard my suit rip," he said.

"That's not what I meant."

"I'm good. How's our date going so far?"

Kat half laughed, leaned close to the ear that wasn't swollen and whispered, "I love you."

"I'll understand if you run far away," he said.

"Not a chance," she said and helped Aileen with gauze. As they patched him up, he started to think back...

LOUIE TWISTED up Joe's Minnesota Twins pajamas into a knot, strangling the boy, lifting him by the bound-up shirt. "Where's your old man?"

"He ran out on us," Joe choked out.

Louie let out a scream so loud it rattled the house.

"Where in fuck you hide it?" Louie shouted at him.

"I SWEAR Louie asked the same thing he did years ago," Joe said. "Did he come looking for something back then?"

"I don't remember anything about that," Aileen said. "Best not to think about Louie and George and those days."

"I think it was after Dad left," Joe said to himself as he noticed the chipped enamel basin she was using. The water was pink. "Didn't you bandage up Louie's hands? Both of 'em? Really mangled and bloody. "

"I don't remember any of that," Aileen said.

"I'm starting to remember it, Ma. His hands looked like they'd been through a meat grinder and..." suddenly he stopped. Louie's hands looked like the fists of someone who had just beaten a man to death.

"You had a nightmare, Joey," Aileen said. "That's all."

"Did he have a lot of childhood nightmares, Mrs. Felcher?" Kat asked, studying Joe.

"Sometimes it seemed like every night," Aileen said.

"They're starting to come back," Kat said. "It's this case he's on."

"I told him over and over that none of it was real," Aileen said. "It didn't happen like his nightmares."

"What didn't happen?" Kat asked.

"Nothing happened. Once his dad left, there was no reason to have nightmares anymore, but he still had 'em."

Aileen was unable to look at them. "Red or blue?"

"We started the evening with red, so red please," Joe said, then saw Kat mouthing 'Blue?' He held a hand up to wait, then grinned as Kat saw the Kool-Aid packet come out. He leaned close to Kat and whispered, "I'm only eight."

"That's no secret," Kat said. "Can I help?"

"There's glasses in the cupboard there," Aileen said.

Kat took down three jelly glasses and gave Joe a meaningful look. "I'm beginning to understand so much."

Soon they sat around the table with red Kool-Aid and cookies and Joe thought this was a momentous occasion.

"Should we call the police?" Kat asked and was shocked when Aileen leapt from her seat in a panic.

"No police, Ma," he said soothingly. "Of course not." He leaned close to Kat and whispered, "When police came, it only got worse afterwards."

This seemed to satisfy Kat until she noticed the lock on the basement door. She had missed it on the way inside. Joe saw her studying it and tried to distract her. He lowered the dish towel and showed off the side of his head. "If the swelling in my ear goes down and I take off this bandage, you think I can pass for halfway respectable?"

"Maybe," Kat conceded. "Not in that suit though."

"I guess I wasn't born to wear a nice suit."

"You looked good in it."

"For the five days I owned it."

Kat inspected the tear in the shoulder with a practiced eye. "My guy might be able to reweave the fabric."

"You have a guy who reweaves?" he said, teasing her.

"Club soda," Aileen said. They both looked at her, then she pointed at the blood stains in Kat's dress. "I used to keep club soda around. Do we have any club soda, Joey?"

"Haven't needed it for years."

"Soak it in that before you go to bed," Aileen said.

First aid, Kool-Aid and cookies finished, they all looked surprised to find themselves together until Joe finally said, "I think I should stay here tonight."

"I think you're right," Kat said as she stood. "Good night, Mrs. Felcher."

Aileen nodded, smiled and suddenly seemed confused by Kat's presence in the house. As Joe escorted Kat to her car, she asked, "What do you think Louie was after?"

"They stole a lot of stuff," Joe said. "Maybe they took something of real value and buried it in the garden." As they hugged, he said, "Not quite the night I envisioned."

"I've had an amazing evening," Kat said. "Your mother confided in me a lot faster than you did."

"What'd she confide?"

"She's not classically agoraphobic. It's almost like she's a sentry. She's guarding her home."

"You learned all that while I was assaulting my uncle?"

Kat nodded and said, "And she doesn't always think you're eight years old. You're in high school sometimes."

"She's kept up with my emotional development," Joe said.

"We have to talk about that basement door when you're ready," Kat said, becoming his therapist again. He nodded, but went back in for another kiss. A far better remedy.

When she drove off, he stood in the empty street a long time before turning back. He hadn't spent the night in his mother's house since high school. It didn't feel good.

When Joe closed the front door, he saw Aileen locking the padlock on the basement door. She was holding a rifle and a handful of shiny brass bullets.

"How many guns you got down there, Ma?"

"Enough to keep Louie from coming inside," she said.

"Louie ran off after he hit me, Ma. He's gone."

She nodded distractedly, then started loading the gun.

She meant business. He grabbed the rifle and angrily knocked the remaining bullets from her hand before she could load them. He was shocked by her instant flash of rage.

"We can't shoot Louie and we can't have loaded guns in the house," Joe said, trying to figure out how to get the bullet out she'd already loaded. She showed him how and then he crept around to find the other bullets. He found drops of blood on the floor. Just like the old days.

With the bullets in hand, he fetched another flashlight and said, "I'm going to figure out what Louie was doing."

"Take the rifle."

"I'm not going to take the rifle," Joe said. "Would you please put it back in the basement while I go outside?"

She glowered at him, but nodded. She pulled the chain with the key on it out from under her house dress, but Joe couldn't watch her unlock the basement door. He escaped into the safety of the night, it felt less dangerous despite there being a known killer lurking about.

He doubted Louie was still there, but he grabbed an axe before he looked around inside the garage. He found a sturdy box with rusty iron straps around it on a work bench. Louie had cracked it open with a hammer and cold chisel which were still on the bench. The box was empty.

When Joe went back inside to ask about the box, Aileen refused to talk. She had her old vacuum out, cleaning the dirt from his suit jacket and drowning him out.

He went to look in the bathroom mirror at the fresh bandage. He felt the throbbing in his ear and the tenderness under the dressing, then finally he stared directly at the scar on his lip.

"*GET THE DOOR,*" *Aileen shouted from the other room.*

Joe dashed out of the bathroom and almost tripped trying to avoid the blood pooled on the wooden floor. He held a blood-soaked dish towel to his lip and blood was spattered all down the front of his pajamas.

He yanked the basement door open, then turned to her and discovered she was barely recognizable through the swelling and bruises.

"Go get yourself some more ice now, Joey," she said.

In the kitchen he dumped out the pink ice, then heard a thump that sounded like Dad stomping up from downstairs.

He slowly peered out of the kitchen to see a long smear of blood. It ran across the living room floor and straight through the basement door. Then another thump resounded from the stairs descending into blackness in the basement.

...AND JOE SAT bolt upright at the horror of what he had just remembered. It hadn't been a bad dream. Had it?

Standing in his bedroom, he couldn't stop long-forbidden thoughts from flooding through him. He felt the scar on his lip and replayed the images before he finally ventured to his door. He opened it and looked into the quiet house.

He girded himself and stepped into his past. He stared down where the pool of blood had once formed. He followed the track of the long bloody smear on the floor and traced his memory directly to the basement door.

The trembling inside shook Joe to his core.

AILEEN CLIMBED BACK up the basement stairs and found Joe staring past her into the black abyss through that door. In the living room she picked up the Louisville Slugger baseball bat from the edge of the bloody red pool.

Its large end was dripping with red.

Joe was silent but quaking as she said, "Don't you ever go down this basement again, Joey. You understand? Ever."

HE EASED himself down the wall and sat in the little hallway. She'd told him thousands of times not to go down there and he had vowed never, ever to touch that door again, never to go down there, never to think about what was down there. Until tonight, with the repeated cajoling of his mother and his own avoidance of the memory, he had succeeded. Now he finally knew why.

Dad was down there.

He hadn't run out, he never completely left. Dad still haunted them both in more than just horrifying memory.

Joe touched the door and, for the first time in two decades, he knew why it tormented him.

JOE COULDN'T TELL how long he sat there, leaning against the wall, staring at the basement door. He now understood why his mother never left the house. Kat had said it was almost as if she were a sentry. She was guarding the gate of their family hell.

A ringing sound cut through the misery and he slowly realized it was his cell phone. As he looked for it, he saw the sun was coming up. Then he found his phone atop the television, but got to it just as it went to voice mail.

When he managed to access it, the message was from Enright, who said, "Get over to the aunt's house a.s.a.p. She's dead and the boy's missing."

26

WEARING HIS TATTERED SUIT, JOE DROVE TO NICOLA'S HOUSE in a daze. He felt as if he were in a bad dream, but reality came back when a policeman stopped him at the gate to Hayden Oak Park. He had to show his ID. Nicola's street was filled with vehicles, so he parked on the access road. The sun was up and it was a glorious morning, but there were policemen going from house to house and others searching the fields outside the Tanovich subdivision.

The first person he saw was Bittinger at Nicola's front door. As Joe put on booties, Bitt ran it down. Billy, Nicola and Senka had gone to a Twins game the previous evening, came home to have a late dinner and there must have been something in the food. Senka woke up from being passed out or drugged, she found Nicola dead and called 911 in a panic. But she couldn't find Billy. There was no note, no sign of a struggle, the boy had simply vanished. Shades of his older sister, Dejana.

"There's hope he's alive, right?" Joe said and Bitt half-nodded. A team was out searching and a lot of energy was being expended, but there was nothing to go on. Joe was torn between screaming at the world and collapsing into inertia.

Bittinger headed inside, but discovered Joe was still stuck at the door. Billy didn't deserve any of this, no one did. Now his aunt was dead and he'd been kidnapped or worse.

"Yeah, we usually don't know them ahead of time," Bittinger said. "It's a tragedy, but to do right by her we gotta catch who did it," he said. "And find the boy."

Bittinger led Joe through the living room, past police and coroner's people and toward the kitchen where they'd all had breakfast. The first thing he saw was Billy's shoes under the table. The shoes Jamal had called 'awe.'

'Please be alive,' went through his mind as he stepped through the doorway and lost his breath. Nicola was still there. She was sprawled out on the kitchen floor where she had slid out of her chair, one leg tucked uncomfortably under her. Her eyes were closed and she looked peaceful, as if she were asleep. She was wearing the same heavy sweater she'd worn at that breakfast. She hadn't been assaulted. She had been sitting and eating, then she was on the floor, dead.

"Coroner says it looks like whatever she ingested put her to sleep, then her heart stopped."

Joe realized it was less than a day since their last interaction – her humiliation from Chesler's cruel attack.

They watched forensic techs putting cartons of Chinese food on the table into evidence bags. Bitt said he'd already informed the techs they'd find his prints, Joe's, Stacy's and Tanovich's, they'd all be there from that recent breakfast. He showed where Billy had sat, there was no sign of violence. He had simply disappeared.

Joe finally tore his eyes away and asked for Enright. Bittinger pointed him to the back of the house. Joe looked into the homey family room which had patio doors to the landscaped back yard, another Tanovich feature.

Enright hurried over to him, then touched his shoulder where the tear in his suit was. "Apology not accepted?" he said, looking closely at Joe's still red ear and the scab under his hairline. "Your girl's stronger than I'd have thought."

"It's not what it looks like."

"Nothing ever is," Enright said and gestured at Stacy who was sitting with Senka while an EMT drew blood. "She's groggy and confused, but she made the 911 call."

"It had to be Tanovich. He hated Nicola."

"His new ironclad alibi has a dozen witnesses."

"He still did it somehow," Joe insisted.

"The guy who butchers one sister doesn't poison the other. Not the same personality at all," Enright said.

"Tanovich is behind this." Joe was adamant.

"You think he poisoned his own daughter?"

"He killed the other one, why not?" Joe said angrily.

"We found Ativan in Nicola's medicine cabinet. Broken tablets so we don't know how much she was taking or even if she was taking it," Enright said. "But it could explain why she died and Senka didn't from eating the same stuff. Mighta been a drug interaction. Coroner put a rush on the blood testing for us," Enright said as the EMT left with Senka's blood in a vial. Another EMT arrived with a gurney for her.

"And Billy ate the same stuff? Would it kill him?"

"My theory? Something just meant to knock them all out was put in the Chinese food they picked up on the way home. How? Why? By whom? No idea," Enright said. "I agree, Tanovich is behind it, but we can't treat it that way. He was with bankers and accountants working out a new financial structure for the company while his personal assets are frozen."

"So his alibi is people who work for him?"

"A dozen people. Much as we don't want it to be true," Enright said, "Tanovich was with that group until four this morning and Nicola was dead by then."

"And Billy was already missing. Where the fuck is he?"

"Best way you and me can help is by thinking nasty."

Joe watched Stacy interviewing Senka. "If something's in the food to make them sleep and Nicola isn't supposed to die then...is Billy kidnapped or killed?"

"Sorry Joe," Enright said, "but this guy...it's logical Tanovich would kill him. The boy is a huge danger. With Billy gone, he's free and clear, no eyewitness."

"But Billy is his legacy, the future of his company, his name, his empire," Joe said. "He offered me millions so he could have the boy. I have to believe Billy is alive."

"Tanovich could have just been trying to corrupt you. Compromise you before the trial."

Enright stepped aside as Senka was wheeled out on the gurney. She was sound asleep. Then Stacy joined them.

"Whatever they ate could have killed her too," she said. "She seemed more confused than alarmed or upset."

"Normal human reactions aren't part of the Tanovich clan's emotional make up," Joe said. "I met her before and she wasn't emotional about Sienna's murder."

Stacy mulled that thought. "She seemed shocked that Mrs. Patterson was actually dead and it did seem strange she wasn't more concerned about her brother." Stacy then looked Joe over and asked, "Is everything all right with you?"

"This case is taking its toll," he admitted.

Stacy pulled out the morning paper and handed him the

'Community' section. His story was on the front page. Twice. There was a photo of his mother and Kat sitting on the front porch talking through the opened screen door. A second photo showed Joe and Kat in tight embrace beside her car. The headline read, 'Life and Love Go On.' Joe and his mother were identified by name and Kat was 'Mystery woman.'

He was pissed and relieved in equal measure. He was still being followed, so his pact with the press was off, but it was the second day in a row his picture was in the paper.

Stacy was not pleased either. "If they get those photos of you and Mrs. Patterson..." she said.

"I don't think Marty would dare. Would he?"

Stacy shrugged, but just then shouting from outside made them all run to the front door. Outside, cops were forming a perimeter containing a horde of news crews flooding the cul-de-sac, all of them shouting. Standing at the center of the throng was Marty Chesler, shaved, preened, prepared and sharp.

He was talking to the reporters as Joe and Enright inched closer, unseen behind the uniformed policemen keeping the noisy press back. Chesler was laying new groundwork, saying that someone had targeted Tanovich and his family. There was an unknown enemy the police and district attorney's offices had ignored. Tanovich was not the criminal, Chesler said, he was the victim. His wife and sister-in-law had been murdered, his son was missing. A forceful assault against his client was being ignored by the city and its representatives.

Then the media crowd parted to reveal Dusan Tanovich. He was haggard, unshaved and believably grieving, trudging blindly ahead, eyes focused solely on the house. The cameras captured it all as he put on what Joe thought must be the performance of a lifetime. Only as he reached him did he seem to notice that Marty Chesler was even there.

Chesler took Tanovich's arm and consoled him and made certain they faced the right way so the house and police were in the shot, which left their backs to Joe and Enright. Stacy was nearby on the phone, but watching.

Looking distraught and unaware of his appearance, Dusan Tanovich spoke in a low voice and exhibited none of the commanding presence and demanding attitude Joe had seen.

"I will pay any ransom," Tanovich said softly. "Whoever has taken my son, please bring him back to me. I will do anything it takes. Everything it takes."

"Anyone with information about these crimes can call the 800 number of my offices," Chesler added.

"I'm offering a ten-million-dollar reward for the return of my son," Tanovich said and the reporters all shouted.

"I have already lost my wife, now my sister-in-law, plus my daughter has been hurt by these, these, animals," Tanovich said, allowing indignant passion to take over.

To a flurry of questions from the press, Tanovich brought himself back to his full stature. "You don't become a wealthy man without creating a few angry people along the way," he said. "Who has done this, I have no idea. I only wish the police and district attorney's offices had been focusing on my enemies instead of me. Maybe they could have prevented these terrible tragedies."

"In light of these horrific events and to allow Mr. Tanovich to focus his energies on the recovery of his son," Chester said, "we are seeking dismissal of the obviously unwarranted indictment against my client. We hope finally the authorities will try to find the real killer or killers."

Chesler started to lead Tanovich away and Joe realized no one was asking the right question, which enemies?

Joe couldn't stop himself. By instinct he submarined.

Under elbows and cameras, Joe found openings as he shoved ahead until he was right in front of Tanovich.

"Tell us your enemies. Who has a vendetta against you?"

In that first instant of eye contact with Tanovich, there was a knowing exchange. Joe saw it was all entirely fake and Tanovich knew at once that Joe understood that. He hated Joe all the more for seeing through him.

But that moment gave way to a rage which brought his voice to a volume to wake the dead and his hatred of Joe to the surface for every camera to capture. "You little bastard," Tanovich shouted belligerently into Joe's face.

"Gentlemen, please," Chesler said trying to intercede.

"It's all your fault," Tanovich shouted and it looked as if he were on the verge of assaulting Joe.

Enright must have thought so too, because he was now at Joe's side pulling him away. Bittinger was on the other side, holding his badge up between the men.

"No one comes to mind?" Joe shouted. "You say you have enemies willing to kill your family but you can't say who?"

"There's no shortage of guys I beat in business," Tanovich said with his usual pride and swagger.

"Then help us find your enemies," Joe said.

"More guys hate me than a losing football coach," Tanovich said, "but if I gotta narrow it down, I'd say you should look at Ziggy Alpman, the Choi Brothers and J. R. Malone and Sons." He was fully calm, all business and his show of pretend human emotions was now long forgotten.

Joe hoped the cameras caught that transformation.

ONCE TANOVICH ALLOWED himself to be led away, Joe was ushered back to the house, but his anger wouldn't go away. Stacy came up and he said, "He's real broken up about his missing son and his daughter. That was all a show."

"We know from Billy's statement he killed Sienna," Stacy said. "No sense in lending credence to this fantasy of the 'real killer.' The first murder led to the second, that much seems clear. We don't need a list of enemies."

"Who will be quickest and happiest to give us every shred of dirt on Dusan Tanovich?" Joe said.

"Cynicism becomes you, Joe," Stacy said, realigning the rip in his suit. The words were meant to be light and cheerful, but the way she looked at Joe was anything but. "But you're not exactly boring the press to death."

"I get the feeling I'll be in the paper a third day in a row." he said with chagrin.

Joe gave Stacy the names of Tanovich's rivals, then talked to Enright as they both drove to the office. He asked him to go through the files on Dejana and anything else he could find about the family at that time. He wanted to know if there had been a significant change in Senka's behavior. "When did she start buying little white statues instead of making friends?" Joe said.

Stacy was in the midst of an intense meeting with Ronald Sheldon, but just pointed to a stack of folders on her side table. They were only a few of the scores of court cases filed against Tanovich Construction.

While Joe changed into his casual clothes in his office, Liza came around to watch and inspect his torn suit jacket.

"You're really hard on clothes...and ears, I see."

"Want to help me sort through Tanovich's enemies?"

Together they read through a litany of unnecessarily cruel and opportunistic behavior by Tanovich. Senka seemed to have no involvement in the financial or competitive aspects of the company, but she gave a lot of sworn statements in his favor. She was no doubt a true believer in the Tanovich empire. And her father's business model seemed clear. It was all-out war and prisoners were not taken.

One case showed what he'd done was legal, though morally bankrupt. It was a takeover by Tanovich of a family-run plumbing company. A father, his adult sons, a cousin and a handful of employees. They wanted to stay independent, but he cut off their sources of work until they had to sell at below market value. In the sales agreement, they had non-compete clauses and at first they all worked for Tanovich. Then he summarily fired them all. Now unable to work as plumbers, they had all dispersed, either going broke, going on public assistance or moving out of state to work.

"Didn't you go to law school with Chuck Demby?" Liza said. "He earned a lot of billable hours on Choi Brothers."

"Perfect," Joe said, took the file and dialed his cell phone. "Joe Brandt calling for Charles Demby."

"Helluva story you tell in the paper, Joe," Chuck said.

"Yeah. Can I buy you a quick coffee?"

"Ten dollar a minute advice for the price of a latte?"

"I want to put Dusan Tanovich away forever."

"Then I got all the time you need. Court Café in ten?"

Joe hurried over to the café which catered to juries on lunch break and made expensive coffees all day.

"You really make six hundred bucks an hour already?"

Chuck ran a finger down his suit, then looked at Joe's polo shirt and khakis and said, "You don't, I'm guessing."

"Tell me about Tanovich."

"I'm not a vindictive man, Joe," Chuck said. "But if Dusan Tanovich were on fire, I wouldn't piss on him to put it out. Remember how we were always taught to be dispassionate? 'Emotions have no place in the law,' all that shit?"

"I was absent that day."

"Yeah, well I bought all of it until I got involved in fighting Tanovich Construction."

"What's he like?"

"Scorched earth. It isn't enough for him to win. He has to destroy anyone who stands up to him, set him on fire and then go fuck the guy's wife," Chuck said in red-faced anger. "I expect Sienna Tanovich's mistake was standing up to him."

"So he chopped her up?"

"Just an escalation from the broken bones he's known for," Chuck said hatefully. "So the kid's missing? You think he's dead now too? That'd vacate the indictment."

"Tanovich seems to see his son as the future."

"You ever studied the thought processes of royalty?" Chuck said. "Think of Tanovich as king. Believe me, he does. He's plundering away, amassing power and property. He's ruthless, savage and primitive, yet also sophisticated. A total sociopath who's built his company into a Fortune 500 enterprise by waging war on everyone. It's all about ego, right? Like the guys who built pyramids as shrines to themselves. It isn't only important to have the power, he has to build an empire to last a thousand years."

"So he needs a prince," Joe said. "What about the daughter? She's pretty involved."

"Kings want sons because they see themselves in them. That and the name, the bloodline."

"You've given this a lot of thought," Joe said.

"Know your enemy," Chuck said. "A king has two duties: preserve the kingdom and produce an heir," Chuck said, thoroughly enjoying his medieval analogy. "It's all ego. He sees himself as Dusan the Great."

"So Billy is alive because he's the future of everything Tanovich built?" Joe said. "I hope you're right."

"It's a habit I have," Chuck said, finishing his latte.

27

When Joe got to RCGC West, he went to Stacy to share his conviction that Billy was still alive. He wanted to brainstorm on how to proceed, but she stopped him from laying out his theory and simply ushered him upstairs to see Mike. Joe thought it was a concession to efficiency so he could fill them both in at the same time. He was wrong.

Ronald Sheldon was part of the same meeting.

It threw Joe off his stride to have Ronald there as he tried to explain his theory about the boy being alive because he was the heir apparent, the prince. Mike and Stacy acknowledged it was an interesting thought, but it didn't help. The real issue, Mike said, was that Tanovich was no longer under indictment. Chesler's petition to vacate the indictment had been granted and the only restriction on Tanovich now was he had agreed not to leave the country.

They had no prospect for resurrecting the case against the father without the son's testimony. And they would be blamed for not looking beyond Tanovich for a killer.

They believed, short of a miracle, Billy was most likely dead. Tanovich's alibi the night of his wife's murder would stick and the two new crimes supported Chesler's claims that Tanovich was the real victim. He appeared to be the target of a campaign against him and his family.

"We know for a fact that Tanovich slaughtered his wife," Joe said angrily. "Billy is a fucking eyewitness."

"But you failed to secure a useful witness statement from the kid," Ronald said, enjoying himself.

Joe fumed and thought of the audio tape Enright made, but saw Stacy shaking her head. He knew she was saying, 'Bring the recording up and Enright loses his job, the two of us get censured and the tape isn't used anyway.'

"We find Billy and we're back in business?" Joe asked.

"We won't get a second indictment with a hearsay deposition," Mike said. "The boy would have to tell it all to the grand jury and then in court."

"Like he should have in the first place," Ronald said.

"He's fucking nine years old, Ronald," Joe said. "And he saw his dad butcher his mother, for Christ's sake."

"Let's bring it down to a simmer," Stacy said. "Joe, we don't have a case against Tanovich at all at this point and we don't have Billy for you to work with."

"We'll find him. He's alive."

"We can hope so, but now we have two new cases, including the boy's kidnapping," Stacy said with sympathy.

"The thing is, Joe, you're directly connected to both of the new victims," Mike said. "So catch Ronald up to speed on the whole case."

"Why?" Joe said in shock. "Billy and Nicola are only victims because they could have put Tanovich in prison," Joe said and discovered he was standing. "They're his victims."

"Sit down, Joe," Mike said, "and keep your job."

"Joe," Stacy said as he sat. "No one disputes that you

worked miracles with Billy, but now we need to look for other suspects. We have maybe gone down the wrong path. Maybe someone else really is responsible for all this."

'This sucks,' Joe said to himself.

"There are photos of you and the murder victim," Stacy said. "They were suppressed as part of discovery in a case that no longer exists. Marty can now publish them."

"We're keeping you on, Joe," Mike said. "Ronald will be first chair on the Patterson murder and Billy's kidnapping. No one knows the entire context better than you. You'll be second chair and you have my absolute support."

Stacy then took the ball, she and Mike were a team who had run this play before. "Ronald has a lot more experience with both murder and kidnapping cases, you two will work together. His presence will severely diminish Chesler's ability to leverage photos or anything else those pricks have come up with in their fear of you," Stacy said. "All of us know how afraid of you Chesler and his team have been. Right Ronald?"

Stacy and Mike both stared impatiently at Ronald until he chimed in. "Yeah, he was terrified you'd deliver the boy."

Until that moment, Joe didn't think anyone could match Chesler for insincerity. Ronald was an inspired rival.

"So we just assume the boy is dead?" Joe asked.

"Of course not," Stacy said. "We want you to continue on the track you're on, keep working with Byron, it's a good match. But work closely with Ronald, bring him up to speed and, with any luck, we'll all still come out with a win."

"We need it, guys. Election year," Mike said, standing to end the discussion. "Whatever hatchets you two have, I expect them to be tossed in the river...today. Work it out. Find the boy and put his old man away forever. Am I understood? Ronald? Joe?"

They both grudgingly grunted their agreement and followed Stacy out. In the hall they got another lecture about teamwork. Neither heard a word. Once the elevator closed behind Stacy, Ronald smiled in triumph at Joe.

JOE TOOK the stairs down to avoid Ronald. On his way, he bumped into Chip Bateman who had a packet of papers. "I am so glad to see you, Joe. I was just at your office," Chip said. "I need to walk you through this because it has to be taken care of right away."

"What is it?"

"The actual sale of the house to the city," Chip said. "That's the most generous offer we're allowed to give your mother on the eminent domain." Joe was surprised by the figure and barely paid attention as Chip showed him where his mother's signature was required. It had to be notarized.

"How soon did you say?" Joe asked.

"She's one of two residents left and they have to be out by Friday," Chip said with a sympathetic smile.

Joe numbly shook hands, took the packet to his office and locked the door. What a mess. Billy was kidnapped and probably dead. Nicola was definitely dead and Tanovich was free. Had he missed anything, he wondered.

Then his eyes fell on the papers on his desk. His mother was being evicted from her house and there was a body in the basement. She would probably get locked up for it.

JOE DIDN'T NOTICE his cell phone until the third ring, then dragged himself out of his pit. "Detective," he said.

"Why in hell am I having to brief this Sheldon guy over at Patterson's house?" Bitt said.

"Consider yourself lucky you didn't have to watch as I was royally fucked," Joe said.

"Ouch. You gonna be there too?" Bitt asked with genuine concern. "You're not off it completely?"

"Not yet."

"Come over, we got real things to talk about and I already worked with Sheldon. He misses everything except the truly irrelevant," Bitt said.

"Have I told you I love you?" Joe said with a laugh.

"Not sure I like that from a guy in your condition."

Joe stuffed the house papers into his briefcase and hurried to his car, hoping there was something worthwhile at Nicola's house. He called Enright, but just got voice mail.

As he entered the kitchen he spotted Ronald staring down at the outline of where Nicola had died. "Oh yeah," he said, "I meant to mention I'd be coming here."

"Thanks for the heads up," Joe said as he shook with Bitt.

"I was just starting to say the preliminary forensics report is back on what was in the food," Bitt said. "Benzo something, it's written down. It's a regular prescription sedative. Half the ladies of a certain age take it."

Bittinger explained it looked to the coroner like the sedative was just meant to make them all fall asleep. If Nicola hadn't been taking Ativan, she wouldn't have died from what she ate. Her death was probably accidental, Bitt said, though still murder, just not premeditated. The sedatives had been stirred into one of the cartons of Chinese food, but not all the way to the bottom. So they knew it had been added after it was cooked.

Bitt said a neighbor with an unhealthy interest in watching Nicola had given them a sketchy timeline. They returned from the baseball game with Senka driving her

Hummer. Not long after they returned, Nicola's car pulled out of the garage and returned in half an hour. The witness' statement more or less fit with the time on the receipt from the Chinese takeout which had been paid in cash. The place had no security cameras. No record.

Senka was in the hospital, but in no danger. Bittinger invited both Joe and Ronald to join him when he interviewed her later. Joe silently thanked him, it looked like Bitt would be his only way to stay in the loop. He asked if Tanovich had visited his daughter yet and the detective shook his head.

"What about her husband?" Ronald asked. "She was getting a divorce, right?"

"Husband was in Miami the last three days," Bitt said. "Joe, I'd like you to take a look at the boy's clothes."

"What the hell is this about, Detective?" Ronald said angrily. "You are aware I'm lead on this case?"

"Extremely aware, but Joe has spent a lot of time with the boy since he moved in here. I don't think you have."

"So what?"

"The neighbor saw what the boy was wearing last night and I'm hoping Mr. Brandt can tell us if he can think of anything he's seen Billy wear that's now missing."

Ronald didn't like it but they both followed Bittinger to the guest room where Billy had moved in his things. There wasn't much besides a small train set and a new basketball in the center of its loop of tracks. The drawers in the dresser were open, but most were empty or nearly so.

"I know he moved out of home in a hurry, but he'd still have more than just these clothes. It looks like whoever kidnapped the boy took some of his clothes too. Changes of underwear and socks would suggest keeping him alive."

"When he came to basketball practice, he wore a blue Timberwolves jersey," Joe said. "Number 14, Pekovic."

They searched the house without finding it. Joe and Bitt thought this was terrific news, maybe Billy really was alive. Ronald wrote it off as insignificant information.

JOE WAS last to drive out of the cul-de-sac, following Ronald's BMW on the drive to St. Joseph's Hospital. He still couldn't reach Enright, so he called Kat, but couldn't bring himself to tell her he'd been demoted and would likely be off the case soon. Instead, he told her why he thought Billy was alive and she bought it. Then she said she'd decided to take vacation days for the rest of the week, because she couldn't begin to concentrate.

"Think you could steal a couple hours away for personal business today?" Kat asked him tentatively.

"I like the sound of that," Joe said.

"I was thinking we should look for places for your mom to live," Kat said. "I've compiled a list from work."

"She won't leave the house."

"If I can get her to go look at places, can I get you to come with us? It's urgent, right?"

"They're going to tear her house down Friday," he said.

She was incredulous. "When were you going to move her?"

It had never crossed his mind it was possible to pry his mother out of that house. She was still guarding the secret that was somewhere down in the basement. By the time he parked at the hospital, he had agreed to Kat's plan.

In deadly silence the three men rode the elevator up and found Senka Tanovich's private room by following the arrays of flowers. Daddy hadn't come to visit but he'd had an assistant spend a couple thousand on floral displays.

Ronald wanted to read Senka's initial statement and the preliminary forensic and coroner reports before they saw her, he didn't want to hear it from them. They went in search of coffee and Bitt launched into an impassioned defense of justifiable homicide. Ronald fit all conditions.

"I still hope to solve this case and find the boy alive, so I need you," Bitt said, then became thoughtful. "One thing I didn't mention at the site, we'll see if Normy-boy picks it up on his own. See, there are no fingerprints on the steering wheel of Nicola's car."

"Wiped clean?"

"We know from the neighbor that the Hummer came back with all three of them in it, then a little later Nicola's car pulled out of the garage – automatic opener, no one got out of the car, darkened windows. It was gone half an hour and came back."

"Only the steering wheel was wiped down?"

"Driver's door handle, gear shift, turn signal."

"My theory is they bought the Chinese food on the way home, but the killer wanted anyone watching to think they went out for it. The question is why?"

"I think Billy was in Nicola's car when it left," Joe said. "Probably unconscious. That's how they moved him."

Bittinger sat in silence mulling it over. Then they worked through possibilities. Maybe the kidnapper had arrived on foot or parked nearby and walked in. Maybe he thought Nicola's car would not be noteworthy coming and going and was the best way to get the boy away. Maybe that meant Billy had been taken less than fifteen minutes away from the house.

"Why bring the car back at all, return to the murder scene, have a second opportunity to be noticed?" Bitt asked.

"This morning I had to walk in from the access road. It'd be easy to sneak in at night behind the houses since there are no fences between yards," Joe said. "Walk in, drug them and grab the unconscious boy, take him someplace nearby, return with the vehicle so it doesn't lead to the drop-off spot, then walk back to the car he came in."

"So he's alive and within fifteen minutes of the site?"

"Unless he's been moved again," Joe said.

"Our fearless leader seems pretty convinced he's dead."

"Ronald's unnaturally anxious to believe it, seems to me," Joe said as they headed back to Senka's room.

Ronald was already inside with her, which irked the hell out of Bittinger as they joined him. Senka was sitting up in bed, surrounded by flowers. The hospital sheet across her lap was creased to perfection and she kept smoothing it as she talked. She seemed pretty alert and cold as ice.

"I don't know any more now than I did when I first woke up," Senka said.

"They came home from the game, shared Chinese food, they all fell asleep right at the kitchen table. She woke up to find...what she found," Ronald summed up for her.

"Mind if I conduct my own interview, counselor?" Bitt asked and Ronald reluctantly stepped aside. "Where did you buy the Chinese food?" Bittinger asked.

"I don't know it. It was in Nicola's neighborhood."

"The Red Dragon?" Bitt prompted but she just gave him a blank look and half a nod as if to say, 'if you say so.'

"So you stopped there on the way back from the game?" Bitt asked but never got an answer.

Ronald pumped Senka for any thoughts on enemies she or Nicola might have, what she knew of Nicola's husband

and the divorce. Joe urged Bitt to step back and let Ronald ask his irrelevant questions. In Senka's view, her family was beloved, the company had never had an unhappy buyer, supplier or sub-contractor and Nicola's divorce was more amicable than most marriages. And her father was on god on this earth. Ronald got nothing useful from her and then he seemed anxious to leave.

Bittinger saw Joe signal behind Ronald's back for him to stay. As Joe blocked Ronald at the door, he heard Bittinger ask again, "So you guys stopped at the Red Dragon on the way home from the game, is that right?"

Ronald wanted to get back in, but Joe stayed in his way.

"Nicola went out for the food while Billy and I waited."

"So she drove her own car and left for how long?"

"I don't know. It can't have been long, I think."

As they left, Joe and Bittinger felt disappointed. She could have opened a door for them and Ronald wouldn't even know it. But she kept the time line in tact and that left the mystery of why the inside of the car was wiped down. Who had been driving it?

Enright was in his office when Joe arrived. "I called you back but your phone was off," Enright said, then added, "You don't look so bad for a guy who's lost a witness, an admirer and a first chair."

"Billy's alive," Joe said as he sat. "What's all this?"

"Senka was pretty, like her sister and mother," Enright said, showing childhood photos from school books and newspaper archives. Long hair, lively eyes. Then Enright laid out the progression of photos he'd found during the protracted search for Dejana. By the end, Senka was dark, severe in hair, dress and outlook. "Amazes me you can think your way into unattractiveness," Enright said.

Enright dug his notebook out and paged through it as a smile grew. "I cross referenced when Dejana disappeared with the houses Tanovich had under construction at that exact time. One jumped out. We've even been inside it."

Enright's smirk was contagious. "Permits list dates for foundation, plumbing and electrical rough-in, framing and all. The most perfect place is Senka's home."

"So the question is, does Senka know it?" Joe asked.

"In that family, anything's possible."

"She seems to believe her father's the center of the universe, the same as he does."

"If a guy like him needed a driver, say, in the middle of the night whilst he was offing the little lady..."

"A true believer would be a good choice."

28

JOE SUNK ANOTHER THREE-POINTER, SHOOTING FROM HIS mother's driveway. He was brooding about his impasse with the Tanovich crime spree, but there was nothing he could do on his own. Ronald stood in his way.

Then he heard Kat yell, "You coming with us, Joey?"

On the front porch Kat was at the railing and standing next to her, clinging to her arm for dear life, was his mother. She was dressed up and Joe thought he saw lipstick.

"You look good, Ma," he said as he took her arm.

She balked at stepping off the stairs, but Kat said calmly, "What did we talk about, Aileen? You let Joe and me share the worry."

To Joe's amazement, they stepped off, walked to the curb and soon had his mother in the car ready for an adventure he never thought could happen. "How'd you do it?" he asked.

"Talking to people is what I do, Joe."

At first their search didn't look too promising. At a modern care facility with multiple levels of independence, Aileen looked at the peaceful wooded setting and refused to get out of the car. They crossed facilities off Kat's list, new was out of the question. Rural was unlikely.

His mother went inside an older, inner city facility, but when she saw a hallway lined with railings, she broke free. More cross-offs, drive-by rejections and a few actual visits. When they found an apartment that appealed to Aileen, Kat thought it looked shabby. Joe knew it had a chance because poor people had lived in it. The furniture was worn, the kitchen laminate was chipped, the wooden floor was scuffed. Aileen sat in an old easy chair facing the television and then came the clincher, the sound of basketballs being dribbled. Out the window was a city park with multiple courts. "That would drive me crazy," Kat said.

"Welcome to my mother's world."

Aileen said yes and Kat reluctantly agreed to start the paperwork. Joe had been waiting for a chance to speak alone with Aileen since his realizations that morning.

"I know where Dad is, Ma."

"No one knows because we never looked for him."

"You can't stay in our house much longer," Joe said. "The city will take the house and dig up the basement. Dad won't be missing anymore. Do you understand?"

She looked him in the eye. "You can fix it, Joey."

He wasn't sure she was acknowledging what he thought she was, but that was all he was going to get.

They signed papers, got two sets of keys and were on their way to a notary. It was not easy establishing her identity with an expired driver's license and no passport, but eventually the house papers were completed and Kat had a nice surprise in store. They stopped at Mickey's Diner.

Aileen recognized the place, became younger and had the first, ear to ear smile Joe ever remembered seeing. It came when she received her chocolate malt in a stemmed glass and the metal container with the extra malt in it. It was just like they used to do when she was a girl. Back when she smiled often. Back before she met George.

Joe marveled that Aileen was going to remember this day the rest of her life. So would he. His mother was actually capable of joy and it was Kat who brought it out.

When they drove home, Aileen was alarmed by a large package on the front porch. It was cardboard boxes and shipping supplies, a gift from Chip Bateman. It took some convincing, but before long she was inside making Kool-Aid, Kat was trying to get her to prioritize the things she wanted to keep and Joe was lugging the boxes into the living room. It felt astonishingly domestic, verging on normal, except that he had to make a sweep of the back yard and garage to be certain there were no signs of his uncle.

That and the fact he still had no idea what to do about the basement. Was Dad going to destroy them from the grave?

Enright called him asking for support because Ronald Sheldon was blocking the investigation. Joe's stolen time was over, but Kat said she'd stay and help pack. She cajoled Aileen to pull out everything from 'Joey's' childhood and he feared it would take him months to wean Kat of calling him Joey.

HE'D NEVER BEEN INVITED to Ronald's office before.

"This isn't a fucking democracy and we're not taking votes on the direction of the investigation," Ronald said angrily from behind his desk that was far too neat.

"Can I at least run it down for you two?" Enright asked. Joe found it immensely gratifying when others detested Ronald.

Enright said he'd watched Senka leaving the hospital. She had a heated private conference with her father between his limo and the taxi waiting for her. There was no hug and he wasn't giving her a ride. They argued, then she rode off in the taxi. Enright wanted surveillance on Senka.

Ronald shook his head and leaned closer to them, "You want to follow a crime victim and potentially jeopardize two cases? You're not doing it. I'm not sanctioning that."

"Something's going on between those two," Enright said.

"You're not following her or her father," Ronald said.

"You do in fact want to solve this case?" Joe asked.

"I haven't gotten my only witness killed," Ronald said. "Mike and Stacy said you can stay on the murder of Sienna Tanovich, so I can't stop you from pursuing that," he said. "But let me be clear, stay away from the murder of Nicola Patterson and the probable murder of Billy Tanovich. You are forbidden to follow either Dusan or Senka Tanovich. Is that clear enough for you two?"

Joe and Enright stayed silent until they were behind a closed door in Joe's office. Then Joe asked a question which had been nagging him, "How far inside this office do you think Tanovich's money could reach?"

Joe explained that Chesler had known about the meeting discussing his future on the case when Don Ward was preparing to smear him. Ronald had been in that meeting. It seemed every action Ronald had taken since he'd gotten control over the case had been to lead away from the Tanovich family. Could Ronald be trying to run interference for them?

"You think he's a mole? Helluva accusation, Joe," Enright said. "Ronald could just be an incompetent prick."

"I know for a fact he's an incompetent prick, it's what else he's doing that worries me."

"That kind of speculation ends careers, Joe," Enright said, then thought a moment. "And doesn't solve cases."

"I'm just being paranoid, I guess," Joe said.

"Ronald believes Billy's dead, right?" Enright said. "If we're merely looking for our living witness and not his dead kidnap victim and as long as we don't follow Senka or Daddy, we're within the bounds he just set." Joe laughed and Enright added, "I get it from my boys, they're experts at splitting hairs."

"What were you suggesting about Senka before Ronald told you to stop?" Joe asked.

"I tailed her," Enright said. He followed her home from the hospital and watched her harangue her gardener. She had the same entitlement issues as her father.

Enright spoke with the gardener and learned Senka had insisted he put covers over the sculptures in her garden. "She only covers them when she leaves town, the gardener said. Until this afternoon, he hadn't heard anything about a trip. He usually gets notified well in advance."

"Where do we think she might be going?" Joe asked.

"The lady takes care of interior design for them and it includes ceramic tiles," Enright said with a note of triumph. "It seems the Tanovichs have hordes of extended family in the old country. Daddy set up a tile making operation back there. Some tiny village in Albania that the old man's parents came from. Cheap labor and cousins to run it. Senka goes there several times a year to check tile designs and make orders."

"So she's going to Albania?" Joe asked.

"If the 'empire and heir apparent' theory is true," Enright said, "then Daddy has a problem. He's kidnapped the young prince, but also had to offer a ten-million-dollar reward to look serious. Now he's gotta keep the boy outa sight for years until he's old enough to run the empire."

"I'd want close family members doing the keeping," Joe said. "A village in Albania where everyone is family and it's easier to keep secrets and iron-fisted control."

"Not a bad thought," Enright said. "Trouble is, I can't find Senka booked on any flight. Sure, Daddy's got a corporate jet but Albania is a lot farther than Cincinnati."

"Can't get a warrant to search her house on what we've got," Joe said. "How's she usually travel to Albania?"

"THERE ARE no direct commercial flights. She usually flies to Rome, but she's not booked from here and I've checked Rome flights through Chicago, New York, Washington."

"And she'd have to get the boy out of the country, which means a serious risk of being caught at passport control."

"I know it'll come as a shock, but rich people can get fake passports that are just as good as real ones," Enright said. "And they make passports in Albania too."

Joe offered to cancel his evening practice with the East Side Sinkers, but Enright didn't think he could use him yet. Enright planned to park outside Senka's house – it wouldn't be 'following' her if she didn't move – and work his phone, see if he could find her overseas booking. They didn't know if she had Billy, but she lived less than fifteen minutes from Nicola. The boy could be there and they would have no way of getting inside to look.

Under orders from Ronald, Bitt had set up a hostage and ransom unit to deal with the missing boy. Tanovich had reluctantly visited, but hadn't even stayed. "He said he had to arrange for a lot of cash to be available in case there was a ransom demand made," Enright told Joe.

"But we don't think he's arranging ransom just in case?"

"They don't know we figured out the village in Albania or that we think Senka's leaving town, but with or without a mole they know we suspect her of something," Enright said.

"Sounds like we gotta keep our heads down," Joe said.

WHAT JOE WANTED MORE than anything was to clear his head by shooting baskets. Maybe it would help him solve the unsolvable problem of what to do about his father. The body, he was now convinced, could only be in one place. But he had his Thursday practice and he didn't feel up to the lies it would take to call the boys and cancel it.

"So Billy probably won't be joining the team," Jamal said as Joe walked up with the bag of balls. He was last to arrive for practice for the first time. They'd all seen Nicola and Billy on the news. Joe led the boys in a discussion about not assuming Billy was dead, but felt he was protesting too much. Even street-tough kids assumed kidnapped meant dead.

Once they started to practice, Joe was off his game, couldn't concentrate on his coaching and his distraction threw everyone off all evening. After practice, Jamal said, "Don't worry, Coach. Your shot will be back on Saturday."

"Thanks," Joe said. "With any luck, so will Billy."

"Good," Jamal said.

IT WAS STILL TWILIGHT as Joe headed for home, but when he passed a house that was being remodeled, it reminded him of Tony's body disposal theories. He pulled over and stared at the construction site. He thought about his mother's house, his father's body being found in the basement and the only punishment the world could exact would be on her. Now that he'd made his family's tortured history into front page news, finding the remains of his father was sure to get headlines. There would be no room for leniency in an election year.

'If the body were never found...' Joe thought.

It wasn't as if there were a definitive moment of decision, but he began looking at houses under construction. He found a site, parked on the next block, walked back trying to look innocent and saw it had the first floor in. He found another and another, then by the time it was completely dark outside, he found the right house. As he looked at it, he thought, 'It's Thursday, they're going to pour cement just hours from now. Am I going to do this?'

As if to delay having to answer, he walked down the alley and almost jumped out of his shoes when a spotlight came on from a motion detector. Once his heart rate calmed and he realized no one came outside to look for an intruder, he went on. The building site had a single light on a temporary electrical service post near the front of the lot. Pallets of lumber and plywood were laid out in the rear area under plastic sheeting and there was a padlocked steel shipping container for tools. Just like Tony had described.

The back of the lot was enclosed with six-foot chain-link fencing. It made a reasonably sturdy barrier, but as Tony had said, it was only designed to discourage vandals. Its metal posts were simply placed into holes in the dirt and wedged with thick wooden shims pounded in around them. Joe knelt and patiently loosened the shims holding the end post in place. The five minutes of work felt like hours as sweat rolled down his face. The wire fencing was still attached to the pole as he lifted it quietly, pulled it aside to enter the site, then put the post back in the hole.

By entering the site, Joe was committing a crime, putting his legal career in serious jeopardy.

The site was open around the foundation, with no trees or bushes for cover. Joe edged toward the foundation under the pale orange light from the lone fixture which left parts of the basement in dark shadow. The floor was dirt, the cinderblock walls had been completed and Joe discovered an egress window which was a wider and taller opening for a fire code exit from below ground level. It would make getting in and out easier. He'd be carrying a body.

He knew at that moment he was actually planning to transfer his father from one basement to another. Somehow.

Tony's theory would work. 'Wouldn't you know,' he thought, 'it had to be a basement.'

His vibrating cell startled him. It was Enright.

Joe squatted down between pallets of lumber to hide, then answered in a whisper. Enright thought it was so he wouldn't wake up Kat. He was calling from outside Senka's and wanted Joe to come watch the house. He had to meet a contact, check out a lead. Joe stared blindly at his watch, trying to figure out if he had time or whether this was a sign that he should abandon his plan.

"I want to be sure we stay on top of Senka," Enright said, "it's the most logical place for them to hold Billy. Maybe you'll see something to give us probable cause."

"So we can finally get a search warrant," Joe said.

"Why'd you lawyers make all these restrictions anyway?" Enright asked and hung up.

29

Joe drove past Senka's house and parked a block away. As he walked up, he could make out the covers on the garden statues, but there wasn't a single light on inside the house. He saw no sign of life as he stood in shadows across the street for a very long hour. It gave him way too much idle time to contemplate his family.

Ma must have killed Dad with the baseball bat. After he beat them and split Joe's lip, it drove her over the line. Then after the killing she'd hidden evidence of the crime.

As he watched, he became fixated on time. How long could he wait and still get Dad out of his mother's basement? At some point it had become a solid, unchangeable decision. He was going to do it, but he didn't have time to waste.

He sneaked up to Senka's front door and saw a blinking red light through the cut glass panel beside the door. The security was on. Did that mean she'd already left or that she turned it on when she was at home? He worked his way around the house, peeking in windows and seeing no movement. He kept an eye out for neighbors and all was quiet. As

Enright said, rich people didn't look out their windows. He threaded through the garden into the back alley, but couldn't see if the Hummer was in the garage.

Joe decided to knock. No one answered at the front door, so he knocked louder. Still no one, so he rang the bell, knocked on windows, the patio door, on the side kitchen service door. The house was empty or Billy was locked up inside while Senka was out making escape arrangements.

'Or it was already too late,' he thought.

"Fuck it," he finally said out loud. He had already committed the first felony of his life an hour earlier.

Joe figured it would take three minutes after he tripped the alarm for the 'armed response' the security company promised. So he gave himself two and a half minutes. If he found the boy, he'd stay and await the police. If he found nothing, he'd do his best to be a Felcher in good standing.

He wrapped his polo shirt around his fist and found it surprisingly easy to shatter the glass in the patio door and let himself inside. Why worry about lights, he figured, the silent alarm was already buzzing somewhere. Then, as he expected, the phone rang. The company was checking to make sure the alarm wasn't a failure by the owner.

Using his shirt, he flipped on lights as he ran. "Billy," he shouted as he opened door after door. Senka's huge bedroom. A guest room decked out in Twins bedspread and posters. The office. A home gym. At the kitchen service door something caught his eye. There was scraping on the paint around one of the security contacts on the door beside the kitchen. It looked like the contact had been moved. Recently. Wishing he had time to contemplate what it meant, but worried about time, Joe abandoned the kitchen door contact unit and raced on in his search.

When he found a door with a lock on the outside, he

rushed in. The bed had been slept in, but the pillows and bedspread were missing. The dresser was completely empty but he spotted a bit of blue beneath the bed. It was Billy's Timberwolves 'away' jersey. Number 14, Pekovic. Proof he had been in the house.

His two and a half minutes were more than up as Joe raced outside with the jersey. He darted out the back patio door and into the garden just as a pair of armed security men from the company arrived at the front of the house.

He worked his way through the garden, but ran into a tall fence. Flashlights shined all around the garden dotted with vaguely human shapes under covers. The lights finally came to rest on the open patio door and broken glass. One man stayed to guard the door and call the police, the other went around the house. While they were focused on the house, Joe scaled the fence and dropped into the neighbor's yard. In less than a minute, he was out on a street, his heart racing as he walked almost casually carrying Billy's jersey and finally pulling his polo shirt back on.

It was all Joe could do to drive away slowly. He was so pumped up he had the awful sense he now knew what went through his father and uncle during their burglaries. The danger and escape had been distressingly exhilarating.

He called Enright and described the Timberwolves jersey, but failed to mention the break-in. "I'm sure Billy is alive; he was at Senka's house, but no one is there now," Joe said. "They must have left before I got there."

"Do I hear a siren?" Enright said.

Once Enright mentioned it, Joe heard it too. In his rearview he saw two police cars heading back the direction he came from. "No idea what that's about," Joe said.

Enright asked how Joe knew all this, but he simply insisted he saw the jersey and it meant Billy was alive. They still had a chance. "Maybe it's not enough for a judge, but it's proof enough for me," Joe said.

"Me too, best news I've heard all day," Enright said.

Enright said he was still working an angle and would get back to Joe. He said this meant they were getting close.

Joe didn't even notice it while he talked to Enright, but he was driving right toward his mother's house.

WHEN HE ARRIVED in front of Aileen's house, Joe felt panicked, Kat's car was parked there. She was still packing up his boyhood memories, all those things he was desperate to leave behind. There were only two things he wanted to come out of that house - his mother and his father. Separate destinations and no looking back.

He thought this might be another sign to abandon his plan and go search for Billy. But where? He hadn't a clue.

Joe needed Kat to leave. He didn't want her implicated in what he planned to do. He parked a block away, walked back and was about to call when he spotted her leaving. She got a hug from his mother and then hurried to her car. Relieved, he watched her drive off before he called.

Kat told him she would have stayed longer, but his mother was so exhausted from the amazing day. She had to leave so Aileen would stop. Joe said he'd better drive over before she went to bed, saying there were things of his own he needed to go through tonight. He told Kat he'd be late, but she made him promise to wake her when he got home.

He watched the lights going out and wanted to give his mother time to be in a very deep sleep. He walked around to look at the demolition and realized many houses were already gone. He could make out silhouettes of heavy excavating and demolition equipment parked amid the half-demolished houses and saw the huge hole for the main building was well under way.

Joe wondered how Billy ended up at Senka's house. How had Tanovich pulled it off? Bittinger's theory they stopped for the Chinese food on the way home from the ball game could be right. Maybe Senka drugged them, took Billy away in Nicola's car after they were asleep, then when she returned, she ate enough of the drugged food to look like a victim. Tanovich could have guarded the boy at Senka's house after his meeting disbanded and they both had alibis. Smart.

He figured Senka was in this all the way, her father's partner in crime. On the night of Sienna's murder, Senka must have driven her father from the hotel to the county road nearest his house and back. Her security system said she was home, but those are meant to keep people out, not in. All she'd need was a screwdriver to remove an alarm contact, leave the two parts together and let herself out without triggering her alarm. Another good alibi.

After his third time around the block he got his car and parked it across from Aileen's house. He put his phone on vibrate, then let himself through the gate. He decided to take a walk through the yard and garage, 'just in case.' By the time he slipped in the back door, he was sweat-soaked again.

His first obstacle was stealing the sole key to the basement lock from his mother. But between the back door and his mother's room there was an obstacle course of boxes, so he fetched a flashlight. He watched his mother sleeping and could see the chain around her neck but the key was under the collar of her nightgown. It took a few nervous attempts to pull the chain out and get it unclasped.

Face to face with the basement door, with the knowledge

of who was down there, Joe toyed with the key and shivered. The only sound he heard was the pounding of his heart.

"S*TOP IT, D*AD," *Young Joe shouted in the living room.*

George's big hand was raised in the air, dripping blood as Joe leapt at the fist and grabbed it with both hands.

On the floor under George, Aileen screamed, "Go back to your room, Joey."

George shook the boy off. But with savage intensity, Joe flung himself forward again, attacking his father. On the back swing George's elbow caught him sharply right in the mouth and sent the boy careening backwards through his bedroom doorway.

Joe collapsed with blood spouting from his severely split lip. Stunned, he watched his hands fill with blood.

WHEN THE LOCK CLICKED OPEN, Joe nearly jumped out of his skin, but somehow he pulled the door open. Ambient city light came through upstairs windows, but down those stairs was the blackest abyss in the universe.

He wiped the sweat from his brow and pulled out the flashlight. The beam was bright and wide and terribly unsteady in his trembling hand. He could see a worn post at the bottom of the steps holding up the floor joists. Below, it looked like a dirt floor. No cement.

He wanted his hands free for the descent, so he pocketed the flashlight and edged toward the top step. With both hands on the rickety handrail, he slipped his foot over the edge and lowered it. He instantly began to feel just as dizzy as he had at Billy's basement. He stepped back to catch his breath and told himself he could do this. He took a breath and lowered his body one step shakily. Then another.

JOE'S BLOOD-FILLED hands trembled more with rage than pain until the sight of his mother receiving another punch drove him to get up. He looked past his baseball glove on his dresser toward his bat. It was a thirty-one-inch Henry Aaron Louisville Slugger.

He picked it up and moment later he stood behind his father, choked up on the bat. "Stop it, Dad," he said with eerie calm.

George looked over his shoulder and there was a murderous look in his eye. He wouldn't stop. He would kill.

Joe took his best batting stance while George lifted his bloody fist higher. They let fire at the same moment.

Joe swung the bat harder than he had ever done before.

There was a horrifying crack as the bat connected perfectly with George's skull.

JOE CRASHED BACKWARD onto the stairs as if he'd just been slammed down. His heart raced as he began to understand.

Ma hadn't been protecting herself all these years.

She'd been protecting him.

Surrounded by impenetrable darkness, Joe held his hands in front of his face recalling far too vividly the blood gushing from his cut lip and the sickening crack of the bat.

His mother had made it her mission to keep him from remembering what happened that night and she had succeeded.

Unfortunately, he now finally understood the truth.

He almost let out a laugh. He had killed his father.

He'd changed from baseball to basketball because he'd bashed his father's head in. All these years she'd whispered it was nightmares and he had worked hard to believe it.

Joe sat for some time halfway down those basement

stairs surrounded by his thoughts, trying to fathom his mother's actions. He was only eight when he had swung that bat to save her life. If the police had been called in, there wouldn't have been charges against him. Nor would they have charged her, he figured. Maybe she was terrified he'd be taken away from her, which was probably quite realistic.

Then he understood. Uncle Louie. It didn't matter what the authorities did, Louie would have killed them both if he'd learned of George's death. His mother had saved them from Louie. She had a mantra, "We protect each other, Joey," which he had always thought was figurative. Until now, he'd never quite put together just how literal it was.

He had no doubt he'd saved his mother's life that night and now it was just as clear, she'd saved them both from Louie. She'd kept them safe for twenty years. He couldn't think of a thing she should have done different.

Did this change anything about his plan tonight? Louie was still a threat and the police still had to be considered. Every way he thought it through, the person who'd pay the highest price was always his mother. She had obstructed justice and no matter how sympathetic her case was, no one could just hide a murder victim in the basement.

"You bury them under the cement floor in someone else's house," Joe said. "We protect each other, Ma."

30

Joe inched farther down into the dull, musty air and realized his feet had hit earth. He felt like a different person from the man who had teetered on the top stair. That guy had thought the worst crime of his life had been to break into a rich woman's house. Now he knew he had killed and conspired to hide that knowledge from himself.

With sudden resolve, Joe fetched the flashlight from his pocket, turned it on and jumped in panic.

Beside the stairs, clothes were drying on lines strung from the joists above. He guessed the dryer had given out over the years. It was a miracle if the washing machine was still working. Certainly no repairman had ever been down to work on it. After he regained his composure, he shined his light around and began to explore.

He'd killed his father. Shouldn't he feel remorse? Yet there was nothing. His mother's indoctrination had been effective, he felt no shame or regret. If that beating were happening right now, he'd swing the bat. Hard.

There was an ancient furnace near the stairs and along the back wall he found a work bench. He discovered stacks of outdated stolen electronic gear out of their boxes and other evidence of George and Louie's past crimes. Then Joe stopped short when he found his baseball glove covered with dust. The ball was still in the webbing, but there was no sign of his bat.

He kept searching, pushing through the drying clothes until he found the washer and dryer. The laundry area had a big tub and a card table for folding clothes. It also had several stacks of crumbling cardboard boxes, the boxes for the electronic gear by the furnace. They bulged strangely. When he touched the cardboard, a box disintegrated and dirt bled out. His mother kept boxes of dirt in the basement.

'She dug a hole here somewhere' he thought. He scanned the floor in every corner of the room, then in the other rooms and even under the stairs, but could find no area that clearly looked like it had been disturbed.

When the basement light came on, Joe jumped in fright.

THEN HE SAW his mother at the bottom of the stairs, turning the bulb in the ceramic fixture. "There's nothing here, Joey," Aileen said.

"I have to get Dad out of here," he said ever so softly.

"Your dad ran out on us when you were eight."

"He ran out, but he didn't really leave the house."

"Your dad ran out, that's all," she said.

Joe studied her as she avoided his gaze. What must she have gone through that night. Beaten nearly to death by her husband, then seeing her son kill him and finally having to decide to hide the body. The long bloody smear to the basement door. The thumping Joe remembered must have been Dad's head hitting the stairs as she dragged him down. She had certainly never brought him

back up. How was he going to find him now? He had
an idea.

"Where's my Henry Aaron Louisville Slugger?"

"Your baseball bat? That's under the dryer," she said.

Joe wrestled the dryer aside, then had to go outside to
the garage to fetch a shovel. What a contrast he realized.
He'd come downstairs filled with terror, now he went up the
steps without hesitation and returned in an instant.

Once he started digging under the spot where the dryer
had been, he soon ran into something hard. He found a
molded plastic suitcase lying on its side which capped a
much deeper hole. When he pulled the suitcase out, he
looked quizzically at his mother, but she remained blank.

The first thing Joe saw when he shined his flashlight into
the hole was a twenty-dollar bill. Soon he found hundreds
of them flowing out of a black plastic yard bag. It had to be
thousands of dollars.

"Your bat's under that," Aileen said impassively.

It took two hands to get the bag of cash out, so he set the
flashlight aside, pulled on the bag and found it surprisingly
heavy. Tens of thousands of dollars. Dad and Louie must
have had a really big score at the end. Now it was clear what
Louie had been looking for, then and recently.

Joe saw what he thought was the end of his bat, reached
down to grab it, then jumped back as if bitten. He shined the
flashlight into the hole and saw it was a bone.

So there he was. Dad.

At that moment, Joe couldn't remember what he thought
he would find, but he hadn't expected to move his dead
father out bone by bone. He shook from the touch, but at
last directed his flashlight farther into the hole for a closer
look. There was still a lot of loose cash, the sleeve of the

plaid shirt he remembered his father wearing that night and, wedged below that, was the end of his baseball bat.

"So my nightmares were all memories, Ma?" he said.

"Nothing happened the way you dreamt it," she said, then started folding the dry clothes to avoid looking at him. He shined the light all around the rather deep hole, trying to form a plan.

Joe reached down and pulled out the bat. It was cracked. It was seriously split right up the wood grain.

"I broke the bat when I hit him, Ma?" Joe said looking at the bat caked with blood and hair.

"The first whack didn't finish it," she said.

Before he could think about that, there was a horrendous crash from upstairs so powerful, it shook the house and sent dust raining down from the joists overhead.

Joe leapt up, signaled his mother to stay where she was. As he ran to the foot of the stairs, he realized the sound was the kitchen door crashing inward. He looked upstairs just as heavy footsteps thundered down toward him.

"What have we here?" Louie said as he descended.

JOE THOUGHT ABOUT THE SHOVEL, but before he could even move, Louie pulled a diamond studded switchblade out of his back pocket and flicked it open. "Stay where I can see you," Louie said as he got to the bottom of the stairs and backed Joe up with the knife. "Where's the old bitch?"

Joe realized that, regardless of age, Louie was still awfully powerful. "You didn't grow much, Kid," he said.

"Was that knife buried out by the garage?" Joe asked. "I should have called the police on you that night."

"Didn't though, did'ja?" Louie said with a snarling smile.

"Wonder why?" Just like his brother, Louie loved the feeling and power of intimidation.

Joe couldn't get his cell phone out of his pocket unseen and now wished he hadn't made his mother put away that rifle. Joe tried to lead him away from the dryer, but Louie stopped him when Aileen emerged through the hanging clothes with the garbage bag brimming over with cash, offering it to Louie.

"This is what you came for."

Louie grabbed it, looked in the bag suspiciously and said, "This ain't all of it, ya crazy old bitch." Without warning, he hit her. It sent her reeling backward, but to Joe's surprise, it didn't knock her over. She had far too much experience at taking a punch. "I spent twenty years in prison because of you."

Louie turned the knife toward Joe who had started to move toward his mother. "Don't get any ideas."

It tore Joe apart to see his mother hit again. "You were in prison because you beat a man to death," Joe said.

"Yeah, well, she snitched on me," Louie said, shaking the knife at Aileen angrily. "Where's the rest of it?"

"That's all there is," Joe said anxiously. He saw a look in Louie's eyes like the one in his dad's that last night. 'He wants the money and he wants revenge.'

Aileen gestured through the hanging clothes toward the laundry room and Joe couldn't fathom why. Was she hoping he could fight his uncle? He couldn't win a fight against Louie even if he didn't have a switchblade.

Louie took a look around the laundry room. The hole, the dirt, the broken baseball bat, a trickle of twenty dollar bills streaming from the hole. He waved the knife at them. "I knew George didn't run out on me," Louie shouted angrily at Aileen. "Ya killed him, ya bitch."

"I killed him," Joe said, stepping in front of Aileen. "I bashed his head in with my baseball bat."

Louie scoffed at him in disbelief.

"Joey stopped him," Aileen said. "I finished it."

Louie raised the knife at her and she stood her ground.

"I killed George and if you don't get out of here, I'll kill you too, Louie Felcher," Aileen said with a force Joe had never heard before. Neither had Louie.

'Could it be true?' Joe wondered.

"The rest of the money's in the hole," Aileen said.

Louie peered into the hole, but it was too dark at the bottom. The flashlight was still shining where Joe left it. Louie bent over to grab the light and shine it in the hole.

The shovel came down on his head with amazing force.

Louie staggered down to his knees and Aileen hit him in the head again so hard he was dead before his face hit the ground.

Louie came to rest draped half over the hole.

She had already raised the shovel to hit him a third time when Joe stopped her.

Until this moment, Joe had kept a hope alive it was possible to get out of this. He might have succeeded in getting rid of one old body, but a new dead body with a bashed-in skull and a ton of cash made escape impossible.

Joe was sick and angry as he looked at Louie, then at the bruises and swelling on her face. "It's all over, Ma."

"George started to wake up," Aileen said. "He'd'a killed us both if he'd gotten back up," Aileen said.

Once he'd stopped his father with a blow to the head, there had been no turning back. She'd protected them when she finished the job, she'd protected them when she convinced him it was nightmares and she'd protected them once again by killing his uncle.

AT FIRST HE barely noticed the vibrating cell phone in his pocket, but then saw it was Enright.

"The Tanovich corporate jet just filed a flight plan for Winnipeg for an hour from now," Enright said.

It took a moment for Joe to bridge the distance from the basement and his family of killers to what Enright was saying. "How'd you find out? What's in Winnipeg?"

"I got a guy at the St. Paul Downtown Airport who promised to let me know about any activity with the corporate jet and, what'd'ya know, he did," Enright said. "Get dressed and call me back when you're on your way."

Joe looked at his uncle draped over the hole, his father below him and the bag of cash nearby, then at his mother.

How could he leave her like this? How could he not?

"There's a kidnapped boy I need to help save, Ma," he said as he escorted her toward the stairs.

"A boy from your basketball team?" she asked.

"Yeah," he said. "We did a good job protecting each other, but it's over now. There's nothing we can do about Dad and Louie anymore. Not this time."

31

JOE SETTLED HIS MOTHER ON THE COUCH AND TURNED ON THE television, then walked out the back door which had been smashed to the floor. He raced out to his car and drove off before calling Enright back.

"Tell me about Winnipeg. What's up there?"

"Not a thing of interest to the Tanovich family," Enright said. "They got no reason to go there, yet they arrange an emergency flight for the dead of night right after the old man's charges are dropped and the boy disappears?"

"You think he's going to run for it?" Joe said. "That doesn't fit for me. He's beating us and he's not going to give up the empire he built. His ego can't let the world believe he's too cowardly to defend what he genuinely believes is his kingdom."

"Good point. But don't snuggle back in with lady love just yet," Enright said. "Flight plans have to be filed for take-off, along with a declaration of international or domestic destination. Bitt tells me flight plans can be amended in the air. The plane could be diverted to Montréal or Toronto.

Both have direct flights to Rome, which is the easiest connection to Albania."

TWENTY MINUTES LATER, Joe drove to the edge of the Downtown Airport which had a panoramic view of the St. Paul skyline across the river. He found Enright peering through powerful binoculars at a gleaming white, hundred-foot-long private jet. In the middle of the night that jet was the only hub of activity at the municipal airport. Enright handed the glasses to Joe while he updated him. Joe watched the uniformed pilot going around the plane inspecting while the co-pilot checked off items on his clipboard. A fuel truck was pumping jet fuel into a wing.

"Naturally Tanovich's jet is the largest private plane allowed here," Enright said. "Any bigger and they'd have to use Minneapolis St. Paul International Airport. Still no sign of the family, but a blue Escalade with tinted windows drove into that hangar. Tanovich owns a blue Escalade."

"Then they're here. But who's going? You think Billy's with them? Where's Bitt?"

"Checking on the fueling."

"What about it?"

"Dunno. Ask him, he knows all that airplane stuff."

Bittinger hurried toward them in the shadow of the main building. "They're putting in every drop she'll hold. That means they're going a lot farther than Winnipeg. That puppy can go six thousand miles."

"Montréal can't be much over a thousand miles," Enright said. "Maybe they're just topping off."

"Pilot wouldn't," Bittinger said. "You take what you need plus a buffer, but only time you're going to fly with every pound of fuel the plane holds is when you need it. The lighter the weight, the better the mileage and handling."

"How far is it to Albania?" Joe asked.

They all looked at each other uncertainly.

"It would be a stretch for any corporate plane, even this one, but I'd wager it's possible they could fly to Albania nonstop," Bittinger said with clear admiration. "Once it's airborne, we're shit out of luck."

"If we see the boy, we can stop them," Joe said.

"He's not on the plane," Enright said definitively. "I saw the pilots first open it up."

"So they have to get him on board and if we see him, he's a kidnap victim being taken aboard an international aircraft," Joe said, "we can swoop in."

"We in a position to swoop?" Enright asked Bittinger. It was just the three of them hiding there in shadows.

"I can't call in the troops on what we got," Bitt said. "We're flying pretty far below the radar here, boys."

"What would it take to block the runway?" Joe asked.

"A court order," Bittinger said.

"What about unofficially?" Joe asked.

"Park a car in the runway and they're stuck on the ground," Bittinger said. "Course the car's driver is headed for federal prison. Airports got all kinds of regulations."

Joe stared across the field as the fuel truck drove away and the pilot walked up the steps right behind the cockpit. "A guy plays fast and loose in any airport in the U.S. of A. and he's asking to be fucked up seventeen ways from Ground Zero," Bitt said in Joe's ear.

"I get your meaning," Joe said, still staring. "What if a guy were to witness a crime being committed?"

"Let me start back at the beginning," Bittinger said. "A crime in an airport isn't local...like breaking and entering," he said with a knowing look at Joe. "We got this thing called a police radio," Bitt said. "Cops talk to other cops..."

'Fuck, they know about Senka's house,' Joe thought.

Bittinger threw up his hands and turned to Enright, "Denser than I thought."

Enright stepped between Joe and his view of the jet. "We have a plane being fueled and a flight plan filed. We got nothing illegal, nothing we can act on. Unless they come out shooting at us, we can't go out there and stop that plane."

"If we see the boy?"

"They parade a kidnap victim in front of us?" Enright looked to Bittinger and they shrugged. "That's do-able."

Joe looked past Enright and pointed. They all watched Senka Tanovich walk from the building the blue Escalade had entered. She was towing a small rolling suitcase and heading right for the stairs up to the plane.

"No crime in her flying to Winnipeg," Enright said. "She wasn't asked or ordered to stay in the country."

The hangar door opened and a workman wheeled out a cart with a wooden crate on it and headed toward the plane. Joe was becoming visibly agitated.

"What's this, an emergency delivery of bathroom tiles to Winnipeg?" Enright said.

The workman parked the cart beside the rear cargo door which was already open. The man went inside the plane and returned with the co-pilot. Together they picked up the crate, which looked heavy, and slid it into the cargo hold.

"Billy's in the box," Joe declared.

"We don't know that," Bitt said.

"The box has holes in the sides."

"Doesn't prove anything, Joe," Enright said.

"Can you access the cargo hold from the passenger cabin once the plane is in the air?" Joe asked Bittinger.

"Sure. Why?"

"Tanovich won't have the boy visible anywhere on the ground," Joe said. "Once it's airborne, they take him out."

"We don't even know Tanovich is here," Enright said.

Just then Senka stepped out of the plane and went to watch the workman securing the crate. There was no more sign of movement from the hangar. Soon the worker closed up the cargo door, then Senka stepped back in the plane.

Joe went crazy when the jet engines started up.

Before Bittinger or Enright could stop him, Joe raced onto the field, shouting and trying to force a showdown.

Just as the workman was about to close the stairs, Joe darted past him and up into the plane.

Joe didn't see it, but behind him Tanovich flew out of the hangar at a sprint.

"Fuck," Enright said.

JOE HADN'T EXPECTED to get this far. He was amazed by the plane's customized luxury and size. It had separate sitting, dining and office areas plus an enclosed bedroom at the back. All of it was paneled in exotic woods, trimmed in gold and the trappings of wealth. A Persian carpet was laid under the walnut dining table.

No one had noticed Joe yet. The pilots were busy at the controls and Senka was in the galley fixing herself a drink. But they all turned around when Tanovich stormed on board and shouted, "Get the fuck off my plane!" The older man's bulk filled the doorway, trapping Joe inside while the startled pilots looked around to see what was going on.

"You got Billy in here," Joe shouted, backing away from the big man who stomped toward him. "He's in the crate."

"How do you..." Senka said.

"Shut up, Senka," Tanovich said with a calm malevolence. He was red with anger as he marched down the middle of the plane. His hands were ready to grab Joe and strangle him. The plane no longer felt very large.

"Call the police!" Joe shouted past Tanovich at the pilots, but the big man spun around.

"Do not make that call," Tanovich yelled.

"Call the police," Joe shouted again. "There is a kidnapped boy on this plane."

"Mr. Tanovich," one pilot said, but Tanovich jutted a finger at him and that shut him right up.

Joe backed past Senka at the galley and she looked with alarm at her father. It was clear she was terrified of Joe being there and what he must know. When Joe started looking around for a hatch to the cargo hold, she figured out what he was looking for. "Daddy..." Senka shouted.

In the cockpit, the pilots shut the engines down.

"Start it back up, you're departing now," Tanovich said to the pilots. But they were frozen and looked too afraid to obey. Tanovich abruptly changed tactics, pointed out the door and shouted at them, "Get the fuck out of my plane."

The shocked pilots looked at Tanovich, then past him toward Joe who had located the hatch door and was frantically trying to get it open. By now Senka was pounding violently on his back and screaming, "Daddy!"

The pilots hurried out and down the steps. The instant they were on the tarmac, Tanovich pushed a button by the door and the stairs started automatically closing into the plane. He was locking Joe inside with him and Senka.

Joe glanced out a window and saw Enright frantically grab the pilots, trying to find out how to open the door from outside. The pilots shook their heads.

Joe felt a presence behind him before he could get the

complicated hatch lock open. He planned to submarine under Tanovich, but then realized it was Senka. She'd left him and had returned with a big knife from the galley. 'A true Tanovich,' Joe thought.

Then he was shocked when the engines started.

He glanced past Senka and saw Tanovich in the open cockpit, starting the engines. 'Holy shit, he flies,' Joe thought just as Senka lunged at him with the knife.

He darted to the side and shoved his shoulder hard into her. She careened against the wood paneling and crumpled to the floor. He stepped over her and ran up the length of the compartment as the plane lurched ahead with a huge bump over the wheel blocks. The jolt knocked him over.

As Joe dragged himself up and struggled ahead toward the cockpit, he could see through the windshield that the plane was heading toward the starting end of the runway. Tanovich knew how to fly this plane. All those circle flights. He had been him learning to fly his own jet.

The plane went too fast around the 180 degree turn onto the runway and it slammed Joe right off his feet against the bulkhead. But when the plane turned onto the runway, it had to stop as Tanovich revved up the engines for take-off.

Joe scrambled frantically into the cockpit and leapt right over the pilot's seat onto Tanovich's head.

A huge elbow slammed hard into him as the revving of the engines escalated. Then Tanovich took his foot off the brakes and the plane heaved forward with such force, it nearly knocked Joe loose from his grasp.

But he held on and pressed on the seatbelt latch to loosen it, trying to drag Tanovich away from the controls.

Then he saw a Crown Victoria parked across the runway. Bittinger's car.

They would never get airborne.

"Car!" Joe screamed and let go of Tanovich. He dove for the co-pilot's controls, trying to turn the speeding plane as hard as he could. When Tanovich saw the car, he slammed on the brakes and yanked back on the throttle, sending the plane into a sideways skid up the runway, skittering toward the car at breakneck speed.

On the tarmac, the pilots sprinted one way, Enright the other and Bittinger, who stood near his car, backed away from his Crown Victoria carrying a rifle as if he could stop the onrushing plane careening down the runway sideways.

Joe and Tanovich fought over the controls as they felt the wheel carriage collapse beneath the plane. The struts had crumpled and the plane now skidded on its belly. But momentum was still driving the out-of-control plane down the runway toward the car, skidding and sending off sparks.

Joe was thrown to the floor of the cockpit when at last the plane lurched to a stop.

From the seat, Tanovich kicked at him.

The radio crackled on, it was Bittinger, "This is the police. Open the door immediately."

Tanovich kicked again before Joe scrambled to his feet.

Outside the windshield, Tanovich saw Bittinger standing on the tarmac in full view of the cockpit. In the distance were the lights of police cars, fire engines and ambulances.

Tanovich seemed incapable of stopping. Backing down was impossible.

In the confines of the cockpit, Joe was within easy reach and Tanovich viciously grabbed him, an arm around his neck, ready to break it.

Joe slammed forward into him as hard as he could and the crowded seats made it hard for Tanovich to keep his footing.

Joe became aware of crazed screaming filling the cabin.

It was Senka, shrieking "Daddy!" as she dove for the two men, that large knife back in her hand.

The blade was headed right for Joe. They were going to kill him together.

Senka brought the knife down with brutal force.

Joe suddenly shoved backwards, away from Tanovich.

And watched as if in slow motion as the big man fell forward on top of him.

That knife plunged right past Joe's face. Hard.

In one instant, all the power that held Joe in its grasp was released and he fell free.

But the screaming only escalated. It looked like Senka was climbing atop her father.

As he regained his footing, Joe could see Senka was insane with terror. She was still holding the knife which was embedded practically to the hilt in her father's throat. He was alive. For the moment.

And she was trying to pull the knife out.

His impenetrable eyes looked beyond his daughter to Joe standing over him. Tanovich knew that life was flowing out of him, but even so, he couldn't believe it as he looked up at the enemy standing over him.

Tanovich gasped his last breath just before Senka yanked the knife free. She turned toward Joe with it. Filled with hate, she dove for Joe with the knife.

He leapt at her, slamming her against the bulkhead.

While she tried desperately to stab him, he spotted the button for the descending door and pressed it.

Senka's screaming rose as they tumbled together out of the plane upon the opening stairs. There they found Enright, his foot firmly planted on Senka's hand with the knife in it.

BITT SCRAMBLED inside the plane with a gun while Enright cuffed Senka just outside it. Even as fire trucks, ambulances and police cars screeched up, Joe leapt back into the plane and raced past Bittinger.

He figured out how to open the hatch to the cargo bay and lowered himself into the tight space. It was dimly lit by small red and green equipment lights. He pressed a green one and the cargo door opened.

Joe crawled around the wooden crate, looking for a way to open it. In less than a minute, he was pulling on the bedding from Senka's house and dragging the boy out of the crate.

Billy was asleep, but very much alive.

32

Billy was taken to St. Joseph's Hospital in an ambulance after being pronounced healthy except for the sedation. Bitt had his hands full overseeing Tanovich's body and Senka's arrest, plus interviews of the pilot, co-pilot and workman.

Joe's litany of potential crimes was beyond his ability to calculate, but as he watched the sun rise over the east side of St. Paul, he thought of his mother. The bodies in the basement, the workmen who would find them and the arrest that would result. He had to get away from here and go help her with the upcoming ordeal.

Joe found Enright enthusiastically giving a run-down of events to a group of policemen and silently beckoned him. Enright broke free and joined Joe, saying, "I may never have to pay for a boilermaker the rest of my life."

"You think it would be okay if I give myself up later?"

"You mean come in for a statement?" Enright, making a clear distinction he hoped Joe could grasp in his present state. The jury was out whether that coin would drop for Joe.

"I've got something urgent to do."

Enright's already happy face grew into an enormous smile. "You were in the middle of make-up sex with lady love when I called? No wonder you been acting crazy."

"I wish that was it," Joe said. "My mother's moving today."

"I'll schedule your statement for this afternoon."

"Think I'll get disbarred?" Joe asked. "Jail?"

"Let's do the math, Joe...you solved a kidnapping and two murders, saved the most famous rich boy in the state, brought in the biggest murder case we've had in years, stopped the killer and now his accomplice is talking up a storm. Mike will get local, state and national headlines for weeks and win re-election by a landslide. One plus one plus one plus one equals...'no.'"

Joe was baffled, but there was Enright grinning and holding out a hand to shake. "Accept the no, Joe."

Joe shook the hand and smiled as hopefully as he could.

PICKUP TRUCKS WERE PARKED all along Forrestal and workmen were finishing coffees as Joe parked. Even as he was heading to the house, he heard the first huge excavator start up in preparation to demolish the remaining nearby houses. To his surprise, the front door of his mother's house wide open.

Inside he saw Kat, then two cops hurry out of the kitchen. It took a moment to register the hand being offered. It was Earl, the cop who had guarded the street during the news crew siege. Joe owed the man a case of Heineken.

Joe blankly shook hands with him, then his partner and felt their pats on the back. He slowly came to recognize they were proud to shake his hand, happy to congratulate him and thrilled the 'Jigsaw Killer' was dead and the boy was alive. News had spread fast.

Next in line was Kat who gave him a ferocious hug and said, "They told me you rescued Billy."

He watched, still confused, as each cop picked up a cardboard box and headed out the front door. He watched through the window as they loaded the boxes in Kat's car which he hadn't even noticed in the driveway.

"Why are police helping move my mother's things?" he asked Kat. 'What the fuck is going on?' he thought.

"They have to certify that each house is empty before it's demolished. This one isn't empty until we have Aileen's things out," Kat said as the police returned, picked up a couple more boxes and happily made another trip. "I think they're thrilled to do it, on this day of all days."

'Yeah, of all days,' Joe thought. It would take a really nasty turn before the day was over. "Where's my ma?"

"She had to get something from the basement," Kat said and started to tape up another box.

"You haven't been down there?" he said with alarm.

"No, she wanted to do it herself," Kat said innocently. "Nasty bruise your Uncle Louie gave her, huh?"

"Yeah. I better go check on her," Joe said and was halfway down the stairs when he realized Kat would have no idea why he was able to do that. He went back and found her staring, gape-mouthed. "I seem to be overcoming my phobia."

"You think?" she said, still dumbstruck.

"I'll tell you about it later," he said, then hurried back downstairs and found his mother in the laundry room.

Nothing was as he had left it. The dryer was back in place and there were no boxes of dirt. His mother was folding dry clothes into piles on the card table; she looked up at him happily. "Kat is such a nice girl."

"Ma? What happened?" Joe said gesturing at the room.

There was no sign of Louie, no trace of Dad, no hole in the floor, no plastic garden bag of cash, no suitcase and it looked like there was a fresh patina of dirt strewn over the entire floor. That must be the dirt from the boxes.

The bodies must be in the hole, capped by the suitcase and the dryer. "I don't think it will work, Ma."

"Louie ran out after he hit me in the face, Joey."

'We're back to that?' Joe thought.

"Everything will turn out okay," she said as she handed him a stack of folded laundry, took a pile herself and headed upstairs. He was alone in the innocent-looking basement. His family crypt. He hurried upstairs after her and put the clothes into a box Kat had ready to tape.

"Your car won't hold any more," Earl said to Kat.

Joe ran to get his car and had a moment to think. The bottom was going to fall out sooner or later, but he realized he might as well let it go as long as it lasted. It wouldn't be worse if they found the bodies on their own and that way his mother wouldn't feel the betrayal she would if he told them himself.

'Let the chips fall,' he thought as he parked and found both Kat and Aileen waiting with boxes. They loaded them in his back seat because his trunk was full of basketballs. Everything fit because Aileen wasn't keeping much.

Joe spotted Earl on the porch beckoning him anxiously. Now the other shoe would drop, Joe figured, as he walked up the stairs to the porch. Earl looked grim and stepped back inside the house with his partner.

"We found something in the basement," Earl said as they hovered just inside the doorway together.

"Yeah?" Joe said, feeling like the ax would now fall.

Before he said another word, the partner showed him his mother's rifle and handful of bullets. "Practically antique but the sucker was loaded, Mr. Brandt."

Joe choked back a laugh. "I doubt she has a permit."

"That's what we were thinking, though with your uncle coming by and hitting her and all, can't really blame her," Earl said. "Thing is, what should we do with it? If we take it, it would have to be destroyed."

"Sounds perfect," Joe said and searched their eyes for signs of other discoveries, but saw none.

AT THE CAR, Kat had called her office and was anxious to go see Billy. He'd asked for both of them when he woke. She had just arranged to become his interim guardian until his grandparents, Sienna and Nicola's parents, arrived to take over guardianship. She hoped she would become a major player in his continued care and wanted to be with him as soon as she could. They decided Joe would take his mother to the new apartment and they'd get the boxes from Kat's car later.

Kat drove away and he was glad she wouldn't be there to watch him sweat through the destruction of the house while fearing every moment would be the end for his mother.

With Aileen in the passenger seat, he parked behind the barricade where the demolition crews insisted they be. An excavator pushed against the house until it collapsed and Joe was surprised how feeble the structure really was. Then another machine with a gaping jaw picked up huge bites and dumped them into a truck. It seemed like only minutes before the one story house didn't exist and there was only the cavernous hole of the basement between them and fate.

Aileen watched in silence and Joe could only guess what she must be thinking as her past disappeared.

He was a nervous wreck waiting for the moment when their secrets were unearthed. The jaws reached into the basement and lifted the furnace. It came back for the work bench. It picked up the washer and then the dryer. It grabbed the stairway itself. Then, to Joe's utter amazement, it backed up on its tracks and headed toward the flattened garage in which Louie had beaten him up.

Joe got out of the car to watch more closely. He saw Chip Bateman wave and give him the thumbs up. Then they both watched while a massive piece of equipment pushed the cinderblock walls of the basement in on themselves. The huge machine took its time as it worked its way around the house, systematically pushing the walls into the hole of the emptied basement.

Then the heavy excavator crisscrossed the land, crushing everything below it, packing it down.

Joe kept thinking it couldn't all end like this.

But as the second huge machine trundled aside, dump trucks came with loads of dirt from the huge hole excavated for the main building. They dumped dirt into the crushed basement as landfill and Joe was awestruck as he watched every detail in disbelief.

He finally trusted it was over when the last machine rolled back and forth, compacting the ground with its weight.

The city was doing what Joe and his mother had not been able to do. It was burying their past forever.

ONCE THE WORKERS WERE DONE, Joe inched past the barricade and found his mother walking along beside him.

Their lot was now nothing but raw, compacted dirt. level and ready for the basketball courts.

Joe escorted her past where the fence had been, over where the sidewalk once was, across the spots where the porch and living room had stood and then they stopped.

Dad and Louie were directly below them. It wasn't exactly by the book, Joe thought, but justice was served.

"They ran out on us, Ma," Joe said quietly.

"And we're not going to look for them."

Want more Joe Brandt?
Click: "The Unraveling Man"

And please take a minute to rate/review
Kindle and Goodreads

ALSO BY DAVID HOWARD

Joe Brandt Thrillers
"RECOLLECTIONS OF MURDER"
"THE UNRAVELING MAN"

Non-fiction
"THE TOOLS OF SCREENWRITING"
St. Martin's Press
"HOW TO BUILD A GREAT SCREENPLAY"
St. Martin's Press

Look for David Howard's author page at:
amazon.com/author/david.howard

Contact the author at:
David@davidhowardbooks.com

ABOUT THE AUTHOR

DAVID HOWARD is an award-winning screenwriter with more than two dozen international film and television productions and several producing credits. He has published two non-fiction books with St. Martin's Press.

His produced feature films have won top prizes at many international festivals, including Berlin and Edinburgh, as well as several best picture awards, the German Film Prize and the Silver Goddess Award. His television writing has garnered such honors as an Emmy Award, a CableACE and the prestigious Humanitas Prize in the US.

His non-fiction includes two seminal books on the art and craft of screenwriting. "The Tools of Screenwriting" is required reading at the top film schools in the US and worldwide, including USC, UCLA, NYU, American Film Institute and Columbia University, plus the Beijing Film Academy, FAMU in Prague and VGIK in Moscow.

He is a tenured full professor at USC where he founded the Graduate Screenwriting Program in the School of Cinematic Arts, which is widely acknowledged as the best film school in the world. His former students are among the world's most well-known film and television writers, producers, directors and series show runners.

He received his BA from the University of Minnesota and his MFA in screenwriting from Columbia University. He lives in Los Angeles with his wife and daughter.

Made in United States
Troutdale, OR
05/12/2025

31281132R00184